Wishing you a very happy birthday,
from your loving sister.

THE SETONS

BY

O. DOUGLAS

AUTHOR OF "PENNY PLAIN," ETC.

THOMAS NELSON AND SONS, Ltd.

LONDON, EDINBURGH, NEW YORK
TORONTO, AND PARIS

THE SETONS

CHAPTER I

" Look to the bakemeats, good Angelica,
Spare not for cost."

Romeo and Juliet.

A NOVEMBER night in Glasgow.
Mr. Thomson got out of the electric tram
which every evening brought him from business,
walked briskly down the road until he came to a
neat villa with *Jeanieville* cut in the pillar, almost
trotted up the gravelled path, let himself in with
his latchkey, shut the door behind him, and cried,
" Are ye there, Mamma ? Mamma, are ye there ? "

After four-and-twenty years of matrimony John
Thomson still cried for Jeanie his wife the moment
he entered the house.

Mrs. Thomson came out of the dining-room and
helped her husband to take off his coat.

" You're home, Papa," she said, " and in nice
time, too. Now we'll all get our tea comfortable in
the parlour before we change our clothes. (Jessie,
tell Annie Papa's in.) Your things are all laid out
on the bed, John, and I've put your gold studs in a
dress shirt—but whit's that you're carrying, John ? "

John Thomson regarded his parcel rather shame-
facedly. " It's a pine-apple for your party, Mamma.

I was lookin' in a fruit shop when I was waitin' for ma car and I just took a notion to get it. Not," he added, " but what I prefer tinned ones maself."

Mrs. Thomson patted her husband's arm approvingly. " Well, that was real mindful of you, Papa. It 'll look well on the table. Jessie," to her daughter, who at that moment came into the lobby from the kitchen, " get down another fruit dish. Here's Papa brought home a pine-apple for your party."

" Tea's in, Mamma," said Jessie ; then she took the parcel from her father, and holding his arm drew him into the dining-room, talking all the time. " Come on, Papa, and see the table. It looks fine, and the pine-apple 'll give it a finish. We've got a trifle from Skinner's, and we're having meringues and an apricot souffle and——"

" Now, Jessie," Mrs. Thomson broke in, " don't keep Papa, or the sausages 'll get cold. Where's Rubbert and Alick ? We'll niver be ready at eight o'clock at this rate."

As she spoke, Alick, her younger son, pranced into the room, and pretended to stand awestruck at the display.

" We're not half doing it in style, eh ? " he said, and made a playful dive at a silver dish of chocolates. Jessie caught him by his coat, and in the scuffle the dish was upset and the chocolates emptied on the cloth.

" Oh, Mamma ! " cried the outraged Jessie. " Look what he's done. He's nothing but a torment." Picking up the chocolates, she glared over her shoulder at her brother with great disapproval. " Such a sight as you are, too. If you can't get your hair to lie straight you're not coming to the party. Mind that."

Alick ruffled up his mouse-coloured locks and

looked in no way dejected. "It's your own fault anyway," he said; "I didn't mean to spill your old sweeties. Come on, Mamma, and give us our tea, and leave that lord alone in her splendour;" and half carrying, half dragging his mother, he left the dining-room.

Jessie put the chocolates back and smoothed the shining cloth.

"He's an awful boy that Alick, Papa," she said, as she pulled out the lace edge of a d'oyley. "He's always up to some mischief."

"Ay, Jessie," said her father, "he's a wild laddie, but he's real well-meaning. There's your mother calling us. Come away to your tea. I can smell the sausages."

In the parlour they found the rest of the family seated at table. Mrs. Thomson was pouring tea from a fat brown teapot; Alick, with four half-slices of bread piled on his plate, had already begun, while Robert sat in his place with a book before him, his elbows on the table, his fingers in his ears. Jessie slid into her place and helped herself to a piece of bread.

"I wish, Mamma," she said, as she speared a ball of butter, "you hadn't had sausages for tea to-night. It's an awful smell through the house."

Mrs. Thomson laid down the cup she was lifting to her mouth.

"I'm sure, Jessie," she said, "you're ill to please. Who'd ever mind a smell of cooking in the house? And a nice tasty smell like sausages, too."

"It's such a common sort of smell in the evening," went on Jessie. "I wish we had late dinner. The Simpsons have it, and Muriel says it makes you feel quite different; more refined."

"Muriel Simpson's daft," put in Alick; "Ewan

says it's her that's put his mother up to send him to an English school. He doesn't want to be made English."

" It's to improve his accent," said Jessie. " Yours is something awful."

Alick laughed derisively and began to speak in a clipt and mincing fashion which he believed to be " English."

" Alick ! Stop it," said his mother. " Don't aggravate your sister."

Jessie tossed her head.

" He's not aggravating me, he's only making a fool of himself."

" Papa," said Alick, appealing to his father, " sure the English are awful silly."

Mr. Thomson's mouth was full, but he answered peaceably, " They haven't had our advantages, Alick, but they mean well."

" They mebbe mean well," said Alick, " but they *sound* gey daft."

Robert had been eating and reading at the same time and paying no attention to the conversation, but he now passed in his cup to his mother and asked, " Who's all coming to-night ? "

" Well," said his mother, lifting the " cosy " from the teapot, " they're mostly Jessie's friends. Some of them I've never seen."

" I wish, Mamma," said Jessie, " that you hadn't made me ask the Hendrys and the Taylors. The Hendrys are so dowdy-looking, and Mr. Taylor's awful common."

" Indeed, Jessie," her mother retorted, " I won-der to hear you. The Hendrys are my oldest friends, and decenter women don't live ; and as for Mr. Taylor, I'm sure he's real joky and a great help at an ' evening.' "

"He'll wear his velveteen coat," said Robert.

"I daresay," said Jessie. "Velveteen coat
indeed! D'you know what he calls it?—his
'splush jaicket.'"

"Taylor's a toffy wee body," said Mr. Thomson,
"but a good Christian man. He's been superintendent of the Sabbath school for twenty years
and he's hardly ever missed a day. Is that all
from the church, Mamma? You didn't think of
asking the M'Roberts or the Andersons?"

"Oh, Papa!" said Jessie, sitting back helplessly.

"What's the matter with them, Jessie?" asked
Mr. Thomson. "Are they not good enough for
you?"

"Uch, Papa, it's not that. But I want this to
be a nice party, like the Simpsons give. They
never have their parties spoiled by dowdy-looking
people. It all comes of going to such a poor church.
I don't say Mr. Seton's not as good as anybody
but the people in the church are no class; hardly
one of them keeps a girl. I don't see why we can't
go to a church in Pollokshields where there's an
organ and society."

"Never heed her," broke in Mrs. Thomson;
"she's a silly girl. Another sausage, Papa?"

"No, Mamma. No, thanks."

"Then we'd better all away and dress," said Mrs.
Thomson briskly. "Your things are laid out on
your bed, Papa, and I got you a nice made-up tie."

"I'm never to put on my swallow-tail?" asked
Mr. Thomson, as he and his wife went upstairs
together.

"'Deed, John, Jessie's determined on it."

Mr. Thomson wandered into his bedroom and
surveyed the glories of his evening suit lying on
the bed, then a thought struck him.

" Here, Mamma," he called. " Taylor hasn't got a swallow-tail and I wouldn't like him to feel out of it. I'll just put on my Sabbath coat—it's wiser-like anyway."

Mrs. Thomson bustled in from another room and considered the question.

" It's a pity, too," she said, " not to let the people see you have dress-clothes, and I don't think Mr. Taylor's the man to mind—he's gey sure of himself. Besides, there'll be others to keep him company ; a lot of them'll not understand it's full dress. I'm sure it would never have occurred to me if it hadn't been for Jessie. She's got ideas, that girl !"

At that moment, Jessie, wrapped in a dressing-gown and with her hair undone, came into the room and asked, " What about my hair, Mamma ? Will I do it in rolls or in a Grecian knot ? "

Mrs. Thomson pondered, with her head on one side and her bodice unbuttoned.

" Well, Jessie, I'm sure it's hard to say, but I think myself the Grecian is more uncommon ; though, mind you, I like the rolls real well. But hurry, there's a good girl, and come and hook me, for that new bodice fair beats me."

" All right, Mamma," said Jessie. " I'll come before I put on my dress."

" I must say, John," said Mrs. Thomson, turning to her husband, " I envy you keeping thin, though I whiles think it's a pity so much good food goes into such a poor skin. I'm getting that stout I'm a burden to myself—and a sight as well."

" Not at all, Mamma," replied her husband ; " you look real comfortable. I don't like those whippin'-posts of women."

" Well, Papa, they're elegant, you must say they're elegant, and they're easy to dress. It's a

thought to me to get a new dress. I wonder if
Jessie minded to tell Annie to have the teapot well
heated before she infused the tea. We're to have
tea at one end and coffee at the other, and that
minds me I promised Jessie to get out the best tea-
cosy—the white satin one with the ribbon-work
poppies. It's in the top drawer of the best wardrobe : I'd better get it before my bodice is on, and
I can stretch ! "

There were sounds of preparation all over the
house, and an atmosphere of simmering excitement.
Alick's voice was heard loudly demanding that some
persons unknown would restore to him the slippers
they had—presumably—stolen ; also his tartan tie.
Annie rushed upstairs to say that the meringues had
come but the cream wasn't inside them, it had
arrived separately in a tin, and could Miss Jessie put
it in, as she couldn't trust herself ; whereupon Jessie,
with her hair in a Grecian knot, but still clad in a
dressing-gown, fled to give the required help.

Presently Mrs. Thomson was hooked into her
tight bodice of black satin made high to the neck
and with a front of pink-flowered brocade. Alick
found his slippers, and his mother helped him with
his stiff, very wide Eton collar, and tied his tie,
which was the same tartan as his kilt. Then she
saw that Mr. Thomson's made-up tie was securely
fastened down behind and that his coat-collar sat
properly ; then, arm in arm, they descended to the
drawing-room.

The drawing-room in Jeanieville was on the left
side of the front door as you entered, a large room
with a bow-window and two side windows. It had
been recently papered and painted and refurnished.
The wall-paper was yellow with a large design of
chrysanthemums, and the woodwork white without

spot or blemish. The thick Axminster carpet of peacock blue was thickly covered with yellow roses. It stopped about two feet from the wall all round, and the hiatus thus made was covered with linoleum which, rather unsuccessfully, tried to look like a parquet floor. There were many pictures on the wall in bright gilt frames, varied by hand-painted plaques and enlarged photographs. The "suite" of furniture was covered with brocade in a shade known as old gold ; and a handsome cabinet with glass doors, and shelves covered with pale blue plush, held articles which in turn held pleasant memories for the Thomsons—objects of art from the *rue de Rivoli* (they had all been in Paris for a fortnight last July), and cow-bells and carved bears from Lucerne.

"There's nothing enlarges the mind like travel," was a favourite saying of Mr. Thomson's, and his wife never failed to reply, "That's true, Papa, I'm sure."

To-night, in preparation for the party, the chairs and tables were pushed back to the wall, and various seats from the parlour and even the best bedroom had been introduced where they would be least noticed ; a few forms with holland covers had also been hired from the baker for the occasion. The piano stood open, with "The Rosary" on the stand ; the incandescent lights in their pink globes were already lit, and a fire—a small one, for the room would get hot presently—burned in the yellow-tiled grate.

Mr. and Mrs. Thomson paused for a moment in the doorway in order to surprise themselves.

"Well, well," said Mr. Thomson, while his wife hurried to the fireside to sweep away a fallen cinder. "You've been successful with your colour scheme,

Mamma, I must say that. The yellow and white's cheery, and the blue of the carpet makes a fine contrast. You've taste right enough."

Mrs. Thomson, with her head on one side, regarded the room which, truth to say, in every detail seemed to her perfect, then she gave a long sigh.

" I don't know about taste, Papa," she said ; " but how ever we'll keep all that white paint beats me. I'm thinking it 'll be either me or Jessie that 'll have to do it. I could not trust Annie in here, poor girl ! She has such hashy ways. Now, Alick," to that youth who had sprung on her from behind, " try and behave well to-night, and not shame your sister before the Simpsons that she thinks so much of. I'm told Ewan Simpson was a perfect gentleman in an Eton suit at their party."

" Haw, haw ! " laughed Alick derisively. " Who's wantin' to be a gentleman ? Not me, anyway. Here, Mamma, are you goin' to ask wee Taylor to sing ? Uch, do, he's a comic——"

" Alick," said his father reprovingly, " Mr. Taylor's not coming here to-night for you to laugh at."

" I know that," said Alick, rolling his head and looking somewhat abashed.

The entrance of Jessie and Robert diverted his parents' attention.

Jessie stood in the middle of the room and slowly turned herself round that her family might see her from all points of view.

" D'you like it, Mamma ? " she asked.

" Yes, Jessie," said her mother slowly, " I do. Miss White's done well. The skirt hangs beautiful, and I must say the Empire style is becoming to you, though for myself I prefer the waist in its natural place. Walk to the door—yes—elegant."

" Very fine, Jessie," said her father.

" Do you like it, Robert ? " asked Jessie.

Robert put down his book for a moment, glanced at his sister, nodded his head and said " Ucha," then returned to it.

" You're awful proud, Jessie," said Alick ; " you think you're somebody."

" Never mind him, Jessie," said Mrs. Thomson. " Are ye sure we've got enough cups ? Nobody 'll be likely to take both tea and coffee, I suppose ? Except mebbe Mr. Taylor—I whiles think that wee man's got both eatin' and drinkin' diabetes. I must say it seems to me a cold-like thing to let them sit from eight to ten without a bite. My way was to invite them at six and give them a hearty set-down tea, and then at ten we had supper, lemonade and jam tartlets and fruit, and I'm sure nothing could have been nicer. Many a one has said to me, ' Mrs. Thomson, they're no ;parties like your parties ; they're that hearty.' How ever 'll they begin the evening when they're not cheered with a cup o' tea ? "

" We'll begin with music, Mamma," said Jessie.

Mrs. Thomson sniffed.

" I do hope Annie 'll manage the showing in all right," went on Jessie. " The Simpsons had one letting you in and another waiting in the bedrooms to help you off with your things."

Mrs. Thomson drew herself up.

" My friends are all capable of taking off their own things, Jessie, I'm thankful to say. They don't need a lady's maid ; nor does Mrs. Simpson, let me tell you, for when I first knew her she did her own washing."

" Uch, Mamma," said Jessie.

" It's five minutes to eight," said Alick, " and I hear steps. I bet it's wee Taylor."

" Mercy ! " said Mrs. Thomson, hunting wildly for her slippers which she had kicked off. " Am I all right, Jessie ? Give me a book—any one—yes, that."

Alick heaved a stout volume — *Shakespeare's Country with Coloured Illustrations* — into his mother's lap, and she at once became absorbed in it, sitting stiffly in her chair, her skirt spread out.

Mr. Thomson looked nervous ; Robert retreated vaguely towards the window curtains ; even Jessie felt a little uncertain, though preserving an outward calm.

" There's the bell," said Alick ; " I'm off."

Jessie clutched him by his coat. " You can't go now," she hissed. " I hear Annie going to the door."

They heard the sound of the front door opening, then a murmur of voices and a subdued titter from Annie, and it closed. Next Annie's skurrying footsteps were heard careering wildly for the best bedroom, followed—a long way behind—by other footsteps. Then the drawing-room door opened prematurely, and Mr. Taylor appeared.

CHAPTER II

"Madam, the guests are come!"
Romeo and Juliet.

MR. TAYLOR was a small man, with legs that did not seem to be a pair. He wore a velveteen coat, a white waistcoat, a lavender tie, and a flower in his buttonhole. In the doorway he stood rubbing his hands together and beaming broadly on the Thomsons.

"The girrl wanted me to wait on Mrs. Taylor coming downstairs, but I says to her, ' No ceremony for me, I'm a plain man,' and in I came. How are you, Mrs. Thomson? And is Jessie a good wee miss? How are you, Thomson—and Rubbert? Alick, you've grown out of recognition."

"Take this chair, Mr. Taylor," said Mrs. Thomson, while *Shakespeare's Country with Coloured Illustrations* slipped unheeded to the floor; and Jessie glared her disapproval of the little man.

"Not at all. I'll sit here. Expecting quite a gathering to-night, Mrs. Thomson?"

"Well, Mr. Taylor, they're mostly young people, friends of Jessie's," Mrs. Thomson explained.

"Quite so. Quite so. I'm at home among the young people, Mrs. Thomson. Always a pleasure

18

to see them enjoy theirselves. Here comes Mrs. Taylor. C'me away, m'dear, into the fire."

"You'd think he owned the house," Jessie muttered resentfully to Robert.

Mrs. Taylor was a tall, thin woman, with a depressed cast of countenance and a Roman nose. Her hair, rather thin on the top, was parted and crimped in careful waves. She was dressed in olive-green silk. In one hand she carried a black beaded bag, and she moved at a run with her head forward, coming very close to the people she was greeting and looking anxiously into their faces, as if expecting to find them suffering from some dire disease.

On this occasion the intensity of her grasp and gaze was almost painful as "How's Mrs. Thomson?" she murmured, and even Mrs. Thomson's hearty "I'm well, thanks," hardly seemed to reassure her. The arrival of some other people cut short her greetings, and she and her husband retired arm in arm to seats on the sofa.

Now the guests arrived in quick succession.

Mrs. Thomson toiled industriously to find something to say to each one, and Jessie wrestled with the question of seats. People seemed to take up so much more room than she had expected. The sofa which she had counted on to hold four looked crowded with three, and of course her father had put the two Miss Hendrys into the two best armchairs, and when the Simpsons came, fashionably late (having only just finished dinner), they had to content themselves with the end of a holland-covered form hired from the baker. They were not so imposing in appearance as one would have expected from Jessie's awe of them. They had both round fat faces and perpetually open mouths, elaborately dressed hair and slightly supercilious

expressions. Their accent was refined, and they
embarrassed Mrs. Thomson at the outset by shaking
her hand and leaving it up in the air.

The moment the Misses Simpson were seated
Jessie sped towards a tall young man lounging
against a window and brought him in triumph to
them.

" I would like to introduce to you Mr. Stewart
Stevenson—the artist, you know. Miss Gertrude
Simpson, Miss Muriel Simpson—Mr. Stevenson."

" Now," she said to herself, as she walked away,
" I wonder if I did that right ? I'm almost sure I
should have said his name first."

" Jessie," said her father in a loud whisper,
clutching at her sleeve, " should we not be doing
something ? It's awful dull. I could ask Taylor
to sing, if you like."

" Uch, no, Papa," said Jessie, " at least not yet.
I'll ask Mr. Inverarity—he's a lovely singer ; " and
shaking herself free, she approached a youth with
a drooping moustache and a black tie who was
standing alone and looking—what he no doubt felt
—neglected.

" Oh, Mr. Inverarity," said Jessie, " I know you
sing. Now," archly, " don't say you haven't
brought your music."

" Well," said Mr. Inverarity, looking cheered,
" as a matter of fact I did bring a song or two.
They're in the hall, beside my coat ; I'll get them."

" Not at all," said Jessie. " Alick ! run out to
the hall and bring in Mr. Inverarity's music. He's
going to give us a song."

Alick went and returned with a large roll of songs.
" Here," he remarked to Jessie in passing, " if he
sings all these we'll do."

Mr. Inverarity pondered over the songs for a few

seconds and then said, " If you would be so kind, Miss Thomson, as to accompany me, I might try this."

" All right," said Jessie, as she removed her jangling bangles and laid them on the top of the piano. " I'll do my best, but I'm not an awfully good accompanist." She gave the piano-stool a twirl, seated herself, and struck some rather uncertain chords, while Mr. Inverarity cleared his throat, stared gloomily at the carpet, and then lustily announced that it was his Wedding Morn Ding Dong.

There was a commendable silence during the performance, and in the chorus of " Thank yous " and " Lovelys " that followed Jessie led the singer to a girl with an " artistic " gown and prominent teeth, whom she introduced as " Miss Waterston, awfully fond of music."

" Pleased to meet you," said Mr. Inverarity. " No," as Miss Waterston tried to make room for him, " I wouldn't think of crowding you. I'll just sit on this wee stool, if nobody has any objections."

Miss Waterston giggled. " That was a lovely song of yours, Mr. Inverarity," she said. " I did enjoy it."

" Thank you, Miss Waterston. D'you sing yourself ? "

" Oh, well," said Miss Waterston, smiling coyly at the toe of her slipper, " just a little. In fact," with a burst of confidence, " I've got a part in this year's production of the Sappho Club. Well, of course, I'm only in the chorus, but it's something to be even in the chorus of such a high-class Club. Don't you think so ? "

" And what," asked Mr. Inverarity, " is the piece to be produced ? "

" Oh ! It's the *Gondoliers*, a kind of old-fashioned thing, of course. I would rather have done something more up to date, like *The Chocolate Box Girl* ; it's lovely."

" It is," Mr. Inverarity agreed, " very tuney ; but d'you know, of all these things my wee favourite's *The Convent Girl*."

" Fency ! " said Miss Waterston, " I've never seen it. I think, don't you, that music's awfully inspiring ? When I hear good music I just feel as if I could—as if I—well, you know what I mean."

" I've just the same feeling myself, Miss Waterston," Mr. Inverarity assured her,—" something like what's expressed in the words ' Had I the wings of a dove I would flee,' eh ? Is that it ? " and Mr. Inverarity nudged Miss Waterston with his elbow.

The room was getting very hot, Mr. Thomson in his nervousness having inadvertently heaped the fire with coals.

A very small man recited " Lasca " on the hearth-rug, and melted visibly between heat and emotion.

" I say," said Mr. Stevenson to Miss Gertrude Simpson, " he looks like Casabianca. By the way, was Casabianca the name of the boy on the ship ? "

" I couldn't say, I'm sure," she replied, looking profoundly uninterested.

" Do you go much to the theatre ? " he asked her sister.

" We go when there's anything good on," she said.

" Such as—— ? "

" Oh ! I don't know——" She looked vaguely round the room. " Something amusing, you know, but quite nice too."

" I see. D'you care for the Repertory ? "

" Oh, well," said Miss Muriel, " they're not bad, but they do such dull things. You remember, Gertrude," leaning across to her sister, " yon awful silly thing we saw ? What was it called ? Yes, *Prunella*. And that same night some friends asked us to go to *Baby Mine*,—every one says it's killing, —but Papa had taken the seats and he made us use them. It was too bad. We felt awfully ' had.' "

" *I* think," said Miss Gertrude, " that the Repertory people are very amateurish."

Mr. Stewart Stevenson was stung.

" My dear young lady," he said severely, " one or two of the Repertory people are as good as any one on the London stage and a long sight better than most."

" Fency," said Miss Gertrude coldly.

Stewart Stevenson looked about for a way of escape, but he was hemmed round by living walls and without doing violence he could not leave his seat. Mrs. Thomson sat before him in a creaking cane chair listening to praise of her drawing-room from Jessie's dowdy friend, Miss Hendry.

" My ! Mrs. Thomson, it's lovely ! *Whit* a carpet —pile near up to your knees ! "

" D'ye like the colouring, Miss Hendry ? " asked Mrs. Thomson.

Miss Hendry looked round at the yellow walls and bright gilt picture frames shining in the strong incandescent light.

" Mrs. Thomson," she said solemnly, " it's *chaste !* "

Mrs. Thomson sighed as if the burden of her magnificence irked her, then : " How d'ye think the evening's goin' ? " she whispered.

" Very pleasant," Miss Hendry whispered back. " What about a game ? "

" I don't know," said poor Mrs. Thomson. " *I*

would say it would be the very thing, but mebbe Jessie wouldn't think it genteel."

A girl stood up beside the piano with her violin, and somebody said " Hush ! " loudly, so Mrs. Thomson at once subsided, in so far as a very stout person can subside in an inadequate cane chair, and composed herself to listen to Scots airs very well played. The familiar tunes cheered the company wonderfully ; in fact, they so raised Mr. Taylor's spirits that, to Jessie's great disgust, and in spite of the raised eyebrows of the Simpsons, he pranced in the limited space left in the middle of the room and invited any one who liked to take a turn with him.

" Jolly thing a fiddle," said Stewart Stevenson cheerily to Miss Muriel Simpson.

" The violin is always nice," primly replied Miss Muriel, " but I don't care for Scotch airs—they're so common. We like high-class music."

" Perhaps you play yourself ? " Mr. Stevenson suggested.

" Oh no," said Miss Muriel in a surprised tone.

" Do you care for reading ? " he asked her sister.

" Oh, I like it well enough, but it's an awful waste of time."

" Are you so very busy, then ? "

" Well, what with calling, and going into town, and the evenings so taken up with dences and bridge parties, it's quite a rush."

" It must be," said Mr. Stevenson.

" And besides," said Miss Gertrude, " we do quite a lot of fency work."

" But still, Gertrude," her sister reminded her, " we nearly always read on Sunday afternoons."

" That's so," said Gertrude ; " but people have got such a way of dropping in to tea. By the way,

Mr. Stevenson, we'll hope to see you, if you should happen to be in our direction any Sunday."

"That is very kind of you," said Mr. Stevenson.

"There!" cried Mrs. Thomson, bounding in her chair, "Miss Elizabeth's going to sing. That's fine!"

Stewart Stevenson looked over his shoulder and saw a girl standing at the piano. She was slight and straight and tall—more than common tall—grey-eyed and golden-haired, and looked, he thought, as little in keeping with the company gathered in the drawing-room of Jeanieville as a Romney would have looked among the bright gilt-framed pictures on the wall.

She spoke to her accompanist, then, clasping her hands behind her, she threw back her head with a funny little gesture and sang.

> " Jock the Piper steps ahead,
>   Taps his fingers on the reed :
>   His the tune to wake the dead,
>   Wile the salmon from the Tweed,
>   Cut the peats and reap the corn,
>   Kirn the milk and fold the flock,—
>   Never bairn that yet was born
>   Could be feared for Heather Jock.
>
>   Jock the Piper wakes his lay
>   When the hills are red with dawn ;
>   You can hear him pipe away
>   After window-blinds are drawn.
>   In the sleepy summer hours,
>   When you roam by scaur or rock,
>   List the tune among the flowers,
>   'Tis the song of Heather Jock.
>
>   Jock the Piper, grave and kind,
>   Lifts the towsy head that drops !
>   Never eyes could look behind
>   When his fingers touch the stops.
>   Bairns that are too tired to play,
>   Little hearts that sorrows mock—
>   ' There are blue hills far away,
>   Come with me,' says Heather Jock.

He will lead them fast and far
Down the hill and o'er the sea,
Through the sunset gates afar
To the land of Ought-to-be !
Where the treasure ships unload,
Treasures free from bar and lock,
Jock the Piper kens the road,
Up and after Heather Jock."

In his enthusiasm Mr. Stevenson turned to the Misses Simpson and cried :

" What a crystal voice ! Who is she ? "

The Misses Simpson regarded him for a moment, then Miss Gertrude replied coldly :

" Her name's Elizabeth Seton, and her father's the Thomsons' minister. It's quite a poor church down in the slums, and they haven't even an organ. Pretty ? D'you think so ? I think there's awfully little *in* her face. Her voice is nice, of course, but she's got no taste in the choice of songs."

Stewart Stevenson was saved from replying, for the door opened cautiously and Annie the servant put her head in and nodded meaningly in the direction of her mistress, whereupon Mrs. Thomson heaved herself from her inadequate seat and gave a hand—an unnecessary hand—to the spare Miss Hendry.

" Supper at last ! " she said. " I'm sure it's time. It niver was my way to keep people sitting wanting food, but there ! What can a body say with a grown-up daughter ? Eh ! I hope Annie's got the tea and coffee real hot, for everything else is cold."

" Never mind, Mrs. Thomson," said Miss Hendry ; " it's that warm we'll not quarrel with cold things."

They were making their way to the door, when Mr. Taylor rushed forward and, seizing Mrs. Thomson's arm, drew it through his own, remarking reproachfully, " Oh, Mrs. Thomson, you were niver goin' in without me ? Now, Miss Hendry," turning playfully to that austere lady, " don't you be jealous ! You know you're an old sweetheart of mine, but I must keep in with Mrs. Thomson to-night—tea and penny-things, eh ? " and he nudged Miss Hendry, who only sniffed and said, " You've great spirits for your age, Mr. Taylor, I'm sure."

Mr. Taylor, who was still hugging Mrs. Thomson's arm, to her great embarrassment, pretended indignation.

" Ma age, indeed ! " he said. " I'm not a day older in spirit than when I was courtin'. Ask Mrs. Taylor, ask her ; " and he jerked his thumb over his shoulder at his wife, who came mincing on Mr. Thomson's arm, then pranced into the dining-room with his hostess.

" Whit is it, Miss Hendry ? " asked Mrs. Taylor, coming very close and looking anxiously into her face. " Are ye feelin' the heat ? "

" Not me, Mrs. Taylor," said Miss Hendry. " It's that man of yours, jokin' away as usual. He says he's as young as when he was courtin'."

" Ay," said Mrs. Taylor mournfully, " he's wonderful ; but ye niver know when trouble 'll come. Lizzy Leitch is down. A-ay. Quite sudden yesterday morning, when she was beginning her fortnight's washin', and I saw her well and bright last Wensday—or was it Thursday ? No, it was Wensday at tea-time, and now she's unconscious and niver likely to regain it, so the doctor says. Ay, trouble soon comes, and we niver——"

" Mrs. Taylor," said Mr. Thomson nervously, " I think we'd better move on. We're keepin' people back. Miss Hendry, who'll we get to take

you in, I wonder ? Is there any young man you
fancy ? "

"Oh, Mr. Thomson," said Miss Hendry, "it's
ower far on in the afternoon for that with me."

"Not at all," said Mr. Thomson politely, looking
about for a squire. "Here, Alick," he cried, catch-
ing sight of his younger son, "come here and take
Miss Hendry in to supper."

Alick had been boring his way supper-wards un-
impeded by a female, but he cheerfully laid hands on
Miss Hendry (his idea of escorting a lady was to
propel her forcibly) and said, "Come on and get a
seat before the rest get in, and we'll have a rare feed.
It's an awful class supper. Papa brought a real
pine-apple, and there's meringues and all."

Half dragged and half pushed, Miss Hendry
reached the dining-room, where Mrs. Thomson,
flushed and anxious, sat ensconced behind her best
teacups, clasping nervously the silver teapot which
was covered by her treasured white satin tea-cosy
with the ribbon-work poppies. The rest of the
company followed thick and fast. There were not
seats for all, so some of the men, having deposited
their partners, stood round the table ready to hand
cups.

Mrs. Thomson filled some teacups and looked
round helplessly. "Where's Rubbert ?" she murmured.

"Can I assist you, Mrs. Thomson ?" said a polite
youth behind her, clad in a dinner jacket, a double
collar, and a white tie.

"Since you're so kind," said Mrs. Thomson.
"That's the salver with the sugar and cream ; it'll
hold two cups at a time. The girl's taking round
the sangwiches, if you'd just follow her."

At the other end of the table sat Jessie with the

coffee-cups, but as most of the guests preferred tea, she had more time than her harassed mother to look about her.

The sight of food had raised every one's spirits, and the hum of conversation was loud and cheerful.

Mr. Inverarity, sitting on the floor at Miss Waterston's feet, a lock of sleek black hair falling in an engaging way over one eye, a cup of tea on the floor beside him and a sandwich in each hand, was being so amazingly witty that his musical companion was kept in one long giggle.

Mrs. Taylor was looking into Mr. Thomson's face as she told him an involved and woeful tale, and the extent of the little man's misery could be guessed by the faces he was making in his efforts to take an intelligent interest in the recital.

Alick had deserted Miss Hendry for the nonce, but his place had been taken by her sister, Miss Flora, a lady as small and fat as Miss Hendry was tall and slim. They had spread handkerchiefs on their brown silk laps, and were comfortably enjoying the good things which Alick, raven-like, brought to them at intervals.

The Simpsons, Jessie regretted to see, had not been as well looked after as their superiority merited. Miss Muriel had been taken in to supper by Robert. He had supplied her with food, but of conversation, of light table-talk, he had nothing to offer her. Neither he nor the lady was making the slightest effort to conceal the boredom each felt in the other's company.

Gertrude Simpson had been unfortunate again in the way of a chair, and was seated on an indifferent wicker one culled from the parlour. Beside her stood Stewart Stevenson, eating a cream-cake, and looking disinclined for conversation.

" Jessie," said Mrs. Thomson, who had left her place behind the teacups in desperation, " Jessie, just look at Annie. The silly girrl's not trying to feed the folk, she's just listening to what they're saying."

Jessie looked across the room to where Annie stood dangling an empty plate and listening with a sympathetic grin to a conversation between Mr. Taylor and a lady friend, then, seizing a plate of cakes, she set off to recall her to her duty.

" It's an awful heat," said poor Mrs. Thomson to no one in particular. Elizabeth Seton, who had crossed the room to speak to some one, stopped.

" Everything's going beautifully, Mrs. Thomson," she said. " Just look how happy every one looks ; it's a lovely party."

" I'm sure," said Mrs. Thomson, " I'm glad you think so, for it's not my idea of a party. But there, I'm old-fashioned, as Jessie often says. Tell me—d'ye think there's enough to eat ? "

Elizabeth Seton laughed. " Enough ! Why, there's oceans. Do let me carry some things round. It's time for the sweets, isn't it ? May I take a meringue on one plate and some of the trifle on another, and ask which they'll have ? "

" I wish you would," said Mrs. Thomson, " for I never think a body gets anything at these stand-up meals." She put a generous helping of trifle on a plate and handed it to Elizabeth. " And mind to say there's chocolate shape as well, and there's a kind of apricot souffley thing too. Papa brought in the pine-apple. Wasn't it real mindful of him ? "

" It was indeed," said Elizabeth heartily, as she set off with her plates.

The first person she encountered was Mr. Taylor, skipping about with his fourth cup of tea.

"Toad, Miss Seton," he cried. "Where are the gemen? No, thanks: not that length yet, Jessie" as the daughter of the house passed with a plate cakes. "Since you're so pressing, I'll take a peny-tling."

"Nice girl, Jessie," he observed, as that affronted damsel passed on. "Papa well, Miss Seton?"

"Quite well, thank you."

"That's right. Yon was a fine sermon on Sabbath mornin'. Niver heard the minister better."

"I'm glad," said Elizabeth. "I shall tell Father."

"Ay, do——we must encourage him." Mr. Taylor put what was left of his cake into his mouth, took a large gulp of tea. "It's a difficult field. Nobody knows that better than me."

"I'm sure no one does," said Elizabeth politely but vaguely. Mr. Taylor blew his nose with a large red silk handkerchief.

"Miss Seton," he said, coming close to her, and speaking confidentially, "our Sabbath-school social's comin' off on Tuesday week, that's the ninth. Would you favour us with a song? Something semi-sacred, you know."

"Of course I shall sing for you," said Elizabeth; "but couldn't I sing something quite secular or quite sacred? I don't like ' semi ' things."

Mr. Taylor stood on tiptoe to put himself more on a level with his tall companion, cocked his head and looked rather like a robin.

"What's the matter with ' The Better Land '?" he asked.

Elizabeth smiled down at him and shook her head.

"Ah, well! I leave it to you, Miss Seton. Here," he caught her arm as she was turning away, "you'll

remind Papa that he's to take the chair t nigh
Tea on the table at seven-thirty."

"Yes, I'll remind him. Keep your mi eas
Mr. Taylor. Father and I'll both be the re.

"Thank you, Miss Seton; that 'll be al right,
then;" and Mr. Taylor took his empty up to his
hostess, while Elizabeth, seeing the two Miss
Hendrys unoccupied for the moment, deposited
with them the meringue and trifle.

She complimented Miss Hendry on her elegant
appearance and admired Miss Flora's hand-made
collar, and left them both beaming. She brought a
pink meringue to Mrs. Taylor and soothed her fears
of the consequences, while that lady hung her head
coyly on one side and said, " Ye're temptin' me ;
ye're temptin' me ! "

Supper had reached the fruit and chocolate stage
when Jessie Thomson brought Stewart Stevenson
and introduced him to Elizabeth Seton.

"I wanted to tell you how much I liked your
song," he began.

"How kind of you ! " said Elizabeth. " I think
myself it's a nice song."

"I don't know anything about music," continued
Mr. Stevenson.

"Was that why you said you liked my song
instead of my singing ? "

"Yes," he said ; and they both laughed.

They were deep in the subject of Scots ballads
when Mr. Inverarity came along with dates on a
majolica dish in one hand, his other hand behind
his back.

"A little historical matter," he said, offering
the dates. "No ? Then," he produced a silver
dish with the air of a conjurer, " a chocolate ? "

Elizabeth chose deliberately.

" I'm looking for the biggest," she said. " You see I'm greedy."

" Not at all," said Mr. Inverarity. " Sweets to the sweet ; " and he passed on his jokesome way.

" Sweets to the sweet," repeated Elizabeth. " Isn't it funny ? Words that were dropped with violets over the drowned Ophelia now furnish witticisms for suburban young men."

" Miss Seton," said Mrs. Thomson, bustling up, " you're here. We're going back to the drawing-room now to have a little more music." She dropped her voice to a hoarse whisper. " Papa's asked Mr. Taylor to sing. Jessie 'll be awful ill-pleased, but he's an old friend."

" Does he want to sing ? " asked Elizabeth.

" Dyin' to," said Mrs. Thomson.

Back to the drawing-room flocked the company, and Mr. Taylor, to use his own words, " took the floor." Jessie was standing beside the Simpsons and saw him do it.

" What a funny little man that is ! " said Miss Simpson languidly. " What's he going to do now ? "

" The dear knows," said Jessie bitterly.

They were not left long in doubt.

Mr. Taylor struck an attitude.

" Ladies and gentlemen," he began, " I have been asked to favour you with a song, but with your kind permission I'll give you first a readin'." He fumbled in his pocket and brought out a newspaper cutting. " It's a little bit I read in the papers," he explained, " very comical."

The " little bit " from the newspapers was in what is known in certain circles as " guid auld Doric," and it seemed to be about a feather-bed and a lodger, but so amused was Mr. Taylor at the joke he had last made, and so convulsed was he at

2

one he saw coming, that very little was heard
except his sounds of mirth.

Laughter is infectious, especially after supper,
and the whole room rocked with Mr. Taylor. Only
Jessie sat glum, and the Simpsons smiled but wanly.
Greatly encouraged by the success of his reading,
Mr. Taylor proceeded with his song, a rollicking
ditty entitled " Miss Hooligan's Christmas Cake."
It was his one song, his only song. It told, at
length, the ingredients of the cake and its effect on
Tim Mooney, who

> " lay down on the sofa
> And said that he wished he was dead."

The last two lines of the chorus ran :

> " It would kill a man twice to eat half a slice
> Of Miss Hooligan's Christmas Cake."

Uproarious applause greeted Mr. Taylor's efforts,
and he was so elated that it was with difficulty Mr.
Thomson restrained him from singing it all over
again.

" You've done fine, man," he whispered. " Mind
you're the superintendent of the Sabbath school."

Mr. Taylor's face sobered.

" Thomson, ye don't think it's unbecoming of me
to sing ' Miss Hooligan ' ? I've often sang it and
no harm thought, but I wouldn't for the world
bring discredit on ma office. I did think of gettin'
up ' Bonnie Mary o' Argyle.' It would mebbe have
been more wise-like."

" No, no, Taylor ; I was only joking. ' Miss
Hooligan's ' fine. I like it better every time I hear
it. There's no ill in it. I'm sorry I spoke."

Meantime Jessie was trying to explain away Mr.

Taylor to the Simpsons, who continued to look disgusted. Elizabeth Seton, standing near, came to her aid.

" Isn't Mr. Taylor delicious ? " she said. " Quite as good as Harry Lauder, and you know "—she turned to Miss Muriel Simpson—" what colossal sums people in London pay Harry Lauder to sing at their parties."

Miss Muriel knew little of London and nothing of London parties, but she liked Elizabeth's assuming she did, so she replied with unction, " That is so."

" Well," said Miss Gertrude, " I never can see why people rave about Harry Lauder. I see nothing funny in vulgarity myself, but look at the crowds ! "

" Perhaps," said Elizabeth, " the crowd has a vulgar mind. I wouldn't wonder ; " and she turned away, to find Stewart Stevenson at her elbow.

" I say, Miss Seton," he said, " I wonder if you would care to see that old ballad-book I was telling you about ? "

" I would, very much," said Elizabeth heartily. " Bring it, won't you, some afternoon ? I am in most afternoons about half-past four."

" Thanks very much—I would like to. . . . Well, good-night."

It seemed to strike every one at the same moment that it was time to depart. There was a general exodus, and a filing upstairs by the ladies to the best bedroom for wraps, and to the parlour on the part of the men, for overcoats and goloshes, or snow-boots as the case might be.

Elizabeth stood in the lobby waiting for her cab, and watched the scene.

As Miss Waterston tripped downstairs in a blue cashmere cloak with a rabbit fur collar Mr. Inverarity emerged from the parlour, with his music sticking out of his coat-pocket.

Together they said good-night to Mr. and Mrs. Thomson, and told Jessie how much they had enjoyed the party. "We've just had a lovely evening, Jessie," said Miss Waterston.

"Awfully jolly, Miss Thomson," said Mr. Inver-arity.

"Not at all," was Jessie's reply; and the couple departed together, having discovered that they both lived "West."

The Simpsons, clad in the smartest of evening cloaks, were addressing a few parting remarks to Jessie, when Mr. and Mrs. Taylor took, so to speak, the middle of the stage. Mrs. Taylor had turned up her olive-green silk skirt and pinned it in a bunch round her waist. Over this she wore a black circular waterproof from which emerged a pair of remarkably thin legs ending in snow-boots. An aged black bonnet—"ma prayer-meeting bonnet" she would have described it—crowned her head.

They advanced arm in arm till they stood right in front of their host and hostess, then Mr. Taylor made a speech.

"A remarkably successful evenin', Mrs. Thomson, as I'm sure everybody 'll admit. You've entertained us well; you've fed us sumptuous; you've——"

"Now, Mr. Taylor," Mrs. Thomson interrupted, "you'll fair affront us. It's you we've to thank for coming, and singing, and I'm sure I hope you'll be none the worse of all—there, there, are you really going? Well, good-night. I'm sure it's real nice to see you and Mrs. Taylor always so affectionate —isn't it, Papa?"

"That's so," agreed Mr. Thomson.

" Mrs. Thomson," said Mr. Taylor solemnly, " me and my spouse are sweethearts still."

Mrs. Taylor looked coyly downwards, murmuring what sounded like " Aay-he " ; then, with her left hand (her right hand being held by her lover-like husband), she seized Mrs. Thomson's hand and squeezed it. " I'll hear on Sabbath if ye're the worse of it," she said hopefully. " It's been real nice, but I sneezed twice in the bedroom, so I doubt I've got a tich of cold. But I'll go home and steam my head, and that 'll mebbe take it in time."

" Yer cab has came," Annie, the servant, whispered hoarsely to Elizabeth.

" Thank you," said Elizabeth. Then a thought struck her : " Mrs. Taylor, won't you let me drive you both home ? I pass your door. Do let me."

" I'm sure, Miss Seton, you're very kind," said Mrs. Taylor.

" Thoughtful, right enough," said her husband ; and, amid a chorus of good-nights, Elizabeth and the Taylors went out into the night.

Half an hour later the exhausted Thomson family sat in their dining-room. They had not been idle, for Mrs. Thomson believed in doing at once things that had to be done. Mr. Thomson and Robert had carried away the intruding chairs, and taken the " leaf " out of the table. Jessie had put all the left-over cakes into a tin box, and folded away the tablecloth and d'oyleys. Mrs. Thomson had herself carefully counted and arranged her best cups and saucers in their own cupboard, and was now busy counting the fruit knives and forks and teaspoons.

" Only twenty-three ! Surely Annie's niver let a teaspoon go down the sink."

"Have a sangwich, Mamma," said her husband.
"The spoon 'll soon turn up."

Mrs. Thomson took a sandwich and sat down on a
chair. "Well," she said slowly, "we've had them,
and we'll not need to have them for a long time
again."

"It's been a great success," said Mr. Thomson,
taking a mouthful of lemonade. "Eh, Jessie?"

"It was very nice," said Jessie, "and as you say,
Mamma, we'll not need to have another for a long
time. Mr. Taylor's the limit," she added.

"He enjoyed himself," said her father.

"He's an awful man to eat," said Mrs. Thomson.
"It's not the thing to make remarks about guests'
appetites, I know, but he fair surpassed himself
to-night. However, Mrs. Taylor, poor body, 's
quite delighted with him."

"He sang well," said Mr. Thomson. "I niver
heard 'Miss Hooligan' better. Quite a lot of talent
we had to-night, and Miss Seton's a treat. Nobody
can sing like her, to my mind."

"That's true," said his wife. "Mr. Stevenson
seems a nice young man, Jessie. What does he
do?"

"He's an artist," said Jessie. "I met him at
the Shakespeare Readings. Muriel Simpson thinks
he's awfully good-looking."

"Muriel Simpson's not, anyway," said Alick,
"She's a face like a scone, and it's all floury too,
like a scone."

"Alick," said his father, "it's high time you were
in bed, my boy. We'll be hearing about this in the
morning. What about your lessons?"

"Lessons!" cried Alick shrilly. "How could I
learn lessons and a party goin' on?"

"Quite true," said Mr. Thomson. "Well, it's

only once in a while. Rubbert,"—to his son who
was standing up yawning,—" you're no great society
man."

Robert shook his head.

" I haven't much use for people at any time," he
said, " but I fair hate them at a party."

And Mr. Thomson laughed in an understanding
way as he went to lift in the mat and lock the front
door and make Jeanieville safe for the night.

CHAPTER III

" When that I was and a little tiny boy,
    With a hey ho hey, the wind and the rain."
                                    Twelfth Night.

THE Reverend James Seton sat placidly eating his breakfast while his daughter Elizabeth wrestled in spirit with her young brother.

" No, Buff, you are *not* to tell yourself a story. You must sup your porridge."

Buff slapped his porridge vindictively with his spoon and said, " I wish all the millers were dead."

" Foolish fellow," said his father, as he took a bit of toast.

" Come away," said Elizabeth persuasively, scooping a hole in the despised porridge, " we'll make a quarry in the middle." She filled it up with milk. " There ! We've made a great deep hole, big enough to drown an army. Now—one sup for the King, and one for the boys in India, and one for—for the partridge in the pear-tree, and one for the poor little starved pussy downstairs."

Buff twisted himself round to look at his sister's face.

" Yes, there is. Ellen found it last night at the kitchen door. If you finish your breakfast quickly, you may run down and see it before prayers."

" What's it like ? " gurgled Buff, as the porridge slid in swift spoonfuls down his throat.

" Grey, with a black smudge on its nose and such a *little* tail."

" Set me down," said Buff, with the air of one who would behold a cherished vision.

Elizabeth untied his napkin, and in a moment they heard him clatter down the kitchen stairs.

Elizabeth met her father's eyes and smiled. " Funny Buff! Isn't it odd his passion for cats ? Oh, Father, you haven't asked about the party ? "

Mr. Seton passed his cup to be filled.

" That is only my second, isn't it ? " he asked. " Well, I hope you had a pleasant evening ? "

Elizabeth wrinkled her brows as she filled her cup. " Pleasant ? Warm, noisy, over-eaten, yes —but pleasant ? And yet, do you know, it was pleasant because the Thomsons were so anxious to please. Dear Mrs. Thomson was so kind, stout and worried, and Mr. Thomson is such an anxious little pilgrim always ; and Jessie was so smart, and Robert—what a nice boy that is !—so obviously hated us all, and Alick's accent was as refreshing as ever. We got the most tremendously fine supper— piles and piles of things, and everybody ate such a lot, especially Mr. Taylor—' keeping up the taber- nacle ' he called it. I was sorry for Jessie with that little man. It is hard to rise to gentility when you are weighted with parents who will stick to their old friends, and our church-people, though they are of such stuff as angels are made, don't look well on the outside. I know Jessie felt they spoiled the look of the party."

" Poor Jessie ! " said Mr. Seton.

" Yes, poor Jessie ! I never saw Mr. Taylor so jokesome. He called her a ' good wee miss,' and shamed her in the eyes of the Simpsons (you don't know them—stupid, vulgar people). And then he sang ! Father, do you think ' Miss Hooligan ' is a fit song for the superintendent of the Sabbath school to sing ? "

Mr. Seton smiled indulgently.

" I don't think there's much wrong with ' Miss Hooligan,' " he said ; " she's a very old friend."

" You mean she's respectable through very age ? Perhaps to us, but I assure you the Simpsons were simply stunned last night at the first time of hearing."

Elizabeth poured some cream into her cup, then looked across at her father with her eyes dancing with laughter. " I laugh whenever I think of Mrs. Taylor," she explained—" *ma spouse*, as Mr. Taylor calls her. I don't think she has any mind really : her whole conversation is just a long tangle of symptoms, her own and other people's. What infinite interest she gets out of her neighbours' insides ! And then the preciseness of her dates— ' would it be Wensday ? No, it was Tuesday—no, Wensday it must ha' been.' "

Her father chuckled appreciatively at Elizabeth's reproduction of Mrs. Taylor's voice and manner, but he felt constrained to remark : " Mrs. Taylor's an excellent woman, Elizabeth. You're a little too given to laughing at people."

" Oh, Father, if a minister's daughter can't laugh, what is the poor thing to do ? But, seriously, I find myself becoming horribly minister's daughter-ish. I'm developing a ' hearty ' manner, I smile and smile, and I have that craving for knowledge of the welfare of absent members of families that is so distinguishing a feature of the female clergy. And I don't in the least want to be a typical ' minister's daughter.' "

" I think," said Mr. Seton dryly, " you might be many a worse thing." He rose as he spoke and brought a Bible from the table in the corner. " Ring the bell, will you ? The child will be late if he doesn't come now."

Even as he spoke the door was opened violently, and Buff came stumbling in, with a small frightened kitten in his arms.

" Father, look ! " he cried breathlessly, casting himself and his burden on his father's waistcoat. " It's a lost kitten, quite lost and very little—see the size of its tail. It's got no home, but Marget says it's got fleas and she won't let it live in her kitchen ; but you'll let it stay in your study, won't you, Father ? It'll sit beside you when you're writing your sermons, and then when I'm doing my lessons it'll cheer me up."

Mr. Seton gently stroked the little shivering ball of fur. " Not so tight, Buff. The poor beastie can scarcely breathe. Put it on the rug now, my son. Here are the servants for prayers." But the little lost kitten clung with sharp frightened claws to Mr. Seton's trousers, and Buff, liking the situation, made no serious effort to dislodge it.

The servants, Marget and Ellen, took their seats, and instantly Marget's wrath was aroused and her manners forgotten.

" Tak' that cat aff yer faither's breeks, David," she said severely.

" Shan't," said Buff, glowering at her over his shoulder.

" Don't be rude, my boy," said Mr. Seton.

" *She* was rude to the little cat, Father ; she said it had fleas."

" Well, well," said his father peaceably ; " be quiet now while I read."

Elizabeth rose and detached the kitten, taking it
and Buff on her knee, while her father opened the
Bible and read some verses from Jeremiah—words
that Jeremiah the prophet spake unto Baruch the
son of Neriah in the fourth year of Jehoiakim, the
son of Josiah, king of Judah. Elizabeth stroked
Buff's mouse-coloured hair and thought how remote
it all sounded. This day would be full of the usual
little busynesses — getting Buff away to school,
ordering the dinner, shopping, writing letters, seeing people—what had all that to do with Baruch,
the son of Neriah, who lived in the fourth year of
Jehoiakim ?

The moment prayers were over Buff leapt to his
feet, seized the kitten, and dashed out of the room.

" He's an ill laddie that," Marget observed, " but
there's wan thing aboot him, he's no' ill-kinded to
beasts."

" Marget," said Elizabeth, " you know quite well
that in your heart you think him perfection."

" No' me," said Marget ; " I think no man perfection. Are ye comin' to see aboot the denner the
noo, or wull I begin to ma front door ? "

" Give me three minutes, Marget, to see the boys
off."

Two small boys with school-bags on their back
came up the gravelled path. " Here comes Thomas
—and Billy following after. Buff ! Buff !—where
is the boy ? "

" Here," said Buff, emerging suddenly from his
father's study. " Where's my bag ? "

He paid no attention to his small companions,
and Thomas and Billy made no sign of recognition
to him.

" Are you boys not going to say good-morning ? "
asked Elizabeth, as she put on Buff's school-bag.

" Don't you know that when gentlefolk meet courtesies are exchanged ? "

The three boys looked at each other and murmured a greeting in a shame-faced way.

" Can you say your lessons to-day, Thomas ? " Elizabeth asked, buttoning the while Buff's overcoat.

" No," said Thomas, " but Billy can say his."

" This is singing day," said Billy brightly.

Billy was round and fat and beaming. Thomas was fat too, but inclined to be pensive. Buff was thin and seemed all one colour—eyes, hair, and complexion. Thomas and Billy were pretty children : Buff was plain.

" Uch ! " said Thomas.

" I thought you liked singing day," said Elizabeth.

" We did," said Buff, " but last day they asked me and Thomas to stop singing cos we were putting the others off the tune."

" Oh ! " said Elizabeth, trying not to smile. " Well, it's time you were off. Here's your Edinburgh rock." She gave each of them half a stick of rock, which they stuck in their mouths cigarwise.

" Be sure and come straight home," said Elizabeth to Buff.

" You'd better not come to tea with us to-day, Buff," said Thomas. " Mamma said yesterday it was about time we had a rest."

" I wasn't coming," said the outraged Buff.

Elizabeth put an arm round him as she spoke to Thomas.

" Mamma has quite enough with her own, Thomas. I expect when Buff joins you you worry her dreadfully. I think you and Billy had better come to tea here to-day, and after you have finished your lessons we'll play at ' Yellow Dog Dingo.' "

" Hurray ! " said Billy.

" And when we've finished ' Yellow Dog Dingo,' " said Buff, " will you play at ' Giantess ' ? "

" Well—for half an hour, perhaps," said Elizabeth. " Now run off, or I'll be Giantess this minute and eat you all up."

They moved towards the door ; then Thomas stopped and observed dreamily :

" I dreamt last night that Satan and his wife and baby were chasing me."

"'Oh, Thomas ! " said Elizabeth. She watched the three little figures in their bunchy little overcoats, with their arms round each other's necks, stumble out of the gate, then she shut the front door and went into her father's study.

Mr. Seton was standing in what, to him, was a very characteristic attitude. One foot was on a chair, his left hand was in his pocket, while in his right he held a smallish green volume. A delighted smile was on his face as Elizabeth entered.

" Aha, Father ! Caught you that time."

Mr. Seton put the book back on its shelf.

" My dear girl, I was only glancing at something that——"

" Only a refreshing glance at Scott before you begin your sermon, Father dear, and ' what for no ' ? Oh ! while I remember—the Sabbath-school social comes off on the ninth : you are to take the chair, and I'm to sing. I shall print it in big letters on this card and stick it on the mantelpiece, then we're bound to remember it."

Mr Seton was already at his writing-table.

" Yes, yes," he said in an absent-minded way. " Run away now, like a good girl. I'm busy."

"Yes, I'm going. Just look at the snug way Buff has arranged the kitten. Father, Thomas has been having nightmares about Satan in his domestic relations. Did you know Satan had a wife and baby——?"

"Elizabeth!"

"I didn't say it; it was Thomas. That boy has an original mind."

"Well, well, girl; but you are keeping me back."

"Yes, I'm going. There's just one thing—about the chapter at prayers. I was wondering—only wondering, you know—if Baruch the son of Neriah had any real bearing on our everyday life?"

Mr. Seton looked at his daughter, then remarked as he turned back to his work: "I sometimes think you are a very ignorant creature, Elizabeth."

But Elizabeth only laughed as she shut the door and made her way kitchenwards.

On the kitchen stairs she met Ellen the housemaid, who stopped her with a "Please, Miss Elizabeth," while she fumbled in the pocket of her print and produced a post card with a photograph on it.

"It's ma brither," she explained. "I got it this mornin'."

Elizabeth carried the card to the window at the top of the staircase and studied it carefully.

"I think he's like you, Ellen," she said. "How beautifully his hair is brushed!"

Ellen beamed. "He's got awful pretty prominent eyes," she said.

"Yes," said Elizabeth. "I expect you're very proud of him, Ellen. Is he your eldest brother?"

"Yes, mum. He's a butcher in the Co-operative and *awful* steady."

Elizabeth handed back the card.

" Thank you very much for letting me see it. How is your little sister's foot ? "

" It's keepin' a lot better, and ma mother said I was to thank you for the toys and books you sent her."

" Oh, that's all right. I'm so glad she's better. When you're doing my room to-day remember the mirrors, will you ? This weather makes them so dim."

" Yes, mum," said Ellen cheerfully, as she went to her day's work.

Elizabeth found Marget waiting for her. She had laid out on the kitchen-table all the broken meats from the pantry and was regarding the display gloomily. Marget had been twenty-five years with the Setons and was not so much a servant as a sort of Grand Vizier. She expected to be consulted on every point, and had the gravest fears about Buff's future because Elizabeth refused to punish him.

" It's no' kindness," she would say ; " it's juist saftness. He *should* be wheepit."

She adored the memory of Elizabeth's mother, who had died five years before, when Buff was a little tiny boy. She adored too " the Maister," as she called Mr. Seton, though deprecating his other-worldly, absent-minded ways. " It wadna dae if we were a' like the Maister," she often reminded Elizabeth. " Somebody maun think aboot washin's and things."

As to the Seton family—Elizabeth she thought well-meaning but " gey impident whiles " ; the boys in India, Alan the soldier and Walter the promising young civilian, she still described as " notorious ill laddies " ; while Buff (David Stuart was his christened name) she regarded as a little soul who, owing to an over-indulgent father and sister, was in danger of straying on the Broad Road were she not there to herd him by threats and admonitions into the Narrow Way.

Truth to say, she admired them all enormously, they were her " bairns," but often her eyes would fill with tears as she said, " They're a' fine, but the best o' them's awa'."

Sandy, the eldest, had died at Oxford in his last summer-term, to the endless sorrow of all who loved him. His mother—that gentle lady—a few months later followed him, crushed out of life by the load of her grief, and Elizabeth had to take her place and mother the boys, be a companion to her father, shepherd the congregation, and bring up the delicate little Buff, who was so much younger than the others as to seem like an only child.

Elizabeth had stood up bravely to her burden, and laughed her way through the many difficulties that beset her—laughed more than was quite becoming, some people said ; but Elizabeth always preferred disapproval to pity.

This morning she noted down all that Marget said was needed, and arranged for the simple meals. Marget was very voluble, and the difficulty was to keep her to the subject under discussion. She mixed up orders for the dinner with facts about the age of her relations in the most distracting way.

" Petaty-soup ! Aweel, the Maister likes them thick. As I was sayin', ma Aunty Marget has worked hard a' her days, she's haen a dizzen bairns, and noo she's ninety-fower an' needs no specs."

" Dear me," said Elizabeth, edging towards the door. " Well, I'll order the fish and the other things ; and remember oatcakes with the potato-soup, please."

She was half-way up the kitchen stairs when

Marget put her head round the door and said,
" That's to say if she's aye leevin', an' I've heard
no word to the contrary."

Elizabeth telephoned the orders, then proceeded
to dust the drawing-room—one of her daily duties.
It was a fairly large room, papered in soft green ;
low white bookcases on which stood pieces of old
china lined three sides ; on the walls were etchings
and prints, and over the fireplace hung a really
beautiful picture by a famous artist of Elizabeth's
mother as a girl. A piano, a table or two, a few large
armchairs, and a sofa covered in bright chintz
made up the furniture of what was a singularly
lovable and home-like room.

Elizabeth's dusting of the drawing-room was
something of a ceremonial : it needed three dusters.
With a silk duster she dusted the white bookcases
and the cherished china ; the chair legs and the
tables and the polished floor needed an ordinary
duster ; then she got a selvyt-cloth and polished the
Sheffield-plate, the brass candlesticks and tinder-
bóxes. After that she shook out the chintz curtains,
plumped up the cushions, and put her dusters in
their home in a bag that hung on the shutter.
" That's one job done," she said to herself, as she
stopped to look out of the window.

The Setons' house stood in a wide, quiet road,
with villas in gardens on both sides. It was an
ordinary square villa, but it was of grey stone and
fairly old, and it had some fine trees round it. Mr.
Seton often remarked that he never saw a house or
garden he liked so well, but then it was James
Seton's way to admire sincerely everything that was
his.

Just opposite rose the imposing structure of three
stories in red stone which sheltered Thomas and

Billy Kirke. Mr. Kirke was in business. Elizabeth suspected him—though with no grounds to speak of—of " soft goods." Anyway, from some mysterious haunt in the city " Papa " managed to get enough money to keep " Mamma " and the children in the greatest comfort, to help the widows and fatherless, and to entertain a large circle of acquaintances in most hospitable fashion. He was a cheery little man with a beard, absolutely satisfied with his lot in life.

Elizabeth looked out at the prospect somewhat drearily. It was a dull November day. Rain was beginning to fall heavily ; the grass looked sodden and dark. A message-boy went past, with his empty basket over his head, whistling a doleful tune. A cart of coal stopped at the Kirkes', and she watched the men carry it round to the kitchen premises. They had sacks over their shoulders to protect them from the rain, and they lifted the wet, shining lumps of coal into hamper-like baskets and staggered with them over the well-gravelled path. What a grimy job for them, Elizabeth thought, but everything seemed rather grimy this morning. Try as she would, she couldn't remember any really pleasant thing that was going to happen ; day after day of dreary doings loomed before her. She sighed, and then, so to speak, shook herself mentally.

Elizabeth had a notion that when one felt depressed the remedy was not to give oneself a pleasure, but to do some hated duty, so she now thought rapidly over distasteful tasks awaiting her. Buff's suit to be sponged with ammonia and mended, old clothes to be looked out for a jumble sale, a pile of letters to reply to. " Oh dear ! " said Elizabeth ; but she went resolutely upstairs, and by the time she had tidied out various drawers and laid out unneeded garments, and had brought brown paper and string and tied them into neat bundles, she felt distinctly more cheerful.

The mending of Buff's suit completed the cheering process ; for, in one of his trouser pockets, she found a picture drawn and coloured by that artist. It was a picture of Noah and the Ark, bold in conception if not very masterly in workmanship. Noah was represented with his head poked out of a skylight, his patriarchal beard waving in the wind, watching for the return of the dove ; but the artist must have got confused in his ornithology, for the fowl coming towards Noah was a fearsome creature with a beak like an eagle. Aloft, astride on a somewhat solid cloud, clad in a crown and a sort of pyjama-suit, sat what was evidently intended to be an angel of sorts—watching with interest the manœuvres of Noah and the eagle-like dove. And as Elizabeth smoothed out the crumpled masterpiece she wondered how she could have imagined herself dull when the house contained the Buffy-boy.

The writing-table in the drawing-room showed a pile of letters waiting to be answered. Elizabeth stirred the fire into a blaze, sniffed at a bowl of violets, and sat down to answer them. " Two bazaar circulars ! and both from people who have helped me. . . . Well, I must just buy things to send." She turned to the next. " How bills do come home to roost ! I wish I had paid this at the time. Now I must write a cheque—and my account so lean and shrunken. What an offence bills are ! "

Very reluctantly she wrote a cheque and looked at it wistfully before she put it into the envelope, and took up a letter from a person unknown, resident in Rothesay, asking her to sing in that town at a charity concert. "*I heard you sing while staying with my sister, Mrs. M'Cubbins, whom you know, and I will be pleased if you can stay the night——*" so ran the letter. "Pleased if I stay the night!" thought Elizabeth wrathfully. "I should just think I would if I went—which I won't, of course. Mrs. M'Cubbins' sister! That explains the impertinence." And she wrote a chill note regretting that she could not give herself the pleasure. An invitation to dinner was declined because it was for "Prayer-meeting night." Then she took up a long letter, much underlined, which she read through carefully before she began to write.

"MOST KIND OF AUNTS,—How can I possibly go to Switzerland with you this Christmas? Have I not a father? also a young brother? It's not because I don't want to go—you know how I would love it; but picture to yourself Father and Buff spending their Christmas alone! Would you not come to us? I propose it with diffidence, for I know you think in Glasgow dwelleth no good thing; but won't you try it? You know you have never given it a chance. A few hours on your way to the North is all you ever give us, and Glasgow can't be judged in an hour or two—nor its people either. I don't say that it would be in the least amusing for you, but it would be great fun for us, and you ought to try to be altruistic, dearest of aunts. You know quite well that Mr. Arthur Townshend will be quite all right without you for a little. He had probably lots of invitations for Christmas, being such a popular young man and——"

The opening of the gate and the sound of footsteps on the gravel made Elizabeth run to the window.

" Buff—*carrying* his coat and the rain pouring !
Of all the abandoned youths ! "

Buff dashed into the house, threw his overcoat
into one corner, his cap into another, and violently
assaulted the study door, kicking it when it failed
to open at the first attempt.

"Boy, what are you about ? " asked his father,
as Buff fell on his knees before the chair on which
lay, comfortably asleep, the little rescued kitten.

CHAPTER IV

" SIR TOBY BELCH. Does not our life consist of four elements ?
SIR ANDREW AGUECHEEK. Faith, so they say, but I think it
rather consists of eating and drinking."

Twelfth Night.

" POO-OR pussy ! " murmured Buff, laying his head beside his treasure on the cushion.

" Get up, boy," said Mr. Seton. " You carry kindness to animals too far."

" And he doesn't carry tidiness any way at all," said Elizabeth, who had followed Buff into the study. " He has strewed his garments all over the place in the most shocking way. Come along, Buff, and pick them up. . . . Father, tell him to come."

" Do as your sister says, Buff."

But Buff clung limpet-like to the chair and ex-postulated. " What's the good of putting things tidy when I'm putting them on again in a minute ? "

" There's something in that," Mr. Seton said, as he put back in the shelves the books he had been using.

" All I have to say," said Elizabeth, " is that if I had been brought up in this lax way I wouldn't be the example of sweetness and light I am now. Do as you are told, Buff. I hear Ellen bringing up luncheon."

Buff stowed the kitten under his arm and stood

up. " I'll pick them up," he said in a dignified way, " if Launcelot can have his dinner with me."

" *Who ?* " asked Elizabeth.

" This is him," Buff explained, looking down at the distraught face of the kitten peeping from under his arm.

" What made you call it Launcelot ? " asked Elizabeth, as her father went out of the room laughing.

" Thomas said to call him Topsy, and Billy said Bull's Eye was a nice name, but I thought he looked more like a Launcelot."

" Well—I'll take it while you pick up your coat and run and wash your hands. You'll be late if you don't hurry."

" Aw ! no sausages ! " said Buff, five minutes later, as he wriggled into his place at the luncheon-table.

" Can't have sausages every day, sonny," said his sister ; " the butcher-man would get tired making them for us."

" Aren't there any sausage-mines ? " asked Buff ; but his father and sister had begun to talk to each other, so his question remained unanswered.

Unless spoken to, Buff seldom offered a remark, but talked rapidly to himself in muffled tones, to the great bewilderment of strangers, who were apt to think him slightly deranged.

Ellen had brought in the pudding when Elizabeth noticed that her young brother was sitting with a tense face, his hands clenched in front of him and his legs moving rapidly.

She touched his arm to recall him to his surroundings. " *Don't touch me,*" he said through his teeth. " I'm a motor and I've lost control of myself."

He emitted a shrill " *Honk Honk*," to the delight of his father, who inquired if he were the car or the chauffeur.

" I'm both," said Buff, his legs moving even more rapidly. Ellen, unmoved by such peculiar table-manners, put his plate of pudding before him, and Buff, hearing Elizabeth remark that Thomas and Billy were in all probability even now on their way to school, fell to, said his grace, was helped into his coat, and left the house in almost less time than it takes to tell.

Mr. Seton and Elizabeth were drinking their coffee when Elizabeth said :

" I heard from Aunt Alice this morning."

" Yes ?   How is she ? "

" Very well, I think.   She wants me to go with her to Switzerland in December.   Of course I've said I can't go."

" Of course," said Mr. Seton placidly.

Elizabeth pushed away her cup.

" Father, I don't mind being noble, but I must say I do hate to have my nobility taken for granted."

" My dear girl !   Nobility——"

" Well," said Elizabeth, " isn't it pretty noble to give up Switzerland and go on plodding here ? Just look at the rain, and I must go away down to the district and collect for Women's Foreign Missions.   There are more amusing pastimes than toiling up flights of stairs and wresting shillings for the heathen from people who can't afford to give. I can hardly bear to take it."

" My dear, would you deny them the privilege ? "

It might almost be said that Elizabeth snorted.

" Privilege !   Oh, well . . . If any one else had said that—but you're a saint, Father, and I believe you honestly think it is a privilege to give. You must, for if it weren't for me I doubt if you would leave yourself anything to live on, but—oh! it's no use arguing. Where are you visiting this afternoon? "

" I really ought to go to Dennistoun to see that poor body, Mrs. Morrison."

" It's such a long way in the rain. Couldn't you wait for a better day? "

James Seton rose from the table and looked at the dismal dripping day, then he smiled down at his daughter. " After twenty years in Glasgow I'm about weather-proof, Lizbeth. If I don't go to-day I can't go till Saturday, and I'm just afraid she may be needing help. I'll see one or two other sick people on my way home."

Elizabeth protested no more, but followed her father into the hall and helped him with his coat, brushed his hat, and ran upstairs for a clean hand-kerchief for his overcoat pocket.

As they stood together there was a striking resemblance between father and daughter. They had the same tall slim figure and beautifully set head, the same broad brow and humorous mouth. But whereas Elizabeth's eyes were grey, and faced the world mocking and inscrutable, her father's were the blue hopeful eyes of a boy. Sorrow and loss had brought to James Seton's table their " full cup of tears," and the drinking of that cup had bent his shoulders and whitened his hair, but it had not touched his expression of shining serenity.

" Are you sure those boots are strong, Father? And have you lots of car-pennies? "

" Yes. Yes."

Elizabeth went with him to the doorstep and patted his back as a parting salutation.

" Now don't try to save money by walking in the rain ; that's poor economy. And oh ! have you the money for Mrs. Morrison ? "

" No, I have not. That's well-minded. Get me half a sovereign, like a good girl."

Elizabeth brought the money.

" We would need to be made of half-sovereigns. Remember Mrs. Morrison is only one of many. It isn't that I grudge it to the poor dears, but we aren't millionaires exactly. Well, good-bye, and now I'm off on the quest of Women's Foreign Mission funds."

Her father from half-way down the gravel-path turned and smiled, and Elizabeth's heart smote her.

" I'll try and go with jubilant feet, Father," she called.

A few minutes later she too was ready for the road, with a short skirt, a waterproof, and a bundle of missionary papers.

Looking at herself in the hall mirror, she made a disgusted face. " I hate to go ugly to the church-people, but it can't be helped to-day. My feet look anything but jubilant ; with these over-shoes I feel like a feather-footed hen."

Ellen came out of the dining-room, and Elizabeth gave her some instructions.

" If Master David is in before I'm back see that he takes off his wet boots at once, will you ? And if Miss Christie comes, tell her I'll be in for tea, and ask her to wait. And, Ellen, if Marget hasn't time —I know she has some ironing to do—you might make some buttered toast and see that there's a cheery fire."

" Yes, mum, I will," said Ellen earnestly.

Once out in the rain, Elizabeth began to tell

herself that there was really something rather nice about a thoroughly wet November day. It made the thought of tea-time at home so very attractive.

She jumped on a tram-car and squeezed herself in between two stout ladies. The car was very full, and the atmosphere heavy with the smell of damp waterproofs. Dripping umbrellas, held well away from the owners, made rivulets on the floor and caught the feet of the unwary, and an air of profound dejection brooded over every one. Generally, Elizabeth got the liveliest pleasure from listening to conversation in the car, but to-day every one was as silent as a canary in a darkened cage.

At Cumberland Street she got off, and went down that broad street of tall grey houses with their air of decayed gentility. Once, what is known as " better-class people " had had their dwellings there, but now the tall houses were divided into tenements, and several families found their home in one house. Soon Elizabeth was in meaner streets—drab, dreary streets which, in spite of witnesses to the contrary in the shape of frequent public-houses and pawn-shops, harboured many decent, hard-working people. From these streets, largely, was James Seton's congregation drawn.

She stopped at the mouth of a close and looked up her collecting book.

" 146. Mrs. Veitch—1s. Four stairs up, of course."

It was a very bright bell she rang when she reached the top landing, and it was a very tidy woman, with a clean white apron, who answered it.

" Good-afternoon, Mrs. Veitch," said Elizabeth.

" It's Miss Seton," said Mrs. Veitch. " Come in. I'll tak' yer umbrelly. Wull ye gang into the room ? I'm juist washin' the denner-dishes."

" Mayn't I come into the kitchen ? It's always so cosy."

" It's faur frae that," said Mrs. Veitch ; " but come in, if ye like."

She dusted a chair by the fireside, and Elizabeth sat down. Behind her, fitted into the wall, was the bed with its curtain and valance of warm crimson, and spotless counterpane. On her right was the grate brilliant from vigorous polishing, and opposite it the dresser. A table with a red cover stood in the middle of the floor, and the sink, where the dinner-dishes were being washed, was placed in the window. Mrs. Veitch could wash her dishes and look down on a main line railway and watch the trains rush past. The trains to Euston with their dining-cars fascinated her, and she had been heard to express a great desire to have her dinner on the train. " Juist for the wance, to see what it's like."

If perfect naturalness be good manners, Mrs. Veitch's manners were excellent. She turned her back on her visitor and went on with her washing-up.

" That's the London train awa' by the noo," she said, as an express went roaring past. " When Kate's in when it passes she aye says, ' There's yer denner awa then, Mither.' It's a kinda joke wi' us noo. It's queer I've aye had a notion to traivel, but traivellin's never come ma gait—except traivellin' up and doon thae stairs to the washin'-hoose."

Elizabeth began eagerly to comfort.

" Yes—travelling always seems so delightful, doesn't it ? I can't bear to pass through a station and see a London train go away without me. But somehow when one is going a journey it's never so nice. Things go wrong, and one gets cross and tired, and it isn't much fun after all."

" Mebbe no'," said Mrs. Veitch dryly, " but a body whiles likes the chance o' finding oot things for theirsel's."

" Of course," said Elizabeth, feeling snubbed.

Mrs. Veitch washed the last dish and set it beside the others to drip, then she turned to her visitor.

" It's money ye're efter, I suppose ? "

Elizabeth held out one of the missionary papers and said in an apologetic voice :

" It's the Zenana Mission. I called to see if you cared to give this year ? "

Mrs. Veitch dried her hands on a towel that hung behind the door, then reached for her purse (Elizabeth's heart nipped at the leanness of it) from its home in a cracked jug on the dresser-shelf.

" What for wud I no' give ? " she asked, and her tone was almost defiant.

" Oh," said Elizabeth, looking rather frightened, " you're like Father, Mrs. Veitch. Father thinks it's a privilege to be allowed to give."

" Ay, an' he's right. There's juist Kate and me, and it's no verra easy for twae weemen to keep a roof ower their heids, but we'll never be the puirer for the mite we gie to the Lord's treasury. Is't a shillin' ? "

" Yes, please. Thank you so much. And how is Kate ? Is she very busy just now ? "

" Ay. This is juist the busy time, ye ken, pairties and such like. She's workin' late near every nicht, and she's awful bad wi' indisgeestion, puir thing. But Kate's no' yin to complain."

" I'm sure she's not," said Elizabeth heartily. " I wonder—some time when things are slacker—if she would make me a blouse or two ? The last were so nice."

" Were they ? " asked Mrs. Veitch suspiciously.

" Ye aye say they fit perfect, and Kate says to me,
' Mither,' she says, ' I wonder if Miss Seton doesna
juist say it to please us ? ' "

" What ! " said Elizabeth, springing to her feet.
" Well, as it happens, I am wearing a blouse of
Kate's making now——" She quickly undid her
waterproof and pulled off the woolly coat she wore
underneath. " Now, Mrs. Veitch, will you dare to
tell that doubting Kate anything but that her
blouse fits perfectly ? "

Mrs. Veitch's face softened into a smile.

" Eh, lassie, ye're awfu' like yer faither," she
said.

" In height," said Elizabeth, " and perhaps in a
feature or two, but not, I greatly fear,"—she was
buttoning her waterproof as she spoke,—" not, Mrs.
Veitch, in anything that matters. Well, will you
give Kate the message, and tell her not to doubt
my word again ? I'm frightfully hurt——"

" Ay," said Mrs. Veitch. " Weel, ye see, she's no'
used wi' customers that are easy to please. Are
ye for aff ? "

" Yes, I must go. Oh ! may I see the room ?
It was being papered the last time I was here. Was
the paper a success ? "

Instead of replying, Mrs. Veitch marched across
the passage and threw open the door with an air.

Elizabeth had a way of throwing her whole
heart into the subject that interested her for the
moment, and it surprised and pleased people to
find this large and beautiful person taking such a
passionate (if passing) interest in them and their
concerns.

Now it was obvious she was thinking of nothing
in the world but this little best parlour with its
newly papered walls.

After approving the new wall-paper, she proceeded to examine intently the old steel engravings in their deep rosewood frames. The subjects were varied : " The Murder of Archbishop Sharp " hung above a chest of drawers ; " John Knox dispensing the Communion " was skyed above the sideboard ; " Burns at the Plough being crowned by the Spirit of Poesy " was partially concealed behind the door ; while over the fireplace brooded the face of that great divine, Robert Murray M'Cheyne. These and a fine old bureau filled with china proclaimed their owner as being " better," of having come from people who could bequeath goods and gear to their descendants. Elizabeth admired the bureau and feasted her eyes on the china.

" Just look at these cups—isn't it a *brave* blue ? "

" Ay," said Mrs. Veitch rather uncertainly ; " they were ma granny's. I wud raither hev hed rosebuds masel'—an' that wide shape cools the tea awfu' quick." She nodded mysteriously toward the door at the side of the fire which hid the concealed bed. " We've got a lodger," she said.

" What ! " cried Elizabeth, startled. " Is she in there now ? "

" Now ! " said Mrs. Veitch in fine scorn. " What for wud she be in the now ? She's at her wark. She's in a shop in Argyle Street."

" Oh ! " said Elizabeth. " Is she a nice lodger ? "

" Verra quiet ; gives no trouble," said Mrs. Veitch.

" And you'll make her so comfortable. Do you bake treacle scones for her ? If you do, she'll never leave you."

" I was bakin' this verra day. Could ye—wud it bother ye to carry a scone hame ? Mr. Seton's terrible fond o' a treacle scone. I made him a cup o' tea wan day he cam' in and he ett yin tae't, and he said he hedna tastit onything as guid sin' he was a callant."

"I know," said Elizabeth. "He told me. Of course I can carry the scones, if you can spare them."

In a moment Mrs. Veitch had got several scones pushed into a baker's bag and was thrusting it into Elizabeth's hands.

"I'll keep it dry under my waterproof," Elizabeth promised her. "My umbrella? Did I leave it at the door?"

"It's drippin' in the sink. Here it's. Good-bye, then."

"Good-bye, and very many thanks for everything—the subscription and the scones—and letting me see your room."

At the next house she made no long visitation. It was washing-day, and the mistress of the house was struggling with piles of wet clothes, sorting them out with red, soda-wrinkled hands, and hanging them on pulleys round the kitchen. Having got the subscription, Elizabeth tarried not an unnecessary moment.

"What a nuisance I am!" she said to herself, as the door closed behind her. "Me and my old Zenana Mission. It's a wonder she didn't give me a push downstairs, poor worried body!"

The next contributor had evidently gone out for the afternoon, and Elizabeth reflected ruefully that it meant another pilgrimage another day. The number of the next was given in the book as 171, but she paused uncertainly, remembering that there had been some mistake last year, and doubting if she had put it right. At 171 a boy was lounging, whittling a stick.

" Is there any one called Campbell in this close ? " she asked him.

" Wait you here," said the boy, " an' I'll rin up and see." He returned in a minute.

" Naw—nae Cam'l. There's a Robison an' a M'Intosh an' twa Irish-lukin' names. That's a'. Twa hooses emp'y."

" Thank you very much. It was kind of you to go and look. D'you live near here ? "

" Ay." The boy jerked his head backwards to indicate the direction. " Thistle Street."

" I see." Elizabeth was going to move on when a thought came to her. " D'you go to any Sunday school ? "

" Me ? Naw ! " He looked up with an impudent grin. " A'm whit ye ca' a Jew."

Elizabeth smiled down at the little snub-nosed face. " No, my son. Whatever you are, you're not that. Listen—d'you know the church just round the corner ? "

" Seton's kirk ? "

" Yes. Seton's kirk. I have a class there every Sunday afternoon at five o'clock—six boys just about your age. Will you come ? "

" A hevna claes nor naething."

" Never mind ; neither have the others. What's your name ? "

" Bob Scott."

" Well, Bob, I do wish you'd promise. We have such good times."

Bob looked sceptical.

" A whiles gang to Sabbath schules," he said, " juist till the swuree comes aff, and then A leave." His tone suggested that in his opinion Sabbath schools and good times were things far apart.

" I see. Well, we're having a Christmas-tree

quite soon. You might try the class till then. You'll come some Sunday? That's good. Now, if I were you I would go home out of the rain."

Bob resumed his whittling, and he looked carefully at his work as he said:

"I canna gang hame for ma faither: he's drunk, and he'll no' let's in."

"Have you had any dinner?"

"Uch, no. A'm no heedin' for't," with a fine carelessness.

Elizabeth tilted her umbrella over her shoulder the better to survey the situation. There was certainly little prospect of refreshment in this grey street which seemed to contain nothing but rain, but the sharp ting-ting of an electric tram passing in the street above brought her an idea, and she caught the boy's arm.

"Come on, Bob, and we'll see what we can get."

Two minutes brought them to a baker's shop, with very good-looking things in the window and a fat, comfortable woman behind the counter.

"Isn't this a horrible day, Mrs. Russel?" said Elizabeth. "And here's a friend of mine who wants warming up. What could you give him to eat, I wonder?"

Mrs. Russel beamed as if feeding little dirty ragged boys was just the thing she liked best to do.

"It's an awful day, as you say, Miss Seton, an' the boy's wet through. Whit would ye say to a hot tupp'ny pie an' a cup o' tea? The kettle's juist on the boil; I've been havin' a cup masel'— a body wants something to cheer them this weather." She laughed cheerily. "He could take it in at the back—there's a rare wee fire."

"That 'll be splendid," said Elizabeth; "won't it, Bob?"

"Ay," said Bob stolidly, but his little impudent starved face had an eager look.

Elizabeth saw him seated before the "rare wee fire" wolfing "tupp'ny pies," then she gathered up her collecting papers and prepared to go.

"Well! Good-bye, Bob; I shall see you some Sabbath soon. Where's that umbrella? It's a bad day for Zenana Missions, Mrs. Russel."

"Is that whit ye're at the day? I thought ye were doin' a bit o' *home* mission work."

She followed Elizabeth to the shop door.

"Poor little chap!" said Elizabeth. "Give him as much as he can eat, will you?"—she slipped some money into her hand,—"and put anything that's over into his pocket. I'm most awfully grateful to you, Mrs. Russel. It was too bad to plant him on you, but if people will go about looking so kind they're just asking to be put upon."

The rain was falling as if it would never tire. The street lamps had been lit, and made yellow blobs in the thick foggy atmosphere. The streets were slippery with that particular brand of greasy mud which Glasgow produces. "I believe I'll go straight home," thought Elizabeth.

She wavered for a moment, then: "I'll do Mrs. Martin and get the car at the corner of the street," she decided. "It's four o'clock, but I don't believe the woman will be tidied."

The surmise was only too correct. The door when Elizabeth reached it was opened by Mr. Martin—a gentleman of infinite leisure—who seemed uncertain what to do with her. Elizabeth tried to solve the difficulty by moving towards the kitchen, but he gently headed her off until a voice from within cried, "Come in, if ye like, Miss Seton, but A'm strippit."

The situation was not as acute as it sounded.
Mrs. Martin had removed her bodice, the better
to comb her hair, and Elizabeth shuddered to see
her lay the comb down beside a pat of butter, as
she cried to her husband, " John, bring ma ither
body here."

She was quite unabashed to be found thus in
deshabille, and talked volubly the while she twisted
up her hair and buttoned her " body." She was
a round robin-like woman with, as Elizabeth put
it, " the sweetest smile and the dirtiest house in
Glasgow."

" An' how's Papa this wet weather ? "

" Quite all right, thank you. And how are
you ? "

" Off and on, juist off and on. Troubled a lot
with the boil, of course." (Elizabeth had to think
for a minute before she realized this was English
for " the bile.") " Many a day, Miss Seton,
nothing 'll lie." Mrs. Martin made a gesture indicating what happened, and continued : " Mr. Martin
often says to me, ' Maggie,' he says, ' ye're no' fit
to work ; let the hoose alane,' he says. Divn't ye,
John ? " she asked, turning to her husband, who had
settled himself by the fire with an evening paper,
and receiving a grunt in reply. " But, Miss Seton,
there's no' a lazy bone in ma body and I canna
see things go. I must be up an' doin' : a hoose
juist keeps a body at it."

" It does," agreed Elizabeth, trying not to see
the unmade bed and the sink full of dirty dishes.

" An' whit are ye collectin' for the day ?
Women's Foreign Missions ? ' Go ye into all the
world.' We canna go oorsel's, but we can send
oor money. Where's ma purse ? "

She went over to the littered dresser and began

to turn things over, until she discovered the purse lurking under a bag of buns and a paper containing half a pound of ham. Elizabeth stood up as a hint that the shilling might be forthcoming, but Mrs. Martin liked an audience, so she sat down on a chair and put a hand on each knee. " Mr. Seton said on Sunday we were to give as the Lord had prospered us. Weel, I canna say much aboot that, we're juist aye in the same bit, but as A often tell ma man, Miss Seton, we must a' help each other, for we're a' gaun the same road—mebbe the heathen tae, puir things ! "

Mr. Martin grunted over his newspaper, and his wife continued : " There's John there—Mr. Martin, A'm meanin'—gits fair riled whiles aboot poalitics. He canna stand Tories by naething, they fair scunner him, but I juist say to him, ' John, ma man,' I says, ' let the Tories alane, for we're a' Homeward Bound.' "

Elizabeth stifled a desire to laugh, while Mr. Martin said with great conviction and some irrelevance, " Lyd George is the man."

" So he is," said his wife soothingly, " though A whiles think if he wud tak' a bit rest to hissel' it wud be a guid job for us a'."

" Well," said Elizabeth, opening her purse in an expectant way, " I must go, or I shall be late for tea."

" Here's yer shillun," said Mrs. Martin, rather with the air of presenting a not quite deserved tip. " An' how's wee David ? Yon's a rale wee favourite o' mine. Are ye gaun to mak' a minister o' him ? "

" Buff ? Oh, I don't think we quite know what to make of him."

Mrs. Martin leaned forward. " Hev ye tried a phrenologist ? " she asked earnestly.

" No," said Elizabeth, rather startled.

" A sister o' mine hed a boy an' she couldna think what to mak' o' him. He had no—no—whit d'ye ca' it ? "

Elizabeth nodded her comprehension.

" Bent ? " she suggested.

" Aweel, she tuk him to yin o' thae phrenologists, an' he said he wud be either an auctioneer or a chimist, and," she finished triumphantly, " a chimist he wus ! "

CHAPTER V

"Truly I would the gods had made thee poetical."

As You Like It.

IN the Setons' drawing-room a company was gathered for tea.

Ellen had remembered Elizabeth's instructions, and a large fire of logs and coal burned in the white-tiled grate. A low round table was drawn up before the fire, and on it tea was laid—a real tea, with jam and scones and cookies, cake and short-bread. On the brass muffin-stool a pile of buttered toast was keeping warm.

James Seton, who dearly loved his tea, was already seated at the table and was playing with the little green-handled knife which lay on his plate as he talked to Elizabeth's friend, Christina Christie. Thomas and Billy sat on the rug listening large-eyed to Buff, who was telling them an entirely apocryphal tale of how he had found an elephant's nest in the garden.

Launcelot lay on a cushion fast asleep.

"Elizabeth is late," said Mr. Seton.

"I think I hear her now," said Miss Christie; and a moment later the drawing-room door opened and Elizabeth put her head in.

"Have I kept you all waiting for tea? Ah!

Kirsty, bless you, my dear. No, I can't come in as I am. Just give me one minute to remove these odious garments—positively only a minute, Father. Yes, Ellen, bring tea, please."

The door closed again.

" And the egg was as big as a roc's egg," went on Buff.

" You never saw a roc's egg," Thomas reminded him, " so how can you know how big they are ? "

" I just know," said Buff, with dignity. " Father, how big is a roc's egg ? "

" A roc's egg," said Mr. Seton thoughtfully. " A great white thing, Sindbad called it, ' fifty good paces round.' As large as this room, Buff, anyway. Ah ! here's your sister."

" Now for tea," said Elizabeth, seating herself behind the teacups. " Sit on this side, Kirsty ; you'll be too hot there. What a splendid fire Ellen has given us. Well, Thomas, my son, what do you want first ? Bread-and-butter ? That's right ! Pass Billy some butter, Buff. I wouldn't begin with a cookie if I were you. No, not jam with the first bit, extravagant youth. Now, Kirsty, do put out your hand, as Marget would say, because, as you know, we have no manners in this house."

" I am having an excellent tea," said Miss Christie. " Ellen said you were collecting this afternoon, Elizabeth."

" Oh, Kirsty, my dear, I was. In the Gorbals, in the rain, begging for shillings for Women's Foreign Missions. And I didn't get them all in either, and I shall have to go back. Father, I'm frightfully intrigued to know what Mr. Martin does. What is his walk in life ? Go any time you like, he's always in the house. Can he be a night-watchman ? "

Mr. Seton helped himself to a scone.

" I had an idea," he said, " that Martin was a cabinetmaker, but he may have retired."

" Perhaps," said Buff, " he's a Robber. Robbers don't go out through the day, only at night with dark lanterns, and come in with sacks of booty."

Elizabeth laughed.

" No, Buff. I don't think that Mr. Martin has the look of a robber exactly. Perhaps he's only lazy. But I'm quite sure Mrs. Martin's efforts don't keep the house. Of all the dirty little creatures ! And so full of religion ! I've no use for people's religion if it doesn't make them keep a clean house. ' We're all Homeward Bound,' she said to me. ' So we are, Mrs. Martin,' said I, ' but you might give your fireside a brush-up in passing ! ' "

" Now, now, Elizabeth," said her father, " you didn't say that ! "

" Well, perhaps I didn't say it exactly, but I certainly thought it," said Elizabeth.

At this moment Buff, who had been gobbling his bread-and-butter with unseemly haste and keeping an anxious eye on a plate of cakes, saw Thomas take the very cake he had set his heart on, and he broke into a howl of rage. " He's taken my cake ! " he shouted.

" Buff, I'm ashamed of you," said his sister. " Remember, Thomas is your guest."

" He's not a *guest*," said Buff, watching Thomas stuff the cake into his mouth as if he feared that it might even now be wrested from him, " he's a pig."

" One may be both," said Elizabeth. " Never mind him, Thomas. Have another cake."

" Thanks," said Thomas, carefully choosing the largest remaining one.

"If Thomas eats so much," said Billy pleasantly, "he'll have to be put in a show. Mamma says so."

"Billy," said Miss Christie, "how is it that you have such a fine accent?"

"I don't know," said Billy modestly.

"It's because," Thomas hastened to explain,— "it's because we had an English nurse when Billy was little. I've a Glasgow accent myself," he added.

"My accent's Peeblesshire," said Buff, forgetting his wrongs in the interest of the conversation.

"Mamma says that's worse," said Thomas gloomily.

Mr. Seton chuckled. "You're a funny laddie, Thomas," he said.

"Kirsty," said Elizabeth, "this is no place for serious conversation; I haven't had a word with you. Oh! Father, how is Mrs. Morrison?"

"Very far through."

"Ah! Poor body. Is there nothing we can do for her?"

"No, my dear, I think not. She never liked taking help, and now she is past the need of it. I'm thankful for her sake her race is nearly run."

Thomas stopped eating. "Will she get a prize, Mr. Seton?" he asked:

James Seton looked down into the solemn china-blue eyes raised to his own and said, seriously and as if to an equal:

"I think she will, Thomas—the prize of her high calling in Jesus Christ."

Thomas went on with his bread-and-butter, and a silence fell on the company. It was broken by a startled cry from Elizabeth.

"Have you hurt yourself, girl?" asked her father.

" No, no. It's Mrs. Veitch's scones. To think I've forgotten them ! She sent them to you, Father, for your tea. Buff, run—no, I'll go myself ; " and Elizabeth left the room, to return in a moment with the paper-bagful of scones.

" I had finished," said Mr. Seton meekly.

" We'll all have to begin again," said his daughter. " Thomas, you could eat a bit of treacle scone, I know."

" The scones will keep till to-morrow," Miss Christie reminded her.

" Yes," said Elizabeth, " but Mrs. Veitch will perhaps be thinking we are having them to-night, and I would feel mean to neglect her present. You needn't smile in that superior way, Kirsty Christie."

" They are excellent scones," said Mr. Seton, " and I'm greatly obliged to Mrs. Veitch. She is a fine woman—comes of good Border stock."

" She's a dear," said Elizabeth ; " though she scares me sometimes, she is so utterly sincere. That's grievous, isn't it, Father ?—to think I live with such double-dealers that sincerity scares me."

Mr. Seton shook his head at her.

" You talk a great deal of nonsense, Elizabeth," he said, a fact which Elizabeth felt to be so palpably true that she made no attempt to deny it.

Later, when the tea-things had been cleared away and the three boys lay stretched on the carpet looking for a picture of the roc's egg in a copy of *The Arabian Nights*, James Seton sat down rather weariedly in one of the big chintz-covered chairs by the fire.

" You're tired, Father," said Elizabeth.

James Seton smiled at his daughter. " Lazy, Lizbeth, that's all—lazy and growing old ! "

" Old ? " said Elizabeth. " Why, Father, you're

the youngest person I have ever known. You're only about half the age of this weary worldling your daughter. You can never say you're old, wicked one, when you enjoy fairy tales just as much as Buff. I do believe that you would rather read a fairy tale than a theological book. He can't deny it, Kirsty. Oh, Father, Father, it's a sad thing to have to say about a U.F. minister, and it's sad for poor Kirsty, who has been so well brought up, to have all her clerical illusions shattered."

" Oh, girl," said her father, " do you never tire talking ? "

" Never," said Elizabeth cheerfully ; " but I'm going to read to you now for a change. Don't look so scared, Kirsty ; it's only a very little poem."

" I'm sure I've no objection to hearing it," said Miss Christie, sitting up in her chair.

Elizabeth lifted a blue-covered book from a table, sat down on the rug at her father's feet, and began to read. It was only a very little poem, as she had said—a few exquisite strange lines. When she finished she looked eagerly up at her father and —" Isn't it magical ? " she asked.

" Let me see the book," said Mr. Seton, and at once became engrossed.

" It's very nice," said Miss Christie ; " but your voice, Elizabeth, makes anything sound beautiful."

" Kirsty, my dear, how pretty of you ! "

Elizabeth's hands were clasped round her knees, and she sat staring into the red heart of the fire as she repeated :

> " Who said ' All Time's delight
> Hath she for narrow bed :
> Life's troubled bubble broken ' ?
> That's what I said."

Kirsty, I love that—' Life's troubled bubble broken.' "

" Say it to me, Lizbeth," said Buff, who had left his book when his sister began to read aloud.

" You wouldn't understand it, sonny."

" But I like the sound of the words," Buff protested.   So Elizabeth said it again.

> " Who said Peacock Pie ?
> The old King to the Sparrow . . ."

" I like it," said Buff, when she had finished. " Say me another."

" Not now, son.   I want to talk to Kirsty now. When you go to bed I shall read you a lovely one about a Zebra called Abracadeebra.   Have you done your lessons for to-morrow ?   No ?   Well, do them now.   Thomas and Billy will do them with you—and in half an hour I'll play ' Yellow Dog Dingo.' "

Having mapped out the evening for her young brother, Elizabeth rose from her lowly position on the hearth-rug, drew forward a chair, and said, " Now, Kirsty, we'll have a talk."

That Elizabeth Seton and Christian Christie should be friends seemed a most improbable thing. They were both ministers' daughters, but there any likeness ended.   It seemed as if there could be nothing in common between this tall golden Elizabeth with her impulsive ways, her rapid heedless speech, her passion for poetry, her faculty for making new friends at every turn, and Christina, short, dark, and neat, with a mind as well-ordered as her raiment, suspicious of strangers and chilling with her nearest—and yet a very true friendship did exist.

" How is your mother ? " asked Elizabeth.

" Mother's wonderful.   Father has been in the house three days with lumbago.   Jeanie has a cold too.   I think it's the damp weather.   This is my month for housekeeping. I wish, Elizabeth, you would tell me some new puddings. Archie says ours are so dull."

Elizabeth immediately threw herself into the subject of puddings.

" I know one new pudding, but it takes two days to make and it's very expensive. We only have it for special people. You know ' Aunt Mag,' of course ? and ' Uncle Tom ' ? That's only ' Aunt Mag ' with treacle. Semolina, sago, big rice—we call those milk things, we don't dignify them by the name of pudding. What else is there ? Tarts, oh ! and bread puddings, and there's that greasy kind you eat with syrup, suet dumplings. A man in the church was very ill, and the doctor said he hadn't any coating or lining or something inside him, because his wife hadn't given him any suet dumplings."

" Oh, Elizabeth ! "

" A fact, I assure you," said Elizabeth. " We always have a suet dumpling once a week because of that. I'm afraid I'm not being very helpful, Kirsty. Do let's think of something quite new, only it's almost sure not to be good. That is so discouraging about the dishes one invents. . . . Apart from puddings, how is Archie ? "

" Oh, he's quite well, and doing very well in business. He has Father's good business head."

" Yes," said Elizabeth. She did not admire anything about the Rev. Johnston Christie, least of all his business head. He was a large pompous man, with a booming voice and a hearty manner, and he had what is known in clerical circles as a " suburban charge." Every Sunday the well-dressed, well-fed congregation culled from villadom to which he ministered filled the handsome new church, and Mr. Christie's heart grew large within him as he looked at it. He was a poor preacher but an excellent organizer : he ran a church as he would have run a grocery establishment. His son Archie was exactly like him, but Christina had something of her mother, a deprecating little woman with feeble health and a sense of humour whom Elizabeth called Chuchundra after the musk-rat in the *Jungle Book* that could never summon up courage to run into the middle of the room.

" Yes," said Elizabeth, " I foresee a brilliant future for Archie, full of money and motor-cars and knighthoods."

" Oh ! I don't know," said Christina, " but I think he has the knack of making money. How are your brothers ? "

" Both well, I'm glad to say. Walter has got a new job—in the Secretariat—and finds it vastly entertaining. Alan seems keener about polo than anything else, but he's only a boy after all."

" You talk as if you were fifty at least."

" I'm getting on," said Elizabeth. " Twenty-eight's a fairly ripe age, don't you think ? "

" No, I don't," said Christina somewhat shortly. Christina was thirty-five.

" Buff asked me yesterday if I remembered Mary Queen of Scots," went on Elizabeth, " and he alluded to me in conversation with Thomas as ' my elderly nasty sister.' "

" Cheeky little thing ! " said Christina. " You spoil that child."

Elizabeth laughed, and by way of turning the conversation asked Christina's advice as to what would sell best at coming bazaars. At all bazaar work Christina was an expert, and she had so many valuable hints to give that long before she had come to an end of them Elizabeth was hauled away to play " Yellow Dog Dingo."

Christina had little liking for children, and it was with unconcealed horror that she watched her friend bounding from *Little God Nqu* (Billy) to *Middle God Nquing* (Buff), then to *Big God Nqong* (Thomas), begging to be made different from all other animals, and wonderfully popular by five o'clock in the afternoon.

It was rather an exhausting game and necessitated much shouting and rushing up and down stairs, and after every one had had a chance of playing in the title rôle, Elizabeth sank breathless, flushed and dishevelled, into a chair.

" Well, I *must* say——" said Christina.

" Come on again," shouted Billy, while Thomas and Buff loped up and down the room.

" No—no," panted Elizabeth, " you're far too hot as it is. What will ' Mamma ' say if you go home looking like Red Indians ? "

Mr. Seton, quite undisturbed by the noise, had been engrossed in the poetry book, but now he laid it down and looked at his watch.

" I must be going," he said.

But the three boys threw themselves on him— " A bit of Willy Wud ; just a little bit of Willy Wud," they pleaded.

James Seton was an inspired teller of tales, and Willy Wud was one of his creations. His adventures—and surely no one ever had stranger and more varied adventures—made a sort of serial story for " after tea " on winter evenings.

" Where did we leave him ? " he asked, sitting down obediently.

" Don't you remember, Father ? " said Buff. " In the Robbers' Cave."

" He was just untying that girl," said Thomas.

" She wasn't a girl," corrected Billy, " she was a princess."

" It's the same thing," said Thomas. " He was untying her when he found the Robber Chief looking at him with a knife in his mouth."

So the story began and ended all too soon for the eager listeners, and Mr. Seton hurried away to his work.

" Say good-night, Thomas and Billy," said Elizabeth, " and run home. It's very nearly bed-time."

" To-morrow's Saturday," said Thomas suggestively.

" So it is. Ask Mamma if you may come to tea, and come over directly you have had dinner."

Thomas looked dissatisfied.

" Couldn't I say to Mamma you would like us to come to dinner ? Then we could come just after breakfast. You see, there's that house we're building——"

" I'm going to buy nails with my Saturday penny," said Billy.

" By all means come to dinner," said Elizabeth, " if Mamma doesn't mind. Good-night, sonnies—now run."

She opened the front door for them, and watched them scud across the road to their own gate—then she went back to the drawing-room.

" I must be going too," said Miss Christie, sitting back more comfortably in her chair.

" It's Band of Hope night," said Elizabeth.

Buff had been marching up and down the room, with Launcelot in his arms, telling himself a story, but he now came and leant against his sister. She stroked his hair as she asked, " What's the matter, Buffy boy ? "

" I wish," said Buff, " that I lived in a house where people didn't go to meetings."

" But I'm not going out till you're in bed. We shall have time for reading and everything. Say good-night to Christina, and see if Ellen has got your bath ready. And, Buff," she said, as he went out of the door, " pay particular attention to your knees—scrub them with a brush ; and don't forget your fair large ears, my gentle joy."

" Those boys are curiosities," said Miss Christie. " What house is this they're building ? "

" It's a Shelter for Homeless Cats," said Elizabeth, " made of orange boxes begged from the grocer. I think it was Buff's idea to start with, but Thomas has the clever hands. Must you go ? "

" These chairs are too comfortable," said Miss Christie, as she rose ; " they make one lazy. If I were you, Elizabeth, I wouldn't let Buff talk to himself and tell himself stories. He'll grow up queer. . . . You needn't laugh."

" I'm very sorry, Christina. I'm afraid we're a frightfully eccentric family, but you'll come and see us all the same, won't you ? "

Miss Christie looked at her tall friend, and a quizzical smile lurked at the corner of her rather dour mouth. " Ay, Elizabeth," she said, " you sound very humble, but I wouldn't like to buy you at your own valuation, my dear."

Elizabeth put her hands on Christina's shoulders as she kissed her good-night. " You're a rude old Kirsty," she said, " but I daresay you're right."

CHAPTER VI

" How now, sir ? What are you reasoning with yourself ?
Nay, I was rhyming; 'tis you that have the reason."
Two Gentlemen of Verona.

ABOUT a fortnight later—it was a Saturday afternoon—an April day strayed into November, and
James Seton walked in his garden and was grateful.

He had his next day's sermon in his hand and as
he walked he studied it, but now and again he would
lift his head to look at the blue sky, or he would
stoop and touch gently the petals of a Christmas-
rose, flowering bravely if sootily in the border.
Behind the hedge, on the drying green, Thomas and
Billy and Buff disported themselves. They had
been unusually quiet, but now the sound of raised
voices drew Mr. Seton to the scene of action. Looking over the hedge, he saw an odd sight. Thomas
lay grovelling on the ground ; Billy, with a fierce
black moustache sketched on his cherubic face, sat
on the roof of the ash-pit ; while Buff, a bulky sack
strapped on his back, struggled in the arms of
Marget the cook.

" Gie me that bag, ye ill laddie," she was saying.

" What's the matter, Marget ? " Mr. Seton asked
mildly.

Buff was butting Marget wildly with his head, but hearing his father's voice, he stopped to explain.

" It's my sins, Father," he gasped.

" It's naething o' the kind, sir ; it's ma bag o' claes-pins. Stan' up, David, this meenit. D'ye no' see ye're fair scrapin' it i' the mud ? "

Thomas raised his head.

" We're pilgrims, Mr. Seton," he explained. " I'm Hopeful, and Buff's Christian. This is me in Giant Despair's dungeon ; " and he rolled on his face and realistically chewed the grass to show the extent of his despair.

" But you've got your facts wrong," said Mr. Seton. " Christian had lost his load long before he got to Doubting Castle."

" Then," said Buff, picking himself up and wriggling out of the straps which tied the bag to his person,—" then, Marget, you can have your old clothes-pins."

" Gently, my boy," said his father. " Hand the bag to Marget and say you're sorry."

" Sorry, Marget," said Buff in a very casual tone, as he heaved the bag at her.

Marget received it gloomily, prophesied the probable end of Buff, and went indoors.

Buff joined Thomas in the dungeon of Doubting Castle.

" Why is Billy sitting up there ? " asked Mr. Seton.

" He's Apollyon," said Thomas, " and he's coming down in a minute to straddle across the way. By rights, I should have been Apollyon——"

Mr. Seton's delighted survey of the guileless fiend on the ash-pit roof was interrupted by Ellen, who came with a message that Mr. Stevenson had called and would Mr. Seton please go in.

In the drawing-room he found Elizabeth conversing with a tall young man, and from the fervour with which she welcomed his appearance he inferred that it was not altogether easy work.

" Father," said Elizabeth, " you remember I told you about meeting Mr. Stevenson at the Thomsons' party ? He has brought us such a treasure of a ballad book to look over. Do let my father see it, Mr. Stevenson."

James Seton greeted the visitor in his kind, absent-minded way, and sat down to discuss ballads with him, while Elizabeth, having, so to speak, laboured in rowing, lay back and studied Mr. Stevenson. That he was an artist she knew. She also knew his work quite well and that it was highly thought of by people who mattered. He had a nice face, she thought ; probably not much sense of humour, but tremendously decent. She wondered what his people were like. Poor, she imagined—perhaps a widowed mother, and he had educated himself and made every inch of his own way. She felt a vicarious stir of pride in the thought.

As a matter of fact she was quite wrong, and Stewart Stevenson's parents would have been much hurt if they had known her thoughts.

His father was a short, fat little man with a bald head, who had dealt so successfully in butter and ham that he now occupied one of the largest and reddest villas in Maxwell Park (Lochnagar was its name), and every morning was whirled in to business in a Rolls-Royce car.

For all his worldly success Mr. Stevenson senior remained a simple soul. His only real passion in life (apart from his son) was for what he called " time-pieces." Every room in Lochnagar contained at least two clocks. In the drawing-room

they had alabaster faces and were supported by
gilt cupids ; in the dining-room they were of
dignified black marble ; the library had one on
the mantelpiece and one on the writing-table—
both of mahogany with New Art ornamentations.
Two grandfather clocks stood in the hall—one on
the staircase and one on the first landing.   Mr.
Stevenson liked to have one minute's difference in
the time of each clock, and when it came to striking
the result was nerve-shattering.   Mrs. Stevenson
had a little nut-cracker face and a cross look which,
as her temper was of the mildest, was most mis-
leading.   Her toque—she wore a toque now instead
of a bonnet—was always a little on one side, which
gave her a slightly distracted look.   Her clothes
were made of the best materials and most expen-
sively trimmed, but somehow nothing gave the little
woman a moneyed look.   Even the Russian sables
her husband had given her on her last birthday
looked, on her, more accidental than opulent.   Her
husband was her oracle and she hung on his words,
invariably capping all his comments on life and
happenings with " Ay.   That's it, Pa."

Their pride in their son was touching.   His
height, his good looks, his accent, his " gentlemanly " manners, his love of books, his talent as
an artist, kept them wondering and amazed.   They
could not imagine how they had come to have such
a son.   It was certainly disquieting for Mr. Stevenson who read nothing but the newspapers on week-
days and *The British Weekly* on the Sabbath, and
for his wife who invariably fell asleep when she
attempted to dally with even the lightest form of
literature, to have a son whose room was literally
lined with books and who would pore with every
mark of enjoyment over the dullest of tomes.

His artistic abilities were not such a phenomenon, and could be traced back to a sister of Mr. Stevenson's called Lizzie who had sketched in crayons and died young.

Had Stewart Stevenson been a poor man's son he would probably have worked long without recognition, eaten the bread of poverty and found his studio-rent a burden, but, so contrariwise do things work, with an adoring father and a solid Ham and Butter business at his back his pictures found ready purchasers.

To be honest, Mr. Stevenson senior was somewhat astonished at the taste shown by his son's patrons. To him the Twopence Coloured was always preferable to the Penny Plain. He could not help wishing that his son would try to paint things with a little more colour in them. He liked Highland cattle standing beside a well, with a lot of purple heather about ; or a snowy landscape with sheep in the foreground and the sun setting redly behind a hill. He was only bewildered when told to remark this " sumptuous black," that " seductive white." He saw " no ' colour ' in the smoke from a chimney, or ' bloom ' in dingy masonry viewed through smoke haze." To him " nothing looked fine " save on a fine day, and he infinitely preferred the robust oil-paintings on the walls of Lochnagar to his son's delicate black-and-white work.

But he would not for worlds have admitted it. . . .

To return. As Elizabeth sat listening to the conversation of her father and Stewart Stevenson, Ellen announced " Mr. Jamieson," and a thin, tall old man came into the room. He was lame and walked with the help of two sticks. When he saw a stranger he hung back, but James Seton sprang up to welcome him, and Elizabeth said as she shook hands :

" You've come at the most lucky moment. We are talking about your own subject, old Scots songs and ballads. Mr. Stevenson is quite an authority."

As the old man shook hands with the young one, " I do like," he said, " to hear of a young man caring for old things."

" And I," said Elizabeth, " do like an old man who cares for young things. I must tell you. Last Sunday I found a small, very grubby boy waiting at the hall door long before it was time for the Sabbath school. I asked him what he was doing, and he said, ' Waitin' for the class to gang in.' Then he said proudly, ' A'm yin o' John Jamieson's bairns.' " She turned to Mr. Stevenson and explained : " Mr. Jamieson has an enormous class of small children and is adored by each of them."

" It must take some looking after," said Mr. Stevenson. " How d'you make them behave ? "

Mr. Jamieson laughed and confessed that sometimes they were beyond him.

" The only thing I do insist on is a clean face, but sometimes I'm beat even there. I sent a boy home twice last Sabbath to wash his face, and each time he came back worse. I was just going to send him again, when his neighbour interfered with, ' Uch here ! he *washt* his face, but he wipit it wi' his bunnet, and he bides in a coal ree.' "

Elizabeth turned to see if her father appreciated the tale, but Mr. Seton had got the little old ballad book and was standing in his favourite attitude with one foot on a chair, lost to everything but the words he was reading.

" Now," he said, " this is an example of what I

mean by Scots practicalness.   It's 'Annan Water'
—you know it, Jamieson?   The last verse is this:

> 'O wae betide thee, Annan Water,
>   I vow thou art a drumly river ;
> But over thee I'll build a brig,
>   That thou true love no more may sever.'

You see?   The last thought is not of the tragedy of
love and death, but of the necessity of preventing
it happen again.   He will build a brig."

He sat down, with the book still in his hand,
smiling to himself at the vagaries of the Scots
character.

"We're a strange mixture," he said, "a mixture
of hard-headedness and romance, common sense
and sentiment, practicality and poetry, business
and idealism.   Sir Walter knew that, so he made
the Gifted Gilfillan turn from discoursing of the
New Jerusalem of the Saints to the price of beasts
at Mauchline Fair."

Mr. Jamieson leaned forward, his face alight with
interest.

"And I doubt, Mr. Seton, the romantic side is
strongest.   Look at our history !   Look at the wars
we fought under Bruce and Wallace !   If we had
had any common sense, we would have made peace
at the beginning, accepted the English terms,
and grown prosperous at the expense of our rich
neighbours."

"And look," said Stewart Stevenson, "at our
wars of religion.   I wonder what other people would
have taken to the hills for a refinement of dogma.
And the Jacobite risings ?   What earthly sense was
in them ?   Merely because Prince Charlie was a
Stuart, and because he was a gallant young fairy-
tale prince, we find sober, middle-aged men risking

their lives and their fortunes to help a cause that
was doomed from the start."

" I'm glad to think," said Mr. Seton, " that with
all our prudence our history is a record of lost causes
and impossible loyalties."

" I know why it is," said Elizabeth. " We have
all of us, we Scots, a queer daftness in our blood.
We pretend to be dour and cautious, but the fact
is that at heart we are the most emotional and
sentimental people on earth."

" I believe you're right," said Stewart Stevenson.
" The ordinary emotional races like the Italians and
the French are emotional chiefly on the surface ;
underneath they are a mercantile, hard-headed
breed. Now we——"

" We're the other way round," said Elizabeth.

" You can see that when you think what type
of man we chiefly admire," said Mr. Jamieson ;
" you might think it would be John Knox——"

" No, no," cried Elizabeth ; " I know Father has
hankerings after him, but I would quake to meet
him in the flesh."

" Sir Walter Scott," suggested Mr. Stevenson.

" Personally I would vote for Sir Walter," said
Mr. Seton.

" Ah, but, Mr. Seton," said John Jamieson, " I
think you'll admit that if we polled the country
we couldn't get a verdict for Sir Walter. I think
it would be for Robert Burns. Burns is the man
whose words are most often in our memories. It is
Burns we think of with sympathy and affection, and
why ? I suppose because of his humanity ; because of his rich humour and riotous imagination ;
because of his *daftness*, in a word——"

" It is odd," said Elizabeth ; " for by rights, as
Thomas would say, we should admire some one

quite different. The *Wealth of Nations* man, perhaps."

"Adam Smith," said Stewart Stevenson.

"You see," said Mr. Seton, "the moral is that he who would lead Scotland must do it not only by convincing the intellect, but above all by firing the imagination and touching the heart. Yes, I can think of a good illustration. In the year 1388, or thereabouts, Douglas went raiding into Northumberland and met the Percy at Otterbourne. We possess both an English and a Scottish account of the battle. The English ballad is called ' Chevy Chase.' It tells very vigorously and graphically how the great fight was fought, but it is only a piece of rhymed history. Our ballad of ' Otterbourne ' is quite different. It is full of wonderful touches of poetry, such as the Douglas's last speech :

> My wound is deep, I fain would sleep :
> Take thou the vanguard of the three ;
> And hide me by the bracken bush
> That grows on yonder lilye lee.
> O bury me by the bracken bush,
> Beneath the blooming briar ;
> Let never living mortal ken
> That ere a kindly Scot lies here ! ' "

James Seton got up and walked up and down the room, as his custom was when moved ; then he anchored before the fire, and continued :

"The two ballads represent two different temperaments. You can't get over it by saying that the Scots minstrel was a poet and the English minstrel a commonplace fellow. The minstrels knew their audience and wrote what their audience wanted. The English wanted straightforward facts ; the Scottish audience wanted the glamour of poetry."

"Father," said Elizabeth suddenly, "I believe

that's a bit of the lecture on Ballads you're writing for the Literary Society."

Mr. Seton confessed that it was.

" I thought you sounded like a book," said his daughter.

Stewart Stevenson asked the date of the lecture and if outsiders were admitted, whereupon Elizabeth felt constrained to ask him to dine and go with them, an invitation that was readily accepted.

Tea was brought in, and John Jamieson was persuaded by Elizabeth to tell stories of his " bairns " ; and then Mr. Stevenson described a walking-tour he had taken in Skye in the autumn, which enchanted the old man. At last he rose to go, remembering that it was Saturday evening and that the Minister must want to go to his sermon. When he shook hands with the young man he smiled at him somewhat wistfully.

" It's fine to be young," he said. " I was young once myself. It was never my lot to go far afield, but I mind one Fair Holiday I went with a friend to Inveraray. To save the fare we outran the coach from Lochgoilhead to St. Catherine's,—I was soople then,—and on the morning we were leaving—the boat left at ten—my friend woke me at two in the morning, and we walked seventeen miles to see the sun rise on Ben Cruachan. We startled the beasts of the forest in Inveraray wood, and I mind as if it were yesterday how the rising sun smote with living fire a white cloud floating on the top of the mountain. My friend caught me by the arm as we watched the moving mist lift. ' Look,' he cried, ' the mountains do smoke ! ' "

He stopped and reached for his sticks. " Well ! it's fine to be young, but it's not so bad to be old as you young folks think."

Elizabeth went with him to the door, and Stewart Stevenson remarked to his host on the wonderful vitality and cheerfulness of the old man.

" Yes," said Mr. Seton, " you would hardly think that he rarely knows what it is to be free of pain. Forty years ago he met with a terrible accident in the works where he was employed. It meant the end of everything to him, but he gathered up the broken bits of his life and made of it—ah, well ! A great cloud of witnesses will testify one day to that. He lives beside the church—not a very savoury district, as you know—but that little two-roomed house of his shines in the squalor like a good deed in a naughty world. Elizabeth calls him ' the Corregidor.' You remember ?

> ' If any beat a horse, you felt he saw :
> 'f any cursed a woman, he took note !
> . . . Not so much a spy
> As a recording Chief-inquisitor.'

And with children he's a regular Pied Piper."

Elizabeth came into the room and heard the last words.

" Is Father telling you about Mr. Jamieson ? He's one of the people who'll be very ' far ben ' in the next world ; but when you know my father better, Mr. Stevenson, you will find that when a goose happens to belong to him it is invariably a swan. His church, his congregation, his house, his servants, his sons——"

" Even his slack-tongued and irreverent daughter," put in Mr. Seton.

" Are pretty nearly perfect," finished Elizabeth. " It is one of the nicest things about Father."

" There is something utterly wrong about the young people of this age," remarked Mr. Seton, as he looked at his watch; "they have no respect for their elders. Dear me! it's late. I must get to my sermon."

"You must come again, Mr. Stevenson," said Elizabeth. "It has been so nice seeing you."

And Mr. Stevenson had, perforce, to take his leave.

"A very nice fellow," said Mr. Seton, when the visitor had departed.

"A very personable young man," said Elizabeth, "but some day he'll get himself cursed, I'm afraid, for he doesn't know when to withdraw his foot from his neighbour's house. Half-past six! Nearly Buff's bed-time!" and as Mr. Seton went to his study Elizabeth flew to see what wickedness Buff had perpetrated since tea.

CHAPTER VII

" How full of briars is this working-day world ! "
As You Like it.

It was Monday morning.

Buff was never quite his urbane self on Monday morning. Perhaps the lack of any other occupation on Sabbath made him overwork his imagination, for certainly in the clear cold light of Monday morning it was difficult to find the way (usually such an easy task) to his own dream-world with its cheery denizens—knights and pirates, aviators and dragons. It was desolating to have to sup porridge, that was only porridge and not some tasty stew of wild-fowl fallen to his own gun, in a dining-room that was only a dining-room, not a Pirate Barque or a Robbers' Cave.

On Monday, too, he was apt to be more than usually oppressed by his conviction of the utter futility of going to school when he knew of at least fifty better ways of spending the precious hours. So he kicked the table-leg and mumbled when his father asked him questions about his lessons.

Ellen coming in with the letters seemed another messenger of Satan sent to buffet him. Time was when he had been Mercury to his family, but having fallen into the pernicious practice of concealing about his person any letters that took his fancy and forgetting about them till bed-time brought them to light, he was deposed. The memory rankled, and he gloomily watched the demure progress of Ellen as she took the letters to Elizabeth.

" Three for you, Father," said Elizabeth, sorting them out, " and three for me. The Indian letters are both here."

" Read them, will you ? " said Mr. Seton, who disliked deciphering for himself.

" I'll just see if they're both well and read the letters afterwards if you don't mind. We'll make Buff late. Cheer up, old son " (to that unwilling scholar). " Life isn't all Saturdays. Monday mornings are bound to come. You should be glad to begin again. Why, the boys "—Walter and Alan were known as " the boys "—" wouldn't have thought of sitting like sick owls on Mondays : they were pleased to have a fine new day to do things in."

Buff was heard to ejaculate something that sounded like " Huch," and his sister ceased her bracing treatment and, sitting down beside him, cut his bread-and-butter into " fingers " to make it more interesting. She could sympathize with her sulky young brother, remembering vividly, as she did, her own childish troubles. Only, as she told Buff, coaxing him the while to drink his milk, it was Saturday afternoon she abhorred. It smelt, she said, of soft soap and of the end of things. Monday was cheery : things began again. Why, something delightful might happen almost any minute : there was no saying what dazzling adventures might lurk round any corner. The Saga of Monday as sung by Elizabeth helped down the milk, cheered the heart of Buff, and sent him off on his daily quest for knowledge in a more resigned

4

spirit than five minutes before had seemed possible. Then Elizabeth gathered up the letters and went into the study, where she found her father brooding absorbed over the pots of bulbs that stood in the study windows. "The Roman hyacinths will be out before Christmas," he said, as he turned from his beloved growing things and settled down with a pleased smile to hear news of his sons.

Alan's letter was like himself, very light-hearted. Everything was delightful, the weather he was having, the people he was meeting, the games he was playing. He was full of a new polo-pony he had just bought and called Barbara, and he had also acquired a young leopard, " a jolly little beast but rank."

" Buff will like to hear about it," said Elizabeth, as she turned to Walter's letter, which was more a tale of work and laborious days. " Tell Father," he finished, " that after bowing in the house of Rimmon for months, I had a chance yesterday of attending a Scots kirk. It was fine to hear the Psalms of David sung again to the old tunes. I have always held that it was not David but the man who wrote the metrical version who was inspired."

" Foolish fellow," said Mr. Seton.

Elizabeth laughed, and began to read another letter. Mr. Seton turned to his desk and was getting out paper when a sharp exclamation from his daughter made him look round.

Elizabeth held out the letter to him, her face tragic.

" Aunt Alice is mad," she said.

" Dear me," said Mr. Seton.

" She must be, for she asks if we can take her nephew Arthur Townshend to stay with us for a week ? "

" A very natural request, surely," said her father.
" It isn't like you to be inhospitable, Elizabeth."

" Oh ! it isn't that.   Any ordinary young man is
welcome to stay for months and months, but this
isn't an ordinary young man.   He's the sort of
person who belongs to all the Clubs—the best ones,
I mean—and has a man to keep him neat, and fares
sumptuously every day, and needs to be amused.
And oh ! the thought of him in Glasgow paralyses me."

Mr. Seton peered in a puzzled way at the letter
he was holding.

" Your aunt appears to say—I wish people would
write plainly—that he has business in Glasgow."

Elizabeth scoffed at the idea.

" Is it likely ? " she asked.   " Why, the creature's
a diplomatist.   There's small scope for diplomatic
talents in the South Side of Glasgow, or ' out West '
either."

" But why should he want to come here ? "

" He *doesn't*, but my demented aunt—bless her
kind heart !—adores him, and she adores us, and it
has always been her dream that we should meet
and be friends ; but he was always away in Persia
or somewhere, and we never met.   But now he is
home, and he couldn't refuse Aunt Alice,—she is
all the mother he ever knew and has been an angel
to him,—and I daresay he is quite good-hearted,
though I can't stand the type."

" Well, well," said Mr. Seton, by way of closing
the subject, and he went over to the window to take
a look at the world before settling down to his
sermon.   " Run away now, like a good girl.   Dear
me ! what a beautiful blue sky for November ! "

" Tut, tut," said Elizabeth, " who can think of
blue skies in this crisis !   Father, have you thought
of the question of *drinks* ? "

" Eh ? "

" Mr. Townshend will want wine—much wine— and how is the desire to be met in this Apollinaris household ? "

" He'll do without it," said Mr. Seton placidly. " I foresee the young man will be a reformed character before he leaves us ; " and he lifted Launcelot from its seat on the blotter, and sat down happily to his sermon.

Elizabeth shook her head at her provokingly calm parent, and picking up the kitten, she walked to the door.

" Write a specially good sermon this week," she advised. " Remember Mr. Arthur Townshend will be a listener," and closed the door behind her before her father could think of a dignified retort.

Mrs. Henry Beauchamp, the " Aunt Alice " who had dropped the bombshell into the Seton household, was the only sister of Elizabeth's dead mother. A widow and childless, she would have liked to adopt the whole Seton family, Mr. Seton included, had it been possible. She lived most of the year in London in her house in Portland Place, and in summer she joined the Setons in the South of Scotland.

Arthur Townshend was her husband's nephew. As he had lived much abroad, none of the Setons had met him ; but now he was home, and Mrs. Beauchamp having failed in her attempt to persuade Elizabeth to join them in Switzerland, suggested he should pay a visit to Glasgow.

Elizabeth was seriously perturbed. Arthur Townshend had always been a sort of veiled prophet to her, an awe-inspiring person for whom people put their best foot foremost, so to speak. Unconsciously her aunt had given her the impression of a young man particular about trifles—" ill to saddle," as Marget would put it. And she had heard so much about his looks, his abilities, his brilliant prospects, that she had always felt a vague antipathy to the youth.

To meet this paragon at Portland Place would have been ordeal enough, but to have him thrust upon her as a guest, to have to feed him and entertain him for a week, her imagination boggled at it.

"It's like the mountain coming to Mahomet," she reflected. "Mahomet must have felt it rather a crushing honour too."

The question was, should she try to entertain him? Should she tell people he was coming, and so have him invited out to dinner, invite interesting people to meet him, attempt elaborate meals, and thoroughly upset the household?

She decided she would not. For, she argued with herself, if he's the sort of creature I have a feeling he is, my most lofty efforts will only bore him, and I shall have bored myself to no purpose; if, on the other hand, he is a good fellow, he will like us best *au naturel*. She broke the news to Marget, who remained unmoved.

"What was guid eneuch for oor ain laddies 'll surely be guid eneuch for him," she said.

Elizabeth explained that this was no ordinary visitor, but a young man of fashion.

"Set him up!" said Marget; and there the matter rested.

Everything went wrong that day, Elizabeth thought, and for all the untoward events she blamed the prospective visitor. Her father lost his address-book—that was no new thing, for it happened at least twice a week, but what was new was Elizabeth's cross answer when he asked her to find it for him. She wrangled with sharp-tongued Marget (where she got distinctly the worse of the encounter), and even snapped at the devoted Ellen. She broke a Spode dish that her mother had prized, and she forgot to remind her father of a funeral till half an hour after the hour fixed.

Nor did the day ring to evensong without a passage-at-arms with Buff.

In the drawing-room she found, precariously perched on the top of one of the white bookcases, a large unwashed earthy pot.

" What on earth——", she began, when Buff came running to explain. The flower-pot was his, his and Thomas's ; and it contained an orange-pip which, if cherished, would eventually become a lovely orange-tree.

" Nonsense," said Elizabeth sharply. " Look how it's marking the enamel ; " and she lifted the clumsy pot. Buff caught her arm, and between them the flower-pot smashed on the floor, spattering damp earth around. Then Elizabeth, sorely exasperated, boxed her young brother's ears.

Buff, grieved to the heart at the loss of his orange-tree, and almost speechless with wrath at the affront offered him, glared at his sister with eyes of hate, but " You—you *puddock* ! " was all he managed to say.

Elizabeth, her brief anger gone, sat down and laughed helplessly.

Thomas grubbed in the earth for the pip. " By rights," he said gloomily, " we would have had oranges growing mebbe in a month ! "

.CHAPTER VIII

" I do desire it with all my heart : I hope it is no dishonest desire to desire to be a woman of the world."

As You Like It.

THERE are many well-kept houses in Glasgow, but I think Jeanieville was one of the cleanest. Every room had its " thorough " day once a fortnight and was turned pitilessly " out." Every " press " in the house was a model of neatness ; the very coal-cellar did not escape. The coals were piled in a neat heap ; the dross was swept tidily into a corner ; the briquettes were built in an accurate pile.

" I must say," Mrs. Thomson often remarked, " I like a tidy coal-cellar ; " and Jessie, who felt this was rather a low taste, would reply, " You're awful eccentric, Mamma."

On the first and fourth Thursdays of the month Mrs. Thomson was " at home " ; then, indeed, she trod the measure high and disposedly.

On these auspicious days Annie the servant, willing but " hashy," made the front door shine, and even " sanded " the pillars of the gate to create a good impression. The white steps of the stairs were washed, and the linoleum in the lobby was polished until it became a danger to the unwary walker. Dinner set agoing, Mrs. Thomson tied a large white apron round her ample person and spent a couple of hours in the kitchen baking scones and pancakes and jam-sandwiches, while Jessie, her share of the polishing done, took the car into town and bought various small cakes, also shortbread and a slab of rich sultana cake.

By half-past two all was ready.

Mrs. Thomson in her second-best dress, and Jessie in a smart silk blouse and skirt, sat waiting. Mrs. Thomson had her knitting, and Jessie some " fancy work." The tea-table with its lace-trimmed cloth and silver tray with the rosy cups (" ma wedding china and only one saucer broken ") stood at one side of the fireplace, with a laden cake-rack beside it, while a small table in the offing was also covered with plates of eatables.

There was never any lack of callers at Jeanieville. It was such a vastly comfortable house to call at. The fire burned so brightly, the tea was so hot and fresh, the scones so delicious, and the shortbread so new and crimpy ; and when Mrs. Thomson with genuine welcome in her voice said, " Well, this is real nice," no matter how inclement the weather outside each visitor felt the world a warm and kindly place.

Mrs. Thomson enjoyed her house and her handsome furniture, and desired—and hoped it was no dishonest desire—to be a social success ; but her kindest smile and heartiest handshake were not for the sealskin-coated ladies of Pollokshields but for such of her old friends as ventured to visit her on her Thursdays, and often poor Jessie's cheeks burned as she heard her mother explain to some elegant suburban lady, as she introduced a friend :

" Mrs. Nicol and me are old friends. We lived for years on the same stair-head."

Except in rare cases, there was no stiffness about the sealskin-ladies, and conversation flowed like a river.

On this particular Thursday four females sat drinking tea with Mrs. Thomson and her daughter out of the rosy cups with the gilt garlands—Mrs. Forsyth and Mrs. Macbean from neighbouring villas, and the Misses Hendry whom we have already met. Mrs. Forsyth was a typical Glasgow woman, large, healthy, prosperous, her face beaming with contentment. She was a thoroughly satisfactory person to look at, for everything about her bore inspection, from her abundant hair and her fresh pink face, which looked as if it were rubbed at least once a day with a nice soapy flannel, to her well-made boots and handsome clothes. Her accent, like Mrs. Thomson's, was Glasgow unabashed.

" Yes, thank you, Mrs. Thomson, two lumps. Did you notice in the papers that my daughter— Mrs. Mason, you know—had had her fourth ? Ucha, a fine wee boy, and her only eight-and-twenty ! I said to her to-day, ' Mercy, Maggie,' I said, ' who asked you to populate the earth ? ' I just said it like that, and she *laughed*. Oh ay, but it's far nicer—just like Papa and me. I don't believe in these wee families."

Mrs. Macbean, a little blurred-looking woman with beautiful sables, gave it as her opinion that a woman was never happier than when surrounded by half a dozen " wee ones."

Mrs. Forsyth helped herself to a scone.

" Home-made, Mrs. Thomson ? I thought so. They're lovely. Speaking about families, I was just saying to Mr. Forsyth the other night that I thought this was mebbe the happiest time of all our married life. It's awful nice to marry young and be able to enjoy your children. I was twenty and Mr. Forsyth was four years older when we started."

"Well, well," said Mrs. Thomson. "You began young, but you've great reason for thankfulness. How's Dr. Hugh?"

"Hugh!" said his mother, with a great sigh of pride; "Hugh's well, thanks."

"He's a cliver young man," said Mrs. Thomson. "It's wonderful how he's got on."

"Mrs. Thomson, his father just said to me this morning, '*Whit* a career the boy's had!' At school he got every prize he could have got, and at College he lifted the Buchanan Prize and the Bailie Medal; then he got the Dixon Scholarship, and—it sounds like boasting, but ye know what I mean—the Professors fair fought to have him for an assistant, and now at his age—at his age, mind you—he's a specialist on—excuse me mentioning it—the stomach and bowels."

Every one in the room murmured their wonder at Dr. Hugh's meteoric career, and Mrs. Macbean said generously, "You should be a proud woman, Mrs. Forsyth."

"Oh! I don't know about that. How are your girls? Is Phemie better?"

"I didn't know she was ill," said Mrs. Thomson.

Mrs. Macbean's face wore an important look, as she said with a sort of melancholy satisfaction, "Yes, she's ill, Mrs. Thomson, and likely to be ill for a long time. And you wouldn't believe how simply it began. She was in at Pettigrew and Stephens', or it might have been Copland and Lye's; anyway, it was one of the Sauchiehall Street shops, and she was coming down the stair quite quietly—Maggie

was with her—when one of the young gentleman
shop-walkers came up the stairs in a kinda hurry,
and whether he pushed against Phemie, I don't
know, and Maggie can't be sure ; anyway, she
slipped. She didn't fall, you know, or anything
like that, but in saving herself she must have given
herself a twist—for I'll tell you what happened."

There was something strangely appetizing in Mrs.
Macbean as a talker : she somehow managed to
make her listeners hungry for more.

" Well, she didn't say much about it at the time.
Just when she came in she said, joky-like, ' I
nearly fell down the stairs in a shop to-day, Mother,
and I gave myself quite a twist.' That was all
she said, and Maggie passed some remark about
the gentleman in the shop being in a hurry, and I
thought no more about it. But about a week later
Phemie says to me, ' D'ye know,' she says, ' I've
got a sort of pain, nothing much, but it keeps
there.' You may be sure I got the doctor quick,
for I'm niver one that would lichtly a pain, as ye
might say, but he couldn't find anything wrong.
But the girl was niver well, and he said perhaps it
would be as well to see a specialist. And I said,
' Certainly, doctor, you find out the best man and
Mr. Macbean won't grudge the money, for he thinks
the world of his girls.' So Dr. Rankine made
arrangements, and we went to see Sir Angus Johnston, a real swell, but sich a nice homely man. I
could have said *anything* to him—ye know what I
mean. And he said to me undoubtedly the trouble
arose from the twist she had given herself that
day."

" And whit was like the matter ? " asked Miss
Hendry, who had listened breathless to the recital.

" Well," said Mrs. Macbean, " it was like this.

When she slipped she had put something out of its place and it had put something else out of *its* place. I really can't tell you right what, but anyway Sir Angus Johnston said to me, ' Mrs. Macbean,' he said, ' your daughter's liver '—well, I wouldn't just be sure that it was her liver—but anyway he said it was as big as a tea-kettle.''

" Mercy ! " ejaculated the awed Miss Hendry, who had no idea what was the proper size of any internal organ.

" Keep us ! " said Mrs. Thomson, who was in a similar state of ignorance. " A tea-kettle, Mrs. Macbean ? "

" A tea-kettle,'' said Mrs. Macbean firmly.

" Oh, I say ! " said Jessie. " That's awful ! "

Mrs. Macbean nodded her head several times, well pleased at the sensation she had made.

" You can imagine what a turn it gave me. Maggie was with me in the room, and she said afterwards she really thought I was going to faint. I just kinda looked at the man—I'm meaning Sir Angus—but I could not say a word. I was speechless. But Maggie—Maggie's real bright—she spoke up and she says, ' Will she recover ? ' she says, just like that. And he was nice, I must say he was awful nice, very reassuring. ' Time,' he says, ' time and treatment and patience '—I think that was the three things, and my ! the patience is the worst thing.''

" But she's improving, Mrs. Macbean ? " asked Mrs. Forsyth.

" Slowly, Mrs. Forsyth, slowly. But a thing like that takes a long time.''

" Our Hugh says that the less a body knows about their inside the better,'' said healthy Mrs. Forsyth.

" That's true, I'm sure,'' agreed Mrs. Thomson.

" Mrs. Forsyth, is your cup out ? Try a bit of this cake."

" Thanks. I always eat an extra big tea here, Mrs. Thomson, everything's that good. Have you a nurse for Phemie, Mrs. Macbean ? "

Mrs. Macbean laid down her cup, motioning Jessie away as she tried to take it to refill it, and said solemnly :

" A nurse, Mrs. Forsyth ? Nurses have walked in a procession through our house this last month. And, mind you, I haven't a thing to say against one of them. They were all nice women, but somehow they just didn't suit. The first one had an awful memory. No, she didn't forget things, it was the other way. She was a good careful nurse, but she could say pages of poetry off by heart, and she did it through the night to soothe Phemie like. She would get Phemie all comfortable, and then she'd turn out the light, and sit down by the fire with her knitting, and begin something about ' The stag at eve had drunk its fill,' and so on and on and on. She meant well, but who would put up with that ? D'you know, that stag was fair getting on Phemie's nerves, so we had to make an excuse and get her away. Then the next was a strong-minded kind of a woman, and the day after she came I found Phemie near in hysterics, and it turned out the nurse had told her she had patented a shroud, and it had given the girl quite a turn. I don't wonder ! It's not a nice subject even for a well body. Mr. Macbean was angry, I can tell you, so *she* went. The next one—a nice wee fair-haired girl—she took appendicitis. Wasn't it awful ? Oh ! we've been unfortunate right enough. However, the one we've got now is all right, and she considers the servants, and that's the main thing—not, mind you, that I ever have much trouble with servants. I niver had what you would call a real bad one. Mine have all been nice enough girls, only we didn't always happen to agree. Ye know what I mean?"

"Ucha," said Mrs. Thomson. "Are you well suited just now, Mrs. Macbean?"

"Fair, Mrs. Thomson, but that's all I'll say. My cook's a Cockney! A real English wee body. I take many a laugh to myself at her accent. I'm quite good at speakin' like her. Mr. Macbean often says to me, 'Come on, Mamma, and give us a turn at the Cockney.' Oh! she's a great divert, but—*wasteful!* It's not, ye know what I mean, that we grudge the things, but I always say that having had a good mother is a great disadvantage these days. My mother brought me up to hate waste and to hate dirt, and it keeps me fair miserable with the kind of servants that are now."

Mrs. Thomson nodded her head in profound agreement; but Mrs. Forsyth said:

"But my! Mrs. Macbean, I wouldna let myself be made miserable by any servant. I just keep the one—not that Mr. Forsyth couldn't give me two if I wanted them, but you can keep more control over one. She gets everything we get ourselves, but she knows better than waste so much as a potato peel. I've had Maggie five years now, and it took me near a year to get her to hang the dishcloths on their nails; but now I have her real well into my ways, and the way she keeps her range is a treat."

Presently Mrs. Forsyth and Mrs. Macbean went away to make other calls, and Mrs. Thomson and her two old friends drew near the fire for a cosy talk.

"Sit well in front and warm your feet, Miss Hendry. Miss Flora, try this chair and turn back your skirt in case it gets scorched. Now, you'll just stay and have a proper tea and see Papa. Yes, yes," as the Misses Hendry expostulated, " you just will. Ye got no tea to speak of, and there's a nice bit of Finnan haddie—— My ! these ' at home ' days are tiring."

" They're awful enjoyable," said Miss Flora, rather wistfully. " Ye've come on, Mrs. Thomson, since we were neighbours, but I must say you don't forget old friends."

" Eh, and I hope I never will. The new friends are all very well, they're kind and all that, but a body clings to the old friends. It was you I ran to when Rubbert took the croup and I thought we were to lose him ; and d'ye mind how you took night about with me when Papa near slipped away wi' pneumonia ? Eh, my, my ! . . . Jessie's awful keen to be grand ; she's young, and young folk havena much sense. She tells me I'm eccentric because I like to see that every corner of the house is clean. She thinks Mrs. Simpson's a real lady because she keeps three servants and a dirty house. Well, Papa's always at me to get another girrl, for of course this is a big house,—we have the nine rooms,—but I'll not agree. Jessie's far better helping me to keep the house clean than trailing in and out of picture-houses like the Simpsons. The Simpsons ! Mercy me, did I not know the Simpsons when they kept a wee shop in the Paisley Road ? And now they're afraid to mention the word shop in case it puts anybody in mind. As I tell Jessie, there's nothing wrong in keepin' a shop, but there's something far wrong in being ashamed of it."

" Bless me," said Miss Hendry, who could not conceive of any one being ashamed of a shop. " A shop's a fine thing—real interesting, I would think. You werena at the prayer-meeting last night ? "

" No. I was real sorry, but there was a touch of fog, if you remember, and Papa's throat was troublesome, so I got him persuaded to stay in. Was Mr. Seton good ? "

" *Fine,*" said Miss Hendry,—" fair excelled himself."

" Papa often says that Mr. Seton's at his best at the prayer-meeting."

" You're a long way from the church now, Mrs. Thomson," said Miss Hendry. " You'll be speakin' about leaving one o' these days."

" Miss Hendry," said Mrs. Thomson solemnly, " that is one thing we niver will do, leave that church as long as Mr. Seton's the minister. Even if I had notions about a Pollokshields church and Society, as Jessie talks about, d'ye think Mr. Thomson would listen to me ? I can do a lot with my man, but I could niver move him on that point—and I would niver seek to."

" Well," said Miss Hendry in a satisfied tone, " I'm glad to hear you say it. Of course *we* think there's not the like of our minister anywhere. He has his faults. He niver sees ye on the street, and it hurts people ; it used to hurt me too, but now I just think he's seeing other things than our streets. And he has a kinda cold manner until ye get used to it. He came in one day when a neighbour was in—a Mrs. Steel, she goes to Robertson's kirk— and she said to me afterwards, ' My ! I wudna like a dry character like that for a minister.' I said to her, ' I daresay no' after the kind ye're used to, but *I* like ma minister to be a gentleman.' Robertson's one o' these joky kind o' ministers."

" Well," said Miss Flora, who seldom got a word

in when her sister was present, " I'm proud of ma minister, and I'm proud of ma minister's family."

" Yes," agreed her sister, " Elizabeth's a fine-lookin' girl, and awful bright, and entertainin'; it's a pity she canna get a man."

" I'm sure," said Mrs. Thomson, " she could get a man any day, if she wanted one. I wouldn't wonder if she made a fine marriage—mebbe an M.P. But what would her father do wanting her? and wee David? She really keeps that house *well*. I've thought an awful lot of her since one day I was there at my tea, and she said to me so innerly-like, ' Would you like to see over the house, Mrs. Thomson?' and she took me into every room and opened every press—and there wasn't a thing I would have changed."

" Well," said Miss Hendry, " they talk about folk being too sweet to be wholesome, like a frosted tattie, and mebbe Elizabeth Seton just puts it on, but there's no doubt she's got a taking way with her. I niver get a new thing either for myself or the house but I wonder what she'll think about it. And she aye notices it, ye niver have to point it out."

" Yes," said Mrs. Thomson. " She's a grand praiser. Some folk fair make you lose conceit of your things, but she's the other way. Did I tell you Papa and me are going away next week for a wee holiday? Just the two of us. Jessie 'll manage the house and look after the boys. Papa says I look tired. I'm sure that it's no' that I work as hard as I used to work; but there, years tell, and I'm no' the Mrs. Thomson I once was. We're going to the Kyles Hydro—it's real homely and nice."

" I niver stopped in a Hydro in my life," Miss

Hendry said. " It must be a grand rest. Nothing to do but take your meat."

" That's so," Mrs. Thomson admitted. " It gives you a kind of rested feeling to see white paint everywhere and know that it's no business of yours if it gets marked, and to sit and look at a fine fire blazing itself away without thinkin' you should be getting on a shovel of dross ; and it's a real holiday-feeling to put on your rings and your afternoon dress for breakfast."

Voices were heard in the lobby. Mrs. Thomson started up to welcome home her husband, while Jessie announced to the visitors that tea was ready in the parlour.

CHAPTER IX

" I have great comfort from this fellow."
The Tempest.

On the afternoon of the Saturday that brought Arthur Townshend to Glasgow Elizabeth sat counselling her young brother about his behaviour to the expected guest. She drew a lurid picture of his everyday manners, and pointed out where they might be improved, so that Mr. Arthur Townshend might not get too great a shock. Buff remained quite calm, merely remarking that he had never seen any one called Townshend quite close before. Elizabeth went on to remind him that any remarks reflecting on the English as a race, or on their actions in history, would be in extreme bad taste. This warning she felt to be necessary, remembering how, when Buff was younger, some English cousins had come to stay, and he had refused to enter the room to greet them, contenting himself with shouting through the keyhole, " *Who killed William Wallace ?* "

Since then, some of his fierce animosity to the " English " had died down, though he still felt that Queen Mary's death needed a lot of explaining.

As his sister continued the lecture, and went into details about clean nails and ears, Buff grew frankly bored, and remarking that he wished visitors would remain at home, went off to find Thomas and Billy.

Mr. Seton, sitting with his sermon, unabatedly cheerful in spite of the fact that a strange young man—a youth " tried and tutored in the world "— was about to descend on his home, looked up and laughed at his daughter.

" Let the boy alone, Lizbeth," he advised. " I see nothing wrong with his manners."

" Love is blind," said Elizabeth. " But it's not only his manners : the boy has a perfect genius for saying the wrong thing. Dear old Mrs. Morton was calling yesterday, and you know what a horror she has of theatres and all things theatrical. Well, when she asked Buff what he was going to be, expecting no doubt to hear that he had yearnings after the ministry, he replied quite firmly, ' An actor-man.' I had to run him out of the room. Then he told Mrs. Orr there was nothing he liked so much as fighting, so he meant to be a soldier. She said in her sweet old voice, ' You will fight with the Bible, darling—the sword of the Spirit.' ' Huh ! ' said Buff, ' queer dumpy little sword that would be.' "

Mr. Seton seemed more amused than depressed by the tale of his son's misdeeds, and Elizabeth continued : " After all, what does it matter what Mr. Arthur Townshend thinks of any of us ? I've done my best for him, and I hope the meals will be decent ; but of course the thought of him has upset Marget's temper. It is odd that when she is cross she *will* quote hymns. I must say it is discouraging to make some harmless remark about vegetables and receive nothing in reply but a muttered

> ' Teach me to live that I may dread
> The grave as little as my bed.' "

" Elizabeth, you're an absurd creature," said her father. " Why you and Marget should allow yourselves to be upset by a visit from an ordinary young man I don't know. Dear me, *I'll* look after him."

" And how do you propose to entertain him, Father ? "

" Well, I might take him one day to see the glasshouses in the Park ; there is a beautiful show of chrysanthemums just now. I greatly enjoyed it as I passed through yesterday. Then one morning we could go to the Cathedral—and the Art Gallery and Municipal Buildings are very interesting in their way."

" *Dear* Father," said Elizabeth.

.   .   .   .

Mr. Arthur Townshend was expected about seven o'clock, and Elizabeth had planned everything for his reception. Buff would be in bed, and Thomas and Billy under the shelter of their own roof-tree. The house would be tidy and quiet, the fires at their best. She herself would be dressed early and ready to receive him.

But it happened otherwise.

Elizabeth, a book in her hand, was sunk in a large armchair, a boy on each of the chair-arms and one on the rug. It was getting dark, but the tale was too breathless to stop for lights ; besides, the fire was bright and she held the book so that the firelight fell on the page.

" Over the rock with them ! " cried the Brigand Chief ; and his men stepped forward to obey his orders.

" Oow ! " squealed Billy in his excitement.

" *Mr. Townshend*," announced Ellen.

No one had heard the sounds of arrival. Elizabeth rose hastily, sending Buff and Billy to the floor, her eyes dazed with firelight, her mind still in the Robbers' Cave.

"But the train isn't in yet," was her none too hospitable greeting.

"I must apologize," said the new-comer. "I came North last night to catch a man in Edinburgh —his ship was just leaving the Forth. I ought to have let you know, but I forgot to wire until it was too late. I'm afraid I'm frightfully casual. I hope you don't mind me walking in like this?"

"Oh no," said Elizabeth, vainly trying to smooth her rumpled hair. "Get up, boys, and let Mr. Townshend near the fire; and we'll get some fresh tea."

"Please don't. I lunched very late. I suppose one of these young men is Buff?"

Ellen, meanwhile, had drawn the curtains and lighted the gas, and the company regarded one another.

"A monocle!" said Elizabeth to herself, feeling her worst fears were being realized, "and *beautifully* creased trousers." (*Had* Ellen remembered to light his bedroom fire?) But, certainly, she had to admit to herself a few minutes later, he knew how to make friends with children. He had got out his notebook and was drawing them a battleship, as absorbed in his work as the boys, who leaned on him, breathing heavily down his neck and watching intently.

"A modern battleship's an ugly thing," he said as he worked.

"Yes," Billy agreed, "that's an ugly thing you're making. I thought a battleship had lovely masts, and lots of little windows, and was all curly."

"He's thinking," said Thomas, "of pictures of ships in poetry books."

"I know," said Arthur Townshend. "Ballad ships that sailed to Norroway ower the faem. This is our poor modern substitute."

"Now a submarine," Buff begged.

Arthur Townshend drew a periscope, and remarked that of course the rest of the submarine was under water.

"Aw!" cried Buff; and the three sprang upon their new friend, demanding further amusements.

But Elizabeth intervened, saying Thomas and Billy must go home, as it was Saturday night. Thomas pointed out that Saturday night made no real difference to him or to Billy, and gave several excellent reasons for remaining where he was; but Elizabeth proving adamant, they went, promising Mr. Townshend that he would see them early the next morning. Buff was told to show the guest to his room (where, finding himself well entertained, he remained till nearly dinner-time, when he was fetched by Ellen, and sent, bitterly protesting, to seek his couch), and Elizabeth was left to tidy away the story books and try to realize her impressions.

Dinner went off quite well. The food, if simple, was well cooked; for Marget, in spite of her temper, had done her best, and Ellen made an efficient if almost morbidly painstaking waitress.

Elizabeth smiled to herself, but made no remark, as she watched her pour water firmly into the guest's glass; and her father, leaning forward, said kindly, "I think you will find Glasgow water particularly good, Mr. Townshend; it comes from Loch Katrine."

Mr. Townshend replied very suitably that water was a great treat to one who had been for so long a dweller in the East. Elizabeth found that with this

guest there was going to be no need of small talk—
no aimless, irrelevant remarks uttered at random
to fill up awkward silences. He was a good talker
and a good listener.

Mr. Seton was greatly interested in his travellers'
tales, and as Elizabeth watched them honesty com-
pelled her to confess to herself that this was not the
guest she had pictured. She liked his manner to
her father, and she liked his frank laugh. After
all, it would not be difficult to amuse him when he
was so willing to laugh.

"I wonder," said Mr. Seton, as he pared an
apple, "if you have ever visited my dream-place?"
He gave his shy boy's smile. "I don't know
why, but the very name spells romance to me—
Bokhara."

"Yes—that 'outpost of the infinite.' I know it
well; or rather I don't, of course, for no stray
Englishman can know a place like that well, but
I have been there several times. . . . I'm just
wondering if it would disappoint you."

"I daresay it might," said Mr. Seton. "But
I'm afraid there is no likelihood of my ever journey-
ing across the desert to find my 'dream-moon-city'
either a delight or a disappointment. But I keep
my vision—and I have a Bokhara rug that is a
great comfort to me."

"When you retire, Father," broke in Elizabeth,
"when we're done with kirks and deacons'-courts
for ever and a day, we shall go to Bokhara, you and
I. It will be such a nice change."

"Well, well," said her father, "perhaps we shall;
but in the meantime I must go to my sermon."

In the drawing-room Elizabeth settled herself in
an armchair with some needlework, and pointed
out the cigarettes and matches to her guest.

" Don't you smoke ? " he asked.

" No.   Father would hate it :   he doesn't ever smoke himself."

" I see.   I say, you have got a lot of jolly prints. May I look at them ? "

He proved very knowledgeable about the prints, and from prints they passed to books, and Elizabeth found him so full of honest enthusiasm, and with so nice a taste in book-people, that the last shreds of distrust and reserve vanished, and she cried in her Elizabethan way : " And actually I wondered what in the world I would talk to you about ! "

Arthur Townshend laughed.

" Tell me," he said, " what subjects you had thought of ? "

" Well," said she, sitting up very straight and counting on her fingers, " first I thought I would start you on Persia and keep you there as long as possible ; then intelligent questions about politics, something really long-drawn-out, like Home Rule or Women's Suffrage ; then—then—I *had* thought of Ella Wheeler Wilcox ! "

Arthur Townshend groaned.

" *What* sort of idea had Aunt Alice given you of me ? "

" Quite unintentionally," Elizabeth said, " she made you sound rather a worm.   Not a crawling worm, you understand, but a worm that reared an insolent head, that would think it a horrid bore to visit a manse in Glasgow—a side-y worm."

" Good Lord," said Mr. Townshend, stooping to pick up Elizabeth's needlework which in her excitement had fallen on the rug, " this is not Aunt Alice——"

" No," said Elizabeth, " it's my own wickedness.

The fact is, I was jealous—Aunt Alice seemed so devoted to you, and quoted you, and admired everything about you so much, and I thought that in praising you she was 'lichtlying' my brothers, so, of course, I didn't like you. Yes, that's the kind of jealous creature I am."

The door opened, and Ellen came in with a tray on which stood glasses, a jug of milk, a siphon, and a biscuit-box. She laid it on a table beside her mistress and asked if anything else was needed, and on being told " No," said good-night and made her demure exit.

" Pretend you've known me seven years, and put a log on the fire," Elizabeth asked her guest.

He did as he was bid, and remained standing at the mantelpiece looking at the picture which hung above it.

" Your mother, isn't it ? " he asked. " She was beautiful ; Aunt Alice has often told me of her."

He looked in silence for a minute, and then went back to his chair and lit another cigarette.

" I never knew my mother, and I only remember my father dimly. I was only her husband's nephew, but Aunt Alice has had to stand for all my home-people, and no one knows except myself how successful she has been."

" She is the most golden-hearted person," said Elizabeth. " I don't believe she ever has a thought that isn't kind and gentle and sincere. I am so glad you had her—and that she had you. One can't help seeing what you have meant to her. . . ." Then a spark of laughter lit in Elizabeth's grey eyes.

" Don't you love the way her sentences never end ? just trail deliciously away . . . and her descriptions of people ?—' such charming people, *such* staunch Conservatives and he plays the violin so beautifully.' "

Arthur Townshend laughed in the way that one laughs at something that, though funny, is almost too dear to be laughed at.

" That is exactly like her," he said. " Was your mother at all like her sister ? "

" Only in heart," said Elizabeth. " Mother was much more definite. People always said she was a ' sweet woman,' but that doesn't describe her in the least. She was gentle, but she could be caustic at times : she hated shams. That picture was painted before her marriage, but she never altered much, and she never got a bit less lovely. I remember once we were all round her as she stood dressed to go to some wedding, and Alan said, ' Are *you* married, Mums ? ' and when she said she was, he cried consolingly, ' But you would do again.' . . . I sometimes wonder now how Mother liked the work of a minister's wife in Glasgow. I remember she used to laugh and say that with her journeys ended in Mothers' Meetings. I know she did very well, and the people loved her. I can see her now coming in from visiting in the district, crying out on the drabness of the lives there, and she would catch up Buff and dance and sing with him and say little French nursery-songs to him, like a happy school-girl. Poor little Buff ! He doesn't know what a dreadful lot he is missing. Sometimes I think I spoil him, and then I remember ' his mother who was patient being dead.' "

The fire had fallen into a hot red glow, and they sat in silence looking into it.

Presently the door opened, and Mr. Seton came in. He came to the fire and warmed his hands, remarking, " There's a distinct touch of frost in the air to-night, and the glass is going up. I hope it means that you are going to have good weather, Mr. Townshend."

He helped himself to a glass of milk and a biscuit.

" Elizabeth, do you know what that brother of yours has done ? I happened to take down *The Pilgrim's Progress* just now, and found that the wretched little fellow had utterly ruined those fine prints by drawing whiskers on the faces of the most unlikely people."

Mr. Seton's mouth twitched.

" The effect," he added, " is ludicrous in the extreme."

His listeners laughed in the most unfeeling way, and Elizabeth explained to Mr. Townshend that when Buff was in fault he was alluded to as " your brother," as if hers was the sole responsibility.

" Well, you know," said Mr. Seton, as he made the window secure, " you spoil the boy terribly."

Elizabeth looked at Arthur Townshend, and they smiled to each other.

CHAPTER X

" If ever you have looked on better days,
  If ever been where bells have knolled to church."
                                    As You Like It.

MR. SETON'S church was half an hour's walk from his house, and the first service began at nine-forty-five, so Sabbath morning brought no " long lie " for the Seton household. They left the house at a quarter-past nine, and remained at church till after the afternoon service, luncheon being eaten in the " interval."

Thomas and Billy generally accompanied them to church, not so much from love of the sanctuary as from love of the luncheon, which was a picnic-like affair. Leaving immediately after it, they were home in time for their two-o'clock Sunday dinner with " Papa."

Elizabeth had looked forward with horror to the prospect of a Sunday shut in with the Arthur Town-shend of her imagination, but the actual being so much less black than her fancy had painted she could view the prospect with equanimity, hoping only that such a spate of services might not prove too chastening an experience for a worldly guest.

Sabbath morning was always rather a worried time for Elizabeth. For one thing, the Sabbath seemed to make Buff's brain more than usually fertile in devising schemes of wickedness, and then, her father *would not* hurry. There he sat, calmly contemplative, in the study while his daughter implored him to remember the " intimations," and to be sure to put in that there was a Retiring Collection for the Aged and Infirm Ministers' Fund.

Mr. Seton disliked a plethora of intimations, and protested that he had already six items.

" Oh, Father," cried his exasperated daughter, " what *is* the use of saying that when they've all to be made ? "

" Quite true, Lizbeth," said her father meekly.

Mr. Seton always went off to church walking alone, Elizabeth following, and the boys straggling behind.

" I'm afraid," said Elizabeth to Mr. Townshend, as they walked down the quiet suburban road with its decorous villa-residences,—" I'm afraid you will find this rather a strenuous day. I don't suppose in Persia—and elsewhere—you were accustomed to give the Sabbath up wholly to ' the public and private exercises of God's worship ' ? "

Mr. Townshend confessed that he certainly had not.

" Oh, well," said Elizabeth cheeringly, " it will be a new experience. We generally do five services on Sunday. My brother Walter used to say that though he never entered a church again, his average would still be higher than most people's. What king was it who said he was a ' sair saunt for the Kirk ' ? I can sympathize with him."

They drifted into talk, and became so engrossed that they had left the suburbs and had nearly reached the church before Elizabeth remembered the boys and stopped and looked round for them.

" I don't see the boys. They must have come

another way. D'you mind going back with me to see if they're coming down Cumberland Street ? "

It was a wide street, deserted save for a small child carrying milk-pitchers, and a young man with a bowler hat hurrying churchwards; but as they watched, three figures appeared at the upper end. Thomas came first, wearing with pride a new overcoat and carrying a Bible with an elastic band. (He had begged it from the housemaid, who, thankful for some sign of grace in such an abandoned character, had lent it gladly.) Several yards behind Billy marched along, beaming on the world as was his wont; and last of all came Buff, deep in a story, walking in a dream. When the story became very exciting he jumped rapidly several times backwards and forwards from the pavement to the gutter. He was quite oblivious of his surroundings till a starved-looking cat crept through the area railings and mewed at him. He stopped and stroked it gently. Then he got something out of his trouser-pocket which he laid before the creature, and stood watching it anxiously.

Elizabeth's eyes grew soft as she watched him.

" Buff has the tenderest heart for all ill-used things," she said, " especially cats and dogs." She went forward to meet her young brother. " What were you giving the poor cat, sonny ? " she asked.

" A bit of milk-chocolate. It's the nearest I had to milk, but it didn't like it. Couldn't I carry it to the vestry and give it to John for a pet ? "

" I'm afraid John wouldn't receive it with any enthusiasm," said his sister. (" John's the beadle," she explained to Mr. Townshend.) " But I expect, Buff, it really has a home of its own—quite a nice one—and has only come out for a stroll; anyway, we must hurry. We're late as it is."

The cavalcade moved again, and as they walked Elizabeth gave Mr. Townshend a description of the meeting he was about to attend.

" It's called the Fellowship Meeting," she told him, " and it is a joint meeting of the Young Men's and the Young Women's Christian Associations. Some one reads a paper, and the rest of us discuss it—or don't discuss it, as the case may be. Some of the papers are distinctly good, for we have young men with ideas. To-day I'm afraid it's a wee young laddie reading his first paper. The president this winter is a most estimable person, but he has a perfect genius for choosing inappropriate hymns. At ten a.m. he gives out ' Abide with me, fast falls the eventide,' or, again, we find ourselves singing

' The sun that bids us rest is waking
Our brethren 'neath the Western sky,'

—such an obvious untruth ! And he chooses the prizes for the Band of Hope children, and last year, when I was distributing them, a mite of four toddled up in response to her name, and I handed her a cheerful-looking volume. I just happened to glance at the title, and it was *The Scarlet Letter*, by Nathaniel Hawthorne. I suppose he must have bought it because it had a nice bright cover ! Don't look at me if he does anything funny to-day ! I am so given to giggle."

The Fellowship Meeting was held in the hall, so Elizabeth led the way past the front of the church and down a side-street to the hall door.

First, they all marched into the vestry, where coats could be left, and various treasures, such as books to read in " the interval," deposited in the cupboard. The vestry contained a table, a sofa,

several chairs, two cupboards, and a good fire ; Mr.
Seton's own room opened out of it.

Billy sat down on the sofa and said languidly
that if the others would go to the meeting he would
wait to help Ellen lay the cloth for luncheon, but
his suggestion not meeting with approval he was
herded upstairs. As it was, they were late. The
first hymn and the prayer were over, and the president was announcing that he had much pleasure in
asking Mr. Daniel Ross to read them his paper on
Joshua when they trooped in and sat down on a
vacant form near the door.

Mr. Daniel Ross, a red-headed boy, rose unwill-
ingly from his seat on the front bench, and taking
a doubled-up exercise-book from his pocket, gave a
despairing glance at the ceiling, and began. It was
at once evident that he had gone to some old divine
for inspiration, for the language was distinctly
archaic. Now and again a statement, boyish,
abrupt, and evidently original, obtruded itself oddly
among the flowery sentences, but most of it had been
copied painfully from some ancient tome. He read
very rapidly, swallowing audibly at intervals, and
his audience was settling down to listen to him when,
quite suddenly, the essay came to an end. The
essayist turned a page of the exercise-book in an
expectant way, but there was nothing more, so he
sat down with a surprised smile.

Elizabeth suppressed an inclination to laugh,
and the president, conscious of a full thirty minutes
on his hands, gazed appealingly at the minister.
Mr. Seton rose and said how pleasant it was to hear
one of the younger members, and that the paper
had pleased him greatly. (This was strictly true,
for James Seton loved all things old—even the
works of ancient divines.) He then went on to talk

5

of Joshua that mighty man of valour, and became so enthralled with his subject he had to stop abruptly, look at his watch, and leave the meeting in order to commune with the precentor about the tunes.

The president asked for more remarks, but none were forthcoming till John Jamieson rose, and leaning on his stick, spoke. An old man, he said, was shy of speaking in a young people's meeting, but this morning he felt he had a right, for the essayist was one of his own boys. Very kindly he spoke of the boy who had come Sabbath after Sabbath to his class : " And now I've been sitting at my scholar's feet and heard him read a paper. It's Daniel Ross's first attempt at a paper, and I think you'll agree with me that he did very well. He couldn't have had a finer subject, and the paper showed that he had read it up." (At this praise the ears of Daniel Ross sitting on the front bench glowed rosily.) " Now, I'm not going to take up any more time, but there's just one thing about Joshua that I wonder if you've noticed. *He rose up early in the morning*. Sometimes a young man tells me he hasn't time to read. Well, Joshua when he had anything to do rose up early in the morning. Another man hasn't time to pray. There are quiet hours before the work of the day begins. The minister and the essayist have spoken of Joshua's great deeds, deeds that inspire ; let me ask you to learn this homely lesson from the great man, to rise up early in the morning."

The president, on rising, said he had nothing to add to the remarks already made but to thank the essayist in the name of the meeting for his " v'ry able paper," and they would close by singing Hymn 493 :

"Summer suns are glowing
Over land and sea ;
Happy light is flowing
Bountiful and free."

As 'they filed out Elizabeth spoke to one and another, asking about ailing relations, hearing of any happenings in families. One boy, with an eager, clever face, came forward to tell her that he had finished Blake's *Songs of Innocence and Experience*, and they were fine ; might he lend the book to another chap in the warehouse ? Elizabeth willingly gave permission, and they went downstairs together talking poetry.

In the vestry Elizabeth paraded the boys for inspection. " Billy, you're to *sit* on the seat to-day, remember, not get underneath it."

" Buff, take that sweetie out of your mouth. It's most unseemly to go into church sucking a toffee-ball."

" *Thomas !* What is that in the strap of your Bible ? "

" It's a story I'm reading," said Thomas.

" But surely you don't mean to read it in church ? "

" It passes the time," said Thomas, who was always perfectly frank.

Mr. Seton caught Arthur Townshend's eye, and they laughed aloud ; while Elizabeth hastily asked the boys if they had their collection ready.

" The ' plate ' is at the church door," she explained to Mr. Townshend. " As Buff used to say, ' We pay as we go in.' Thomas, put that book in the cupboard till we come out of church. Good boy : now we'd better go in. You've got your intimations, Father ? "

" Seton's kirk," as it was called in the district,

was a dignified building, finely proportioned, and plain to austerity. Once it had been the fashionable church in a good district. Old members still liked to tell of its glorious days, when " braw folk " came in their carriages and rustled into their cushioned pews, and the congregation was so large that people sat on the pulpit steps.

These days were long past. No one sat on the pulpit steps to hear James Seton preach, there was room and to spare in the pews. Indeed, " Seton's kirk " was now something of a forlorn hope in a neighbourhood almost entirely given over to Jews and Roman Catholics. A dreary and disheartening sphere to work in, one would have thought, but neither Mr. Seton nor his flock were dreary or disheartened. For some reason, it was a church that seemed difficult to leave. Members " flitted " to the suburbs and went for a Sabbath or two to a suburban church, then they appeared again in " Seton's kirk," remarking that the other seemed " awful unhomely somehow."

Mr. Seton would not have exchanged his congregation for any in the land. It was so full of character, he said ; his old men dreamed dreams, his young men saw visions. That they had very little money troubled him not at all. Money was not one of the things that mattered to James Seton.

Arthur Townshend sat beside Elizabeth in the Manse seat. Elizabeth had pushed a Bible and Hymnary in his direction, and never having taken part in a Presbyterian service, he awaited further developments with interest, keeping an eye the while on Billy, who had tied a bent pin to a string and was only waiting for the first prayer to angle in the next pew. As the clock struck eleven the beadle carried the big Bible up to the pulpit, and descending, stood at the foot of the stairs until the minister had passed up. Behind came the precenter, distributing before he sat down slips with the psalms and hymns of the morning service, round the choir.

Mr. Seton entered the pulpit. A hush fell over the church. " Let us pray," he said.

A stranger hearing James Seton pray was always struck by two things—the beauty of his voice, or rather the curious arresting quality of it which gave an extraordinary value to every word he said, and the stateliness of his language. There was no complacent camaraderie in his attitude towards his Maker. It is true he spoke confidently as to a Father, but he never forgot that he was in the presence of the King of kings.

" Almighty and merciful God, who hast begotten us again unto a living hope by the resurrection of Jesus Christ from the dead, we approach Thy presence that we may offer to Thee our homage in the name of our risen and exalted Saviour. Holy, holy, holy art Thou, Lord God Almighty. The whole earth is full of Thy glory. Thou art more than all created things, and Thou givest us Thyself to be our portion. Like as the hart pants after the waterbrooks, so make our souls to thirst for Thee, O God. Though Abraham acknowledge us not and Israel be ignorant of us, we are Thy offspring. . . ."

Mr. Seton had a litany of his own, and used phrases Sabbath after Sabbath which the people looked for and loved. The Jews were prayed for with great earnestness—" Israel beloved for the Father's sake " ; the sick and the sorrowing were " the widespread family of the afflicted." Again, for those kept at home by necessity he asked, " May they who tarry by the brook Bezor divide the spoil " ; and always he finished, " And now, O Lord, what wait we for ? Our hope is in Thy word."

There was no " instrument " in " Seton's kirk," not even a harmonium. They were an old-fashioned people and liked to worship as their fathers had done. True, some of the young men, yearning like the Athenians after new things, had started a movement towards a more modern service, but nothing had come of it. At one time psalms alone had been sung, not even a paraphrase being allowed, and when " human " hymns were introduced it well-nigh broke the hearts of some of the old people. One old man, in the seat before the Setons, delighted Elizabeth's heart by chanting the words of a psalm when a hymn was given out, his efforts to make the words fit the tune being truly heroic.

Mr. Seton gave out his text :

" The kingdom of heaven is like unto a certain king who made a marriage for his son, and he sent forth his servants, saying, Tell them which are bidden, and they would not come. Again he sent forth other servants, saying, Behold, I have prepared my dinner ; my oxen and fatlings are killed, and all things are ready. *But they made light of it.*"

To Arthur Townshend Mr. Seton's preaching came as a revelation. He had been charmed with him as a gentle saint, a saint kept human by a sense of humour, a tall daughter, and a small, wicked son. But this man in the pulpit, his face stern and sad as he spoke of the unwilling guests, was no gentle saint, but a " sword-blade man."

He preached without a note, leaning over the pulpit, pouring out his soul in argument, beseeching his hearers not to make light of so great a salvation. He seemed utterly filled by the urgency of his message. He told no foolish anecdotes, he had few quotations, it was simple what he said : one felt that nothing mattered to the preacher but his message.

The sermon only lasted a matter of twenty minutes (even the restless Buff sat quietly through it), then a hymn was sung. " Before singing this hymn, I will make the following intimations," Mr. Seton announced. After the hymn, the benediction, and the service was over.

To reach the vestry, instead of going round by the big door, the Manse party went through the choir-seat and out of the side-door. The boys, glad to be once again in motion, rushed down the passage and collided with Mr. Seton before they reached the vestry.

" Gently, boys," he said. " Try to be a little quieter in your ways ; " and he retired into his own room to take off his gown and bands.

Luncheon had been laid by Ellen, and Marget was pouring the master's beef-tea into a bowl.

" I've brocht as much as 'll dae him tae," she whispered to Elizabeth, as she departed for the small hall, where tea and sandwiches were provided for people from a distance. The " him " referred to by Marget was standing with his monocle in his eye watching Buff and Billy who, clasped in each other's arms, were rolling on the sofa like two young bears, while Thomas hung absorbed over the cocoa-tin.

" Mr. Townshend, will you have some beef-tea, or cocoa ? And do find a chair. The boys can all sit on the sofa, if we push the table nearer them."

" I don't want any hot water in my cup," said Thomas, who was stirring cocoa, milk, and sugar into a rich brown paste. "Try a lick," he said to Buff ; "it's like chocolate."

Mr. Townshend found a chair, and said he would like some beef-tea, but refused a sausage-roll, to the astonishment of the boys.

"The sausage-rolls are because of you," said Elizabeth reproachfully. "They are Marget's speciality, and she made them as a great favour. However, have a sandwich. Thomas,"—to that youth, who was taking a sip of chocolate and a bite of sausage-roll turn about,—"Thomas, you'll be a very sick man before long."

"Aw, well," said Thomas, "if I'm sick I'll not can go to school, and I'm happy just now, anyway."

"Thomas is a philosopher," said Arthur Townshend.

Mr. Seton had put his bowl of beef-tea on the mantelpiece to cool (it was rather like the Mad Tea-party, the Setons' lunch), and he turned round to ask which (if any) of the boys remembered the text.

"Not me," said Thomas, always honest.

"Something about oxes," said Buff vaguely, "and a party," he added.

Billy looked completely blank.

"Mrs. Nicol wasn't in church," said Thomas, who took a great interest in the congregation, and especially in this lady, who frequently gave him peppermints, "and none of the Clarks were there. Alick Thomson winked at me in the prayer."

"If your eyes had been closed, you wouldn't have seen him," said Elizabeth, making the retort obvious. "Come in," she added in response to a knock at the door. "Oh ! Mr. M'Auslin, how are you ? Let me introduce—Mr. Townshend, Mr. M'Auslin."

Arthur Townshend found himself shaking hands with the president of the Fellowship Meeting, who said " Pleased to meet you," in the most friendly way, and proceeded to go round the room shaking hands warmly with every one.

" Sit down and have some lunch," said Mr. Seton.

" Thank you, Mr. Seton, no. I just brought in Miss Seton's tracts." He did not go away, however, nor did he sit down, and Arthur Townshend found it very difficult to go on with his luncheon with this gentleman standing close beside him ; no one else seemed to mind, but went on eating calmly.

" A good meeting this morning," said Mr. Seton.

" Very nice, Mr. Seton. Pleasant to see the younger members coming forward as, I think, you observed in your remarks."

" Quite so," said Mr. Seton.

" How is your aunt ? " Elizabeth asked him.

" Poorly, Miss Seton ; indeed I may say very poorly. She has been greatly tried by neuralgia these last few days."

" I'm so sorry. I hope to look in to see her one day this week."

" Do so, Miss Seton ; a visit from you will cheer Aunt Isa, I know. By the way, Miss Seton, I would like to discuss our coming Social Evening with you, if I may."

" Yes. Would Thursday evening suit you ? "

" No, Miss Seton. I'm invited to a cup of tea on the Temperance Question on Thursday."

" I see. Well, Saturday ? "

" That would do nicely. What hour is most convenient, Miss Seton ? "

" Eight—eight-thirty ; just whenever you can come."

"Thank you, Miss Seton. Good-morning. Good-morning, Mr. Seton." He again went round the room, shaking hands with every one, and withdrew.

"Did you recognize the chairman of the Fellowship Meeting?" Elizabeth asked Arthur Townshend. "Isn't he a genteel young man?"

"He has very courtly manners," said Arthur.

"Yes; and his accent is wonderful, too. He hardly ever falls through it. I only once remember him forgetting himself. He was addressing the Young Women's Bible Class on Jezebel, and he got so worked up he cried, 'Oh, girrls, girrls, Jezebel was a bad yin, girrls.' I wonder why he didn't talk about the Social here and now? He will come trailing up to the house on Saturday and put off quite two hours."

"My dear," said her father, "don't grudge the time, if it gives him any pleasure. Remember what a narrow life he has, and be thankful little things count for so much to him. To my mind, Hugh M'Auslin is doing a very big thing, and the fine thing about him is that he doesn't see it."

"But, Father, what is he doing?"

"Is it a small thing, Lizbeth, for a young man to give up the best years of his life to a helpless invalid? Mr. M'Auslin," Mr. Seton explained to Arthur Townshend, "supports an old aunt who cared for him in his boyhood. She is quite an invalid and very cantankerous, though, I believe, a good woman. And—remember this, you mocking people, when you talk of courtly manners—his manners are just as 'courtly' when his old aunt upbraids him for not spending every minute of his sparse spare time at her bedside."

"I never said that Mr. M'Auslin wasn't the best

of men," said Elizabeth, " only I wish he wouldn't be so coy. Well, my district awaits me, I must go. I wonder what you would like to do, Mr. Townshend? I can lend you something to read—*The Newcomes* is in the cupboard—and show you a quiet cubby-hole to read it in, if you would like that."

" That will be delightful, but—is it permitted to ask what you are going to do? "

" I? Going with my tracts. That's what we do between services. I have two ' closes,' with about ten doors to each close. Come with me, if you like, but it's a most unsavoury locality."

Thomas and Billy were getting into their overcoats preparatory to going away. Buff asked if he might go part of the way with them, and permission being given, they set off together.

Elizabeth looked into the little square looking-glass on the mantelpiece to see if her hat was straight, then she threw on her fur, and went out with Arthur Townshend into the street.

The frost of the morning had brought a slight fog, but the pavements were dry, and it was pleasant walking. " It's only a few steps," said Elizabeth,— " not much of a task after all. One Sunday I sent Ellen, and Buff went with her. She had a formula which he thought very neat. At every door she said, ' This is a tract. Chilly, isn't it? '"

Arthur Townshend laughed. " What do you say? " he asked.

" At first I said nothing, simply poked the tract at them. When Father prayed for the ' silent messengers '—meaning, of course, the tracts—I took it to mean the tract distributors! I have plucked up courage now to venture a few remarks, but they generally fall upon stony ground."

At a close-mouth blocked by two women and

several children Elizabeth stopped and announced that this was her district. It was very dirty and almost quite dark, but as they ascended the light got better.

Elizabeth knocked in a very deprecating way at each door. Sometimes a woman opened the door and seemed pleased to have the tract, and in one house there was a sick child for whom Elizabeth had brought a trifle. On the top landing she paused. " Here," she said, " we stop and ponder for a moment. These two houses are occupied respectively by Mrs. Conolly and Mrs. O'Rafferty. I keep on forgetting who lives in which."

" Does it matter ? "

" Yes, a lot. You see, Mrs. Conolly is a nice woman and Mrs. O'Rafferty is the reverse. Mrs. Conolly takes the tract and thanks me kindly ; Mrs. O'Rafferty, always gruff, told me on my last visit if I knocked again at her door she would come at me with a fender. So you see it is rather a problem. Would you like to try and see what sort of ' dusty answer ' you get ? Perhaps, who knows, the sight of you may soothe the savage breast of the O'Rafferty. I'll stand out of sight."

Arthur Townshend took the proffered tract from Elizabeth's hand, smiling at the mischief that danced in her eyes, and was about to knock when one of the doors opened suddenly. Both of the tract distributors started visibly ; then Elizabeth sprang forward, with a relieved smile.

" Good-morning, Mrs. Conolly. I was just going to knock. I hope you are all well."

Mrs. Conolly was understood to say that things were moderately bright with her, and that close being finished, Elizabeth led the way downstairs.

" What quite is the object of giving out these

things?" asked Arthur Townshend, as they emerged into the street. "D'you think it does good?"

"Ah! 'that I cannot tell, said he,'" returned Elizabeth. "I expect the men light their pipes with them, but that isn't any business of mine. My job is to give out the tracts and leave the results in Higher Hands, as Father would say."

.   .   .   .   .   .

The afternoon service began at two and lasted an hour. Mr. Seton never made the mistake of wearying his people with long services. One member was heard to say of him: "He needs neither specs nor paper, an' he's oot on the chap o' the hour."

The attendance was larger in the afternoons, and the sun struggled through the fog and made things more cheerful. Mr. Seton preached on Paul. It was a subject after his own heart, and his face shone as he spoke of that bond-slave of Jesus Christ —of all he gave up, of all he gained. At the church door, the service ended, people stood in groups and talked. Elizabeth was constantly stopped by somebody. One stolid youth thrust himself upon her notice, and when she said pleasantly, "How are you all, Mr. . . . ?" (she had forgotten his name), he replied, "Fine, thanks. Of coorse ma faither's deid and buried since last I saw ye."

"Why 'of course'?" Elizabeth asked Arthur. "And there is another odd thing—the use of the word 'annoyed.' When I went to condole with a poor body whose son had been killed in an explosion, she said, 'Ay, I'm beginnin' to get over it now, but I was real annoyed at first.' It sounds so *inadequate.*"

"It reminds me of a Hindu jailer," said Arthur, "in charge of a criminal about to be hung. Commenting on his downcast look, the jailer said, ' He says he is innocent, and he will be hung to-morrow, therefore he is somewhat peevish.' "

Arthur Townshend found himself introduced to many people who wrung his hand and said " V'ry pleased to meet you." Little Mr. Taylor, hopping by the side of his tall wife, asked him if he had ever heard Mr. Seton preach before, and being told " No," said, " Then ye've had a treat the day. Isn't he great on Paul ? "

The Taylors accompanied them part of the way home. Mr. Taylor's humour was at its brightest, and with many sly glances at Mr. Townshend he adjured Elizabeth to be a " good wee miss " and not think of leaving " Papa." Finding the response to his witticisms somewhat disappointing, he changed the subject, and laying a hand on Buff's shoulder, said, " Ye'll be glad to hear, Mr. Townshend, that this boy is going to follow his Papa and be a minister."

Buff had been " stotting " along the road, very far away from Glasgow and Mr. Taylor and the Sabbath Day. He had been Cyrano de Bergerac, and was wiping his trusty blade after having accounted for his eighty-second man, when he was brought rudely back to the common earth.

He turned a dazed eye on the speaker. What was he saying ? " This boy is going to be a minister."

And he had been Cyrano ! The descent was too rapid.

" Me ? " cried Buff. " Not likely ! I'm going to fight and kill *hundreds of people*."

" Oh, my, my," said Mrs. Taylor. " That's not a nice way for a Christian little boy to speak. That's like a wee savage ! "

Buff pulled his sister's sleeve.

" Was Cyrano a savage ? " he whispered.

Elizabeth shook her head.

" Well," said Buff, looking defiantly at Mrs. Taylor, " Cyrano fought a hundred men one after another and *he* wasn't a savage."

Mrs. Taylor shook her head sadly. " Yer Papa would be sorry to think ye read about sich people."

" Haw ! " cried Buff, " it was Father read it to me himself,—didn't he, Lizbeth ?—and he laughed —he *laughed* about him fighting the hundred men."

They had come to the end of the street where the Taylors lived, and they all stopped for a minute, Buff flushed and triumphant, Mrs. Taylor making the bugles of her Sabbath bonnet shake with disapproval, and Mr. Taylor still brimful of humour.

" It's as well we're leavin' this bloodthirsty young man, Mrs. Taylor," he said. " It's as well we're near home. He might feel he wanted to kill us." (Buff's expression was certainly anything but benign.)

Elizabeth shook hands with her friends, and said :

" It would be so nice if you would spend an evening with us. Not this week—perhaps Tuesday of next week ? "

The Taylors accepted with effusion. There was nothing they enjoyed so much as spending an evening, and this Elizabeth knew.

" That 'll be something to look forward to," Mr. Taylor said ; and his wife added, " Ay, if we're here and able, but ye niver can tell."

As they walked on Elizabeth looked at her companion's face and laughed.

" Mr. Taylor is a queer little man," she said. " He used to worry me dreadfully. I simply couldn't stand his jokes—and then I found out that he wasn't the little fool I had been thinking him, and I was ashamed. He is rather a splendid person."

Mr. Townshend and Buff both looked at her.

"Yes; Father told me. It seems that years ago he had a brother who was a grief to him, and who did something pretty bad, and went off to America, leaving a wife and three children. Mr. Taylor wasn't a bit well-off, but he set himself to the task of paying off the debts his brother had left, and helping to keep the family. For years he denied himself everything but the barest necessities—no pipe, no morning paper, no car-pennies—and he told no one what he was doing. And his wife helped him in every way, and never said it was hard on her. The worst is over now, and he told Father. But I think it must have been in those hard days that he learned the joking habit, to keep himself going, you know, and so I don't find them so silly as I did, but brave, and rather pathetic somehow."

Arthur Townshend nodded. "'To know all,'" he quoted. "It seems a pity that there aren't always interpreters at hand."

"And what do you think of the Scots Kirk?" Elizabeth asked him presently.

"In the Church of England a man who could preach like your father would be a bishop."

"I daresay. We have no bishops in our Church, but we have a fairly high standard of preaching. Do you mean that you think Father is rather thrown away in that church, preaching to the few?"

"It sounds impertinent—but I think I did mean that."

"Yes. Oh! I don't wonder. I looked round this morning and wondered how it would strike you. A small congregation of dull-looking, shabby people ! But as Father looks at them they aren't dull or shabby. They are the souls given him to shepherd into the Fold. He has a charge to keep. He simply wouldn't understand you if you talked to him of a larger sphere, more repaying work, and so on. People often say to me, ' Your father is thrown away in that district.' They don't see . . ."

" You must think me a blundering sort of idiot——" Arthur began.

" Oh no ! I confess I have a leaning towards your point of view. I know how splendid Father is, and I rather want every one else to know it too. I want recognition for him. But he doesn't for himself. ' Fame i' the sun ' never vexes his thoughts. I expect, if you have set your face steadfastly to go to Jerusalem, these things seem very small. And I am quite sure Father could never be a really popular minister. At times he fails lamentably. Yes ; he simply can't be vulgar, poor dear, not even at a social meeting. He sees in marriage no subject for jesting. Even twins leave him cold. Where another man would scintillate with brilliant jokes on the subject Father merely says, ' Dear me ! ' Sometimes I feel rather sorry for the people—the happy bridegroom and the proud father, I mean. They are standing expecting to be, so to speak, dug in the ribs—and they aren't. I could do it quite well,—it is no trouble to me to be all things to all men,—but Father can't."

Arthur Townshend laughed. " No, I can't see your father being jocose. I was thinking when I listened to him what a tremendous thing for people to have a padre like that. His very face is an inspiration. His eyes seem to see things beyond. He makes me think of—who was it in *The Pil-*

grim's Progress who had ' a wonderful innocent smile ' ? "

Elizabeth nodded.

" I know. Isn't it wonderful, after sixty odd years in this world ? There is something so oddly joyous about him. And it isn't that sort of provoking fixed brightness that some Christian people have—people who have read Robert Louis and don't mean to falter in their task of happiness. When you ask them how they are, they say ' *Splendid* ' ; and when you remark, conversationally, that the weather is ghastly beyond words, they pretend to find pleasure in it, until, like Pet Marjorie, you feel your birse rise at them. Father knows just how bad the world is, the cruelty, the toil, the treason ; he knows how bitter sorrow is, and what it means to lay hopes in the grave, but he looks beyond and sees something so ineffably lovely—such an exceeding and eternal weight of glory—that he can go on with his day's work joyfully."

" Yes," said Arthur, " the other world seems extraordinarily real to him."

" Oh ! Real ! Heaven is much the realest place there is to Father. I do believe that when he is toiling away in the Gorbals he never sees the squalor for thinking of the streets of gold."

Elizabeth's grey eyes grew soft for a moment with unshed tears, but she blinked them away and laughed.

" The nicest thing about my father is that he is full of contradictions. So gentle and with such an uncompromising creed ! The Way is the Way to Father, narrow and hard and comfortless. And he is so good, so purely good, and yet never righteous over much. There is a sort of ingrained humility and lovableness in him that attracts the sinners as

well as the saints. He never thinks that because
he is virtuous there should be no more cakes and ale.
And then, though with him he carries gentle peace,
he is by no means a pacific sort of person. He
loves to fight ; and he hates to be in the majority.
Minorities have been right, he says, since the days
of Noah. When he speaks in the Presbytery it is
always on the unpopular side. D'you remember
what a fuss they made about Chinese labour in
South Africa ? Father made a speech defending
it ! Some one said to me that he must have an
interest in the Mines ! Dear heart ! He doesn't
even know what his income is. The lilies of the
field are wily financiers compared to him."

Half an hour later—at four o'clock, to be precise
—the Setons and their guest sat down to dinner.

" I often wonder," said Mr. Seton, as he meditatively carved slices of cold meat, " why on Sabbath
we have dinner at four o'clock and tea at seven.
Wouldn't it be just as easy to have tea at four and
dinner at seven ? "

" ' Sir,' " said Elizabeth, " in the words of Dr.
Johnson, ' you may wonder ! ' All my life this
has been the order of meals on the Sabbath Day,
and who am I that should change them ? Besides,
it's a change and makes the Sabbath a little
different. Mr. Townshend, I hope you don't
mind us galumphing through the meal ? Father
and I have to be back at the church at five
o'clock."

" You don't mean," protested Arthur Townshend,
" that you are going back to church again ? "

" Alas ! yes.—Have some toast, won't you ?—
Father has his Bible class, and I teach a class in
the Sabbath school. Buff, pass Mr. Townshend the
butter."

" Thank you. But, tell me, do you walk all the way again ? "

" Every step," said Elizabeth firmly. " We could get an electric car, but we prefer to trudge it."

" But why ? "

" Oh ! just to make it more difficult."

Elizabeth smiled benignly on the puzzled guest. " You see," she explained, " Father is on the Sabbath Observance Committee, and it wouldn't look well if his daughter ruffled it on Sabbath-breaking cars. Isn't that so, Father ? "

Mr. Seton shook his head at his daughter, but did not trouble to reply ; and Elizabeth went on :

" It's more difficult than you would think to be a minister's family. The main point is that you must never do anything that will hurt your father's ' usefulness,' and it is astonishing how many things tend to do that—dressing too well, going to the play, laughing when a sober face would be more suitable, making flippant remarks—their name is legion. Besides, try as one may, it is impossible always to avoid being a stumbling-block. There are little ones so prone to stumble that they would take a toss over anything."

" That will do, Elizabeth," said Mr. Seton.

" Sorry, Father." She turned in explanation to Mr. Townshend. " When Father thinks I am flippant and silly he says ' Elizabeth ! ' and his eyes twinkle ; but when I become irreverent—I am apt to be often—he says ' That will do,' and I stop. So now you will understand. To change the subject—perhaps the most terrible experience I have had, as yet, in my ministerial career was being invited to a christening party and having to sit down in a small kitchen to a supper of tripe and kola. Alan says the outside edge was reached with him when a man who picked his ears with a pencil asked him if he were saved."

"Elizabeth," said her father, "you talk a great deal of nonsense."

"I do," agreed Elizabeth; "I'm what's known as vivacious—in other words, 'a nice bright girl.' And the funny thing is it's a thing I simply hate being. I admire enormously strong, still people. Won't it be awful if I go on being vivacious when I'm fifty? Or do you think I'll be arch then? There is something so resuscitated about vivacious spinsters." She looked gaily round the table, as if the dread future did not daunt her greatly.

Ellen had removed the plates and was handing round the pudding. Elizabeth begged Mr. Townshend not to hurry, and to heed in no way the scrambling table manners of his host and hostess. She turned a deaf ear to his suggestion that he would like to hear her instruct her class, assuring him that he would be much better employed reading a book by the fire. Buff, she added, would be pleased to keep him company after he had learned his Sabbath evening task, eight lines of a psalm.

"Aw," said Buff. "Must I, Father?"

"Eight lines are easily learned, my son."

"Well, can I choose my own psalm?"

His father said "Certainly"; but Elizabeth warned him: "Then make him promise to learn a new one, or he'll just come with 'That man hath perfect blessedness.'"

"I won't," said Buff. "I know a nice one to learn: quite new, about a worm."

"Dear me," said his father, "I wonder what psalm that is? Well, Lizbeth, we must go. You'll find books in the drawing-room, Mr. Townshend; and see that the fire is good."

Elizabeth's class consisted of seven little bullet-headed boys. To-night there was an extra one, whom she welcomed warmly—Bob Scott, the small boy whom she had befriended while collecting in the rain. She found, however, that his presence was not conducive to good conduct in the class. Instead of lapping up the information served out to him without comment, as the other boys did, he made remarks and asked searching questions. Incidents in the Bible lesson recalled to him events, generally quite irrelevant, which he insisted on relating. For instance, the calling forth of evil spirits from the possessed reminded him of the case of a friend of his, one Simpson, a baker, who one morning had gone mad and danced on the bakehouse roof, singing, " Ma sweetheart hes blue eyes," until he fell through a skylight, with disastrous results.

Bob's manners, too, lacked polish. He attracted Elizabeth's attention by saying " Hey, wumman ! " he contradicted her flatly several times ; but in spite of it all, she liked his impudent, pinched little face, and at the end of the hour kept him behind the other boys to ask how things were going with him. He had no mother, it seemed, and no brothers or sisters : he went to school (except when he " plunk't "), ran messages for shops, and kept house—such keeping as it got. His father, he said, was an extra fine man, except when he was drunk.

Before they parted it was arranged that Bob should visit the Setons on Saturday and get his dinner ; he said it would not be much out of his way, as he generally spent his Saturday mornings having a shot at " fitba' " in the park near. He betrayed no gratitude for the invitation, merely saying " S'long, then," as he walked away.

On Sabbath evenings the Setons had prayers at

eight o'clock, and Buff stayed up for the event.
Marget and Ellen were also present, and Elizabeth
played the hymns and led the singing.

"First," said Mr. Seton, "we'll have Buff's
psalm."

Buff was standing on one leg, with his ill-used
Bible bent back in his hand, learning furiously.

"Are you ready?" asked his father.

Buff took a last look, then handed the Bible to
his father.

"It's not a psalm," he said; "it's a paraphrase."

He took a long breath, and in a curious chant,
accentuating such words as he thought fit, he recited:

> "Next, from the *deep*, th' Almighty King
>   Did *vital* beings frame;
> Fowls of the *air* of ev'ry wing,
>   And fish of every name.
> To all the various *brutal* tribes
>   He *gave* their wondrous birth;
> At once the lion *and* the worm
>   *Sprung* from the teeming earth."

He only required to be prompted once, and when he
had finished he drew from his pocket a paper which
he handed to his father.

"What's this?" said Mr. Seton. "Ah, I see."
He put his hand up to his mouth and appeared to
study the paper intently.

"It's not my best," said Buff modestly.

"May I see it?" asked Elizabeth.

Buff was fond of illustrating the Bible, and this
was his idea of the Creation so far as a sheet of note-
paper and rather a blunt pencil could take him. In
the background rose a range of mountains on the
slopes of which a bird, some beetles, and an elephant
(all more or less of one size) had a precarious foot-
hold. In the foreground a dishevelled lion glared

at a worm which reared itself on end in a surprised way. Underneath was printed "At once the lion and the worm"—the quotation stopped for lack of space.

" Very fine, Buff," said Elizabeth, smiling widely. " Show it to Mr. Townshend."

" He's seen it," said Buff. " He helped me with the lion's legs, but I did all the rest myself—didn't I ? " he appealed to the guest.

" You did, old man. We'll colour it to-morrow, when I get you that paint-box."

" Yes," said Buff, crossing the room to show his picture to Marget and Ellen, while Mr. Seton handed Arthur Townshend a hymn-book and asked what hymn he would like sung, adding that every one chose a favourite hymn at Sabbath evening prayers. Seeing Arthur much at a loss, Elizabeth came to his help with the remark that English hymn-books were different from Scots ones, and suggesting " Lead, kindly Light," as being common to both.

Marget demanded " Not all the blood of beasts," while Ellen murmured that her favourite was " Sometimes a light surprises."

" Now, Buff," said his father.

" Prophet Daniel," said Buff firmly.

Both Mr. Seton and Elizabeth protested, but Buff was adamant. The " Prophet Daniel " he would have and none other.

" Only three verses, then," pleaded Elizabeth.

" It all," said Buff.

The hymn in question was a sort of chant. The first line ran " Where is now the Prophet Daniel ? " This was repeated three times, and the fourth line was the answer : " Safe in the Promised Land."

The second verse told the details : " He went through the den of lions " (repeated three times), " Safe to the Promised Land."

After the prophet Daniel came the Hebrew children, then the Twelve Apostles. The great point about the hymn was that any number of favourite heroes might be added at will. William Wallace Buff always insisted on, and to-night as he sang " He went up from an English scaffold " he gazed searchingly at the English guest to see if no shade of shame flushed his face ; but Mr. Townshend sat looking placidly innocent, and seemed to hold himself entirely guiltless of the death of the patriot. The Covenanters came after William Wallace, and Buff with a truly catholic spirit wanted to follow with Graham of Claverhouse ; but this was felt to be going too far. By no stretch of imagination could one picture the persecutor and the persecuted, the wolf and the lamb, happily sharing one paradise.

" That will do now, my son," said Mr. Seton ; but Buff was determined on one more, and his shrill treble rose alone in " Where is now Prince Charles Edward ? " until Elizabeth joined in, and lustily, almost defiantly, they assured themselves that the Prince who had come among his people seeking an earthly crown had attained to a heavenly one and was " Safe in the Promised Land."

Mr. Seton shook his head as he opened the Bible to read the evening portion. " I hope so," he said, and his tone was dubious,—" I hope so."

" Well ! " said Elizabeth, as she said good-night to her guest, " has this been the dullest day of your life ? "

Arthur Townshend looked into the mocking grey eyes that were exactly on a level with his own, and " I don't think I need answer that question," he said.

" The only correct answer is, ' Not at all.' But

I'm quite sure you never sang so many hymns or met so many strange new specimens of humanity all in one day before."

Mr. Seton, who disliked to see books treated lightly, was putting away all the volumes that Buff had taken out in the course of the evening and left lying about on chairs and on the floor. As he locked the glass door he said :

"Lizbeth turns everything into ridicule, even the Sabbath Day."

His daughter sat down on the arm of a chair and protested.

"Oh no, I don't. I don't indeed. I laugh a lot, for ' werena ma hert licht I wad dee.' I have, how shall I say ? a heart too soon made glad. But I'm only stating a fact, Father, when I say that Mr. Townshend has sung a lot of hymns to-day and seen a lot of funnies. . . . Oh ! Father, *don't turn out the lights*. Isn't he a turbulent priest ! My father, Mr. Townshend, has a passion for turning out lights. You will find out all our peculiarities in time—and the longer you know us the odder we'll get."

"I have six more days to get to know you," said Mr. Townshend. And he said it as if he congratulated himself on the fact.

CHAPTER XI

"As we came in by Glasgow town
We were a comely sight to see."
Old Ballad.

ARTHUR TOWNSHEND was what Elizabeth called a repaying guest. He noticed and appreciated things done for his comfort, he was easily amused; also he had the air of enjoying himself. Mr. Seton liked him from the first, and when he heard that he reread several of the Waverley Novels every year he hailed him as a kindred spirit.

He won Buff's respect and admiration by his knowledge of aeroplanes. Even Marget so far unbent towards him as to admit that he was " a wise-like man "; Ellen thought he looked " noble." As for Elizabeth—" You're a nice guest," she told him; " you don't blight."

" No? What kind of guest blights? "

" Several, but *the* Blight devastates. Suppose I've had the drawing-room done up and am filled with pride of it, open the door and surprise myself with it a dozen times in the day—you know, or rather I suppose you don't know, the way of a house-proud woman with a new room. The Blight enters, looks round, and says, ' You've done something to this room, haven't you? Very nice. I've just

155

come from the Puffington-Whalleys, and their draw-ing-rooms are too delicious.   I must describe them to you, for I know you are interested in houses,' and so on and so on, and I have lost conceit of my cherished room.   Sometimes the Blight doesn't say anything, but her glance seems to make one's be-longings shrivel.   And she is the same all the time. You stay her with apples and she prattles of necta-rines ; you drive her in a hired chaise and she talks of the speed of So-and-so's Rolls-Royce.''

" A very trying person," said Arthur Townshend. " But it isn't exactly fulsome flattery to compli-ment me on not being an ill-bred snob.   Do you often entertain a Blight ? ''

" Now that I think of it," Elizabeth confessed, " it only happened once.   Real blights are rare. But we quite often have ungracious guests, and they are almost as bad.   They couldn't praise anything to save their lives.   Everything is taken, as the Scotsman is supposed to have taken his bath, for granted.   When you say, ' I'm afraid it is rather a poor dinner,' they reply, ' Oh, it doesn't matter,' —the correct answer, of course, being, ' What *could* be nicer ? ' ''

" I shall remember that," said Arthur Town-shend ; " and I'm glad that so far you find me a fairly satisfactory guest, only I wish the standard had been higher.   I only seem white because of the blackness of those who went before."

Mr. Seton carried out his plan of showing Mr. Townshend the sights of Glasgow, and on Monday morning they viewed the chrysanthemums in the Park, in the afternoon the Cathedral and the Muni-cipal Buildings ; and whatever may have been the feelings of the guest, Mr. Seton drew great enjoyment from the outing.

On Tuesday Elizabeth became cicerone, and announced at the breakfast-table her intention of personally conducting Mr. Townshend through Glasgow on the top of an electric car.

Buff was struggling into his overcoat, watched (but not helped) by Thomas and Billy, but when he heard of his sister's plan he at once took it off again and said he would make one of the party.

Thomas looked at his friend coldly.

" Mamma says," he began, " that it's a very daft-like thing the way you get taken to places and miss school. By rights I should have got staying at home to-day with my gumboil."

" Poor old Thomas ! " said Elizabeth. " Never mind. You and Buff must both go to school and grow up wise men, and you will each choose a chocolate out of Mr. Townshend's box for a treat."

The sumptuous box was produced, and diverted Buff's mind from the expedition ; and presently the three went off to school, quite reconciled to attempting another step on the steep path to knowledge.

" Isn't Thomas a duck ? " said Elizabeth, as she returned to the table after watching them go out of the gate. " So uncompromising."

" ' Mamma ' must be a frank and fearless commentator," said Mr. Townshend.

" Thomas makes her sound so," Elizabeth admitted. " But when I meet her—I only know her slightly—she seems the gentlest of placid women. Well, can you be ready by eleven-thirty ? *Of course* I want to go. I'm looking forward hugely to seeing Glasgow through your eyes. Come and write your letters in the drawing-room while I talk to Marget about dinner."

Punctually they started. It was a bright, frosty morning, and the trim villas with their newly cleaned doorsteps and tidily brushed-up gardens looked pleasant, homely places as they regarded them from the top of a car.

"This is much nicer than motoring," said Elizabeth. "You haven't got to think of tyres, and it only costs twopence-ha'penny all the way."

She settled back in her seat, and "You've to do all the talking to-day," she said, nodding her head at her companion. "On Sunday I *deaved* you, and you suffered me gladly, or at least you had the appearance of so doing, but it may only have been your horribly good manners; anyway, to-day it is your turn. And you needn't be afraid of boring me, because I am practically unborable. Begin at the beginning, when you were a little boy, and tell me all about yourself." She broke off to look down at a boy riding on a lorry beside the driver. "Just look at that boy! He's being allowed to hold the whip and he's got an apple to eat! What a thoroughly good time he's having—and playing truant too, I expect."

Arthur Townshend glanced at the happy truant, and then at Elizabeth smiling unconsciously in whole-hearted sympathy. She wore a soft blue homespun coat and skirt, and a hat of the same shade crushed down on her hair which burned golden where the sun caught it. Some nonsensical half-forgotten lines came into his mind:

> " Paul said and Peter said,
> And all the saints alive and dead
> Vowed that she had the sweetest head
> Of yellow, yellow hair."

Aloud he said, " You're fond of boys ? "

" Love them," she said. " Even when they're at their roughest and naughtiest and seem all

tackety boots. What were you like when you
were little ? "

" Oh ! A thoroughly uninteresting child. Ate a
lot, and never said or did an original thing. Aunt
Alice cherishes only one *mot*. Once, when the
nursery clock stopped, I remarked, ' No little clock
now to tell us how quickly we're dying,' which
seems to prove that besides being commonplace I
was inclined to be morbid. I went to school very
early, and Aunt Alice gave me good times in my
holidays ; then came three years at Oxford—three
halcyon years—and since then I have been very
little in England. You see, I'm a homeless, wandering sort of creature, and the worst of that sort
of thing is, that when the solitary, for once in a
way, get set in families, they don't understand
the language. Explain to me, please, the meaning
of some of your catch-words. For instance—*Fish
would laugh.*"

" You mean our ower-words," said Elizabeth.
" We have a ridiculous lot ; and they must seem
most incomprehensible to strangers. *Fish would
lawff.* It is really too silly to tell. When Buff was
tiny, three or four or thereabouts, he had a familiar
spirit called Fish. Fish was a loofah with a boot-
button for an eye, and, wrapped in a duster or anything that happened to be lying about, he slept in
Buff's bed, sat in his chair, ate from his plate, and
was unto him a brother. His was an unholy influence. When Buff did anything wicked, Fish said
' Good,' or so Buff reported. When any one did
anything rather fine or noble, Fish ' lawffed,'—you
know the funny way Buff says words with ' au ' ?
Fish was a Socialist and couldn't stand Royalties,
so when we came to a Prince in a fairy tale he had
to call him Brother. He whispered nasty things

about us to Buff : his mocking laughter pursued us ;
his boot-button eye got loose and waggled in the
most sinister way.　He really was a horrid creature
—but how Buff loved him !　Through the day he
alluded to him by high-sounding titles,—Sir John
Fish, Admiral Fish, V.C., Brigadier-General Fish,
—but at night, when he clutched him to his heart
in bed, he murmured over him, ' *Fishie beastie !* '
He lost his place in time, as all favourites do ; but
the memory of him still lives with us, and whenever
any one bucks unduly, or too obviously stands
forth in the light, we say, *Fish would lawff !* ''

The thought of Fish so intrigued Arthur that he
wanted to hear more of him, but Elizabeth begged
him to turn his eyes to the objects of interest around
him.

" Now," she said, " we are on the Broomielaw
Bridge, and that is Clyde's ' wan water.'　I'm told
Broomielaw means ' beloved green place,' so it can't
always have been the coaly hole it is now.　I don't
know what is up the river—Glasgow Green, I think,
and other places, but "—pointing down the river—
" there lies the pathway to the Hebrides.　It always
refreshes me to think that we in Glasgow have a
' back-door to Paradise.' ''

" Yes," said Mr. Townshend, leaning forward to
look at the river.　" Edinburgh, of course, has the
Forth.　I've been reading *Edinburgh Revisited,*—
you know it, I suppose ?—and last week when I was
there I spent some hours wandering about the
' lands ' in the Old Town.　I like Bone's description
of the old rooms filled with men and women of
degree dancing minuets under guttering sconces.
You remember he talks of a pause in the dance,
when the musicians tuned their fiddles, and ladies
turned white shoulders and towering powdered

heads to bleak barred windows to meet the night wind blowing saltly from the Forth ? I think that gives one such a feeling of Edinburgh."

" I know. I remember that," said Elizabeth. " Doesn't James Bone make pictures with words ? "

" Oh ! It's extraordinary. The description of George Square as an elegant old sedan-chair gently decaying, with bright glass still in its lozenge-panels ! I like the idea of the old inhabitants of the Square one after another through the generations coming back each to his own old grey-brown house—such a company of wit and learning and bravery."

" And Murray of Broughton," she cried, her grey eyes shining with interest, " Murray, booted and cloaked and muffled to the eyes, coming down the steps of No. 25 and the teacup flying after him, and the lame little boy creeping out and picking up the saucer, because Traitor Murray meant to him history and romance ! Yes. . . . But it isn't quite tactful of you to dilate on Edinburgh when I am trying to rouse in you some enthusiasm for Glasgow. You think of Edinburgh as some lovely lady of old years draped as with a garment by memories of unhappy far-off things. But you haven't seen her suburbs ! No romance there. Rows and rows of smug, well-built houses, each with a front garden, each with a front gate, and each front gate remains shut against the casual caller until you have rung a bell—and the occupants have had time to make up their minds about you from behind the window curtains —when some mechanism in the vestibule is set in motion, the gate opens, and you walk in. That almost seems to me the most typical thing about Edinburgh. Glasgow doesn't keep visitors at the gate. Glasgow is on the doorstep to welcome them in. It is just itself—cheerful, hard-working, shrewd,

kindly, a place that, like Weir of Hermiston, has no
call to be bonny : it gets through its day's work.
Edinburgh calls Glasgow vulgar, and on the surface
we are vulgar.   We say ' Ucha,' and when we meet
each other in July we think it is funny to say ' A
good New Year ' ; and always our accent grates on
the ears of the genteel.   I have heard it said that
nothing could make Glasgow people gentlefolks,
because we are ' that weel-pleased ' ; and the less
apparent reason there seems for complacency the
more ' weel-pleased ' we are.   As an Edinburgh
man once said to me in that connection, ' If a
Glasgow man has black teeth and bandy legs he
has cheek enough to stand before the King.'   But
we have none of the subtle vulgarity that pretends :
we are plain folk and we know it. . . . I am boring
you.   Let's talk about something really interesting.
What do you think of the Ulster Question ? "

The car went on its way, up Renfield Street and
Sauchiehall Street, till it left shop-windows behind,
and got into tracts of terraces and crescents, rows of
dignified grey houses stretching for miles.

Elizabeth and her companion got out at a stop-
ping-place, and proceeded to walk back to see the
University.   Arthur, looking round, remarked that
the West End of one city was very like the West
End of any other city.

" It's the atmosphere of wealth, I suppose," he
said.

Elizabeth agreed that it was so.   " What do you
think wealth smells like ? " she asked him.   " To me
it is a mixture of very opulent stair-carpets and a
slight suspicion of celery.   I don't know why, but the
houses of the most absolutely rolling-in-riches-people
that I know smell like that—in Glasgow, I mean."

" It is an awesome thought," Arthur said, as he

looked round him, " to think that probably every one of those houses is smelling at this moment of carpets and celery."

" This," said Elizabeth, " is where the City gentlemen live—at least the more refined of the species. We in the South Side have a cruder wealth."

" There is refinement, then, in the West End ? "

Elizabeth made a face.

" The refinement which says ' preserves ' instead of ' jam.' "

Then she had one of her sudden repentances.

" I didn't mean that nastily—but of course, you know, where one is in the process of rising one is apt to be slightly ridiculous. There is always a striving, an uneasiness, a lack of repose. To be so far down as to fear no fall, and to be so securely up as to fear no fall, tends to composure of manner. You who have, I suppose, lived always with the ' ups,' and I who consort almost entirely with the ' downs,' know that for a fact. It is an instructive thing to watch the rise of a family. They rise rapidly in Glasgow. In a few years you may see a family ascend from a small villa in Pollokshields and one servant—known as ' the girrl '—to a ' place ' in the country and a pew in the nearest Episcopal church ; and if this successful man still alludes to a person as a ' party ' and to his wife in her presence as ' Mistress So-and-so here,' his feet are well up the ladder. A few years more and he will cut the strings that bind him to his old life : his boys, educated at English schools, will have forgotten the pit from whence they were dug, his daughters will probably have married well, and he is ' county ' indeed. But you mustn't think Glasgow is full of funnies or that I am laughing at the dear place—not that it would care if I did, it can stand a bit of laughing at. I have the most enormous respect for Glasgow people for all they have done, for their tremendous capacity for doing, for their quite perfect taste in things that matter, and I love them for their good-nature and ' well-pleasedness.'   A very under-sized little man —one whose height might well have been a sore point—said to me once, ' They tell me my grand-father was six-foot-four—he would laugh if he saw me.' And he thoroughly enjoyed the joke."

" But tell me," said Arthur, " have you many friends in Glasgow ? "

" Heaps, but I haven't much time for seeing them. The winter is so crowded with church-work ; then in spring, when things slacken off, I go to London to Aunt Alice ; and in summer we are at Etterick. But I do dine out now and again, and sometimes we have little parties. Would you care to meet some people ? "

He hastily disclaimed any such desire, and assured her he was more than content with the company he had. " But," he added, " I should like to see more of the church people."

" You shall," Elizabeth promised him.

One o'clock found them again in Sauchiehall Street, and Arthur asked Elizabeth's advice as to the best place for luncheon.

" This is my day," she reminded him. " You will have lunch with me, please. If you'll promise not to be nasty about it, I'll take you to my favourite haunt. It's a draper's shop, but don't let that prejudice you."

He found himself presently in a large sunny room carpeted in soft grey and filled with little tables. The tablecloths were spotless, and the silver and glass shone. Elizabeth led the way to a table in the window, and picked up a menu card.

" This," she said, " is where Glasgow beats every other town. For one-and-sixpence you get four courses. Everything as good as can be, and daintily served." She nodded and smiled to a knot of waitresses. " I come here quite often, so I know all the girls ; they are such nice friendly creatures, and never forget one's little likes and dislikes. Let's choose what we'll have. What do you say to asparagus soup, fish cakes, braised sweetbreads, fruit salad, and coffee ? "

" What ! All that for one-and-sixpence ? "

" All except the coffee, and seeing that this is no ordinary day we shall commit the extravagance. It's a poor heart that never rejoices."

One of the smiling waitresses took the order, and conveyed it down a speaking-tube to the kitchen far below.

" I always sit here when I can get the table," Elizabeth confided to Arthur. " I like to hear them repeating the orders. Listen."

A girl was speaking. " Here, I say ! Hurry up with another kidney : that one had an accident. Whit's that ? The kidneys are finished ! Help ! "

The luncheon-room, evidently a very popular one, was rapidly filling up. Arthur Townshend fixed his monocle in his eye and surveyed the scene. The majority of the lunchers were women—women in for the day from the country, eagerly discussing purchases, purchases made and purchases contemplated ; women from the suburbs lunching in town because their men-folk were out all day ; young girls in town for classes—the large room buzzed like a beehive on a summer's day. A fat, prosperous-looking woman in a fur coat sat down at a table near and ordered—" No soup, but a nice bit of fish."

" Isn't her voice nice and fat ? " murmured Elizabeth,—" like turtle-soup."

A friend espied the lady, and sailing up to the table, greeted her with " Fency seeing you here ! " and they fell into conversation.

" And what kind of winter are you having ? " asked one.

" Fine," said the other. " Mr. Jackson's real well, his indigestion is not troubling him at all, and the children are all at school, and I've had the drawing-room done up—Wylie and Lochhead—handsome. And how are you all ? "

" Very well. I was just thinking about you the other day and minding that you had never seen our new house. I've changed my day to first Fridays, but just drop a p.c. and come any day."

" Aren't the shops nice just now ? And it's lovely to see the sun shining. . . . Are you going ? Well, be sure you come soon. Awful pleased to have met you. Good-bye."

" An example of ' weel-pleasedness,' " said Elizabeth.

" I find," said Arthur, " that I like the Glasgow accent. There is something so soft and—and——"

" Slushy ? " she suggested. " But I know what you mean : there is a cosy feeling about it, and it is kindly. But don't you think this is a wonderfully good luncheon for one-and-sixpence ? "

" Quite extraordinarily good. I can't think how they do it."

" An Oxford friend of Alan's once stayed with us, and the only good thing he could find to say of Glasgow was that in the tea-shops you could make a beast of yourself for ninepence."

Elizabeth laid down her coffee-cup with a sigh.

" I'm always sorry when meals are over," she

said. " I like eating, though Mrs. Thomson would say, in her frank way, that I put good food into a poor skin—meaning that I'm a thin creature. I don't mind a bit at home—I am quite content with what Marget gives us—but when I am, say, in Paris, where cooking is a fine art, I revel."

" And so ethereal-looking ! " commented Arthur.

" That's why I can confess to being greedy, of course," said she. " Well, Ulysses, having seen yet another city, would you like to go home ? "

Arthur stooped to pick up Elizabeth's gloves and scarf which had fallen under the table, and when he gave them to her he said he would like to do some shopping, if she were agreeable.

" I promised Buff a paint-box, for one thing," he said.

" Rash man ! He will paint more than pictures. However, shopping of any kind is a delight to me, so let's go."

The paint-box was bought (much too good a one, Elizabeth pointed out, for the base uses it would almost certainly be put to), also sweets for Thomas and Billy. Then a book-shop lured them inside, and browsing among new books, they lost count of time. Emerging at last, Arthur was tempted by a flower-shop, but Elizabeth frowned on the extravagance, refusing roses for herself. In the end she was prevailed upon to accept some flowering bulbs in a quaint dish to take to a sick girl she was going to visit.

" What is the use," she asked, " of us having a one-and-sixpenny luncheon if you are going to spend pounds on books and sweets and flowers ? But Peggy will love these hyacinths."

" Are you going to see her now ? "

" Yes. Will you take the purchases home ? Or

wait—would it bore you very much to come with
me ? If Peggy is able to see people, it would please
her, and we'd only stay a short time."

Arthur professed himself delighted to go anywhere, and meekly acquiesced when Elizabeth
vetoed the suggestion of a taxi as a thing unknown
in church visitation. " It isn't far," she said, " if
we cross the Clyde by the suspension bridge."

The sun was setting graciously that November
afternoon, gilding to beauty all that, in dying, it
touched. They stopped on the bridge to look at the
light on the water, and Arthur said, " Who is Peggy ? "

" Peggy ? " Elizabeth was silent for a minute,
then she said, " Peggy Donald is a bright thing
who, alas ! is coming quick to confusion. She is
seventeen and she is dying. Sad ? Yes—and yet
I don't know. She has had the singing season,
and she is going to be relieved of her pilgrimage
before sorrow can touch her. She is such an eager,
vivid creature, holding out both hands to life—
horribly easy to hurt : and now her dreams will
all come true. My grief is for her parents. They
married late, and are old to have so young a
daughter. They are such bleak, grey people, and
she makes all the colour in their lives. They adore
her, though I doubt if either of them has ever
called her ' dear.' She doesn't know she is dying,
and they are not at all sure that they are doing
right in keeping it from her. They have a dreadful
theory that she should be ' prepared.' Imagine a
child being ' prepared ' to go to her Father ! . . .
This is the place. Shall I take the hyacinths ? "

As they went up the stair (the house was on the
second floor) she told him not to be surprised at
Mrs. Donald's manner. " She has the air of not
being in the least glad to see one," she explained ;

" but she can't help her sort of cold, grudging manner. She is really a very fine character. Father thinks the world of her."

Mrs. Donald herself opened the door—a sad-faced woman, very tidy in a black dress and silk apron. In reply to Elizabeth's greeting, she said that this happened to be one of Peggy's well days, that she was up and had hoped that Miss Seton might come.

Arthur Townshend was introduced and his presence explained, and Mrs. Donald took them into the sitting-room. It was a fairly large room with two windows, solidly furnished with a large mahogany sideboard, dining-table, chairs, and an American organ.

A sofa heaped with cushions was drawn up by the fire, and on it lay Peggy ; a rose-silk eiderdown covered her, and the cushions that supported her were rose-coloured with dainty white muslin covers. She wore a pretty dressing-gown, and her two shining plaits of hair were tied with big bows.

She was a " bright thing," as Elizabeth had said, sitting in that drab room in her gay kimono, and she looked so oddly well with her geranium-flushed cheeks and her brilliant eyes.

Elizabeth put down the pot of hyacinths on a table beside her sofa, a table covered with such pretty trifles as one carries to sick folk, and kneeling beside her, she took Peggy's hot fragile little hands into her own cool firm ones, and told her all she had been doing. " You must talk to Mr. Townshend, Peggy," she said. " He has been to all the places you want most to go to, and he can tell stories just like *The Arabian Nights*. He brought you these hyacinths. . . . Come and be thanked, Mr. Townshend."

Arthur came forward and took Peggy's hand very gently, and sitting beside her tried his hardest to be amusing and to think of interesting things to tell her, and was delighted when he made her laugh.

While they were talking, Mrs. Donald came quietly into the room and sat down at the table with her knitting.

Arthur noticed that in the sick-room she was a different woman. The haggard misery was banished from her face, and her expression was serene, almost happy. She smiled to her child and said, " Fine company now ! This is better than an old dull mother." Peggy smiled back, but shook her head ; and Elizabeth cried :

" Peggy thinks visitors are all very well for an hour, but Mothers are for always."

Elizabeth sat on the rug and showed Peggy patterns for a new evening dress she was going to get. They were spread out on the sofa, and Peggy chose a vivid geranium red.

Elizabeth laughed at her passion for colour and owned that it was a gorgeous red. But what about slippers ? she asked. The geranium could never be matched.

" Silver ones," said Peggy's little, weak voice.

" What a splendid idea ! Of course, that's what I'll get."

" I should like to see you wear it," whispered Peggy.

" So you shall, my dear, when you come to Etterick. We shall all dress in our best for Peggy. And the day you arrive I shall be waiting at the station with the fat white pony, and Buff will have all his pets—lame birds, ill-used cats, mongrel puppies—looking their best. And Father will show you his dear garden. And Marget will bake scones and shortbread, and there will be honey for tea. . . . Meanwhile, you will rest and get strong, and I shall go and chatter elsewhere. Why, it's getting quite dark!"

Mrs. Donald suggested tea, but Elizabeth said they were expected at home.

"Sing to me before you go," pleaded Peggy.

"What shall I sing? Anything?" She thought for a moment. "This is a song my mother used to sing to us. An old song about the New Jerusalem, Peggy;" and sitting on the rug, with her hand in Peggy's, with no accompaniment, she sang:

> "There lust and lucre cannot dwell,
>   There envy bears no sway;
> There is no hunger, heat nor cold,
>   But pleasure every way.
>
> Thy walls are made of precious stones,
>   Thy bulwarks diamonds square;
> Thy gates are of right Orient pearls,
>   Exceeding rich and rare.
>
> Thy gardens and thy gallant walks
>   Continually are green!
> There grow such sweet and pleasant flowers
>   As nowhere else are seen.
>
> Our Lady sings Magnificat,
>   In tones surpassing sweet;
> And all the virgins bear their part,
>   Sitting about her feet."

Mrs. Donald came with them to the door and thanked them for coming. They had cheered Peggy, she said.

Elizabeth looked at her wistfully.

"Do you think it unseemly of me to talk about new clothes and foolish things to little Peggy? But if it gives her a tiny scrap of pleasure? It can't do her any harm."

" Mebbe no'," said Peggy's mother. " But why do you speak about her going to visit you in summer ? She is aye speaking about it, and fine you know she'll never see Etterick." Her tone was almost accusing.

Elizabeth caught both her hands, and the tears stood in her eyes as she said, " Oh ! dear Mrs. Donald, it is only to help Peggy over the hard bits of the road. Little things, like bright ribbons and dresses, and things to look forward to, help when one is a child. If Peggy is not here when summer comes, we may be quite sure it doesn't vex her that she is not seeing Etterick. She "— her voice broke—" she will have far, far beyond anything we can show her—the King in His beauty and the land that is very far off."

CHAPTER XII

" They confessed that they were strangers and pilgrims."

" LET's walk home," suggested Arthur, as they came out into the street. " It's such a ripping evening."

Elizabeth agreed, and they started off through the busy streets.

After weeks of dripping weather the frost had come, and had put a zest and a sparkle into life. In the brightly lit shops, as they passed, the shop-men were serving customers briskly, with quips and jokes for such as could appreciate badinage. Wives, bare-headed, or with tartan shawls, ran down from their stair-heads to get something tasty for their men's teas—a kipper, maybe, or a quarter of a pound of sausage, or a morsel of steak. Children were coming home from school ; lights were lit and blinds were down—life in a big city is a cheery thing on a frosty November evening.

Elizabeth, generally so alive to everything that went on around her, walked wrapped in thought. Suddenly she said :

" I'm *horribly* sorry for Mrs. Donald. Inarticu-late people suffer so much more than their noisy sisters. Other mothers say, ' Well, it must just have been to be : everything was done that could

173

be done,' and comfort themselves with that. She says nothing, but looks at one with those suffering eyes. *My dear little Peggy!* No wonder her mother's heart is nearly broken."

Arthur murmured something sympathetic, and they walked on in silence, till he said:

"I want to ask you something. Don't answer unless you like, because it's frightful cheek on my part. . . . Do you really believe all that?"

"All what?"

"Well, about the next world. Are you as sure as you seem to be?"

Elizabeth did not speak for a moment, then she nodded her head gravely.

"Yes," she said, "I'm sure. You can't live with Father and not be sure."

"It seems to me so extraordinary. I mean to say, I never heard people talk about such things before. And you all know such chunks of the Bible—even Buff. Why do you laugh?"

"At your exasperated tone! You seem to find our knowledge of the Bible almost indecent. Remember, please, that you have never lived before in Scots clerical circles, and that ministers' children are funny people. We are brought up on the Bible and the Shorter Catechism—at least the old-fashioned kind are. In our case, the diet was varied by an abundance of poetry and fairy tales, which have given us our peculiar daftness. But don't you take any interest in the next world?"

Arthur Townshend screwed his short-sighted eyes in a puzzled way, as he said:

"I don't know anything about it."

"As much as anybody else, I daresay," said Elizabeth. "Don't you like that old song I sang to Peggy?—

One has a vision of smooth green turf, and ladies ' with lace about their delicate hands' walking serenely; and gentlemen ruffling it with curled wigs and carnation silk stockings. Such a deliciously modish Heaven! Ah well! Heaven will be what we love most on earth. At Etterick——"

" Tell me about Etterick," begged Arthur. " It's a place I want very much to see. Aunt Alice adores it."

" Who wouldn't! It's only a farmhouse with a bit built on, and a few acres of ground round it, but there is a walled garden where old flowers grow carelessly, and the heather comes down almost to the door. And there is a burn—what you would call a stream—that slips all clear and shining from one brown pool to another; and the nearest neighbours are three good miles away, and the peeweets cry, and the bees hum among the wild thyme. You can imagine what it means to go there from a Glasgow suburb. The day we arrive Father swallows his tea and goes out to the garden, snuffing the wind, and murmuring like Master Shallow, ' Marry, good air.' Then off he goes across the moor, and we are pretty sure that the psalm we sing at prayers that night will be ' I to the hills will lift mine eyes.' "

" Etterick belongs to your father ? "

" Yes, it is our small inheritance. Father's people have had it for a long time. We can only be there for about two months in the summer, but we often send our run-down or getting-better people for a week or two. The air is wonderful, but it is dull for them, lacking the attractions of Millport or Rothesay—the contempt of your town-

bred for the country-dwellers is intense, and
laughable. I was going to tell you about the old
man who along with his wife keeps it for us. He
has the softest, most delicious Border voice, and
he remarked to me once, 'A' I ask in the way o'
Heaven is juist Etterick—at a raisonable rent.' I
thought the ' raisonable rent ' rather nice. Nothing wanted for nothing, even in the Better
Country."

Arthur laughed, and said the idea carried too
far might turn Heaven into a collection of Small
Holdings.

" But tell me one thing more. What do you do
it for ? I mean visiting the sick, teaching Sunday
schools, handing people tracts. Is it because you
think it is your duty as a parson's daughter ? "

Elizabeth turned to look at her companion's
face to see if he were laughing ; but he was looking
quite serious, and anxious for an answer.

" Do you know," she asked him, " what the Scots
girl said to the Cockney tourist when he asked her
if all Scots girls went barefoot ? No ? Then I'll
tell you. She said, ' Pairtly, and pairtly they mind
their ain business.' "

" I deserve it," said Arthur. " I brought it on
myself."

" I'm not proud, like the barefoot girl," said
Elizabeth. " I'll answer your questions as well as
I can. I think I do it ' pairtly ' from duty and
' pairtly ' from love of it. But oh ! isn't it best
to leave motives alone ? When I go to see Peggy
it is a pure labour of love, but when I go to see
fretful people who whine and don't wash I am
very self-conscious about myself. I mean to say,
I can't help saying to myself, ' How nice of you,
my dear, to come into this stuffy room and spend

your money on fresh eggs and calf's-foot jelly for this unpleasant old thing.' Then I walk home on my heels. You've read *Valerie Upton* ? Do you remember the loathly Imogen and her 'radiant goodness,' and how she stood 'forth in the light' ? I sometimes have a horrid thought that I am rather like that."

"Oh no," said Arthur consolingly. "You will never become a prig. If your own sense of humour didn't save you I know what would—the knowledge that *Fish would lawff.*"

Their walk was nearly over : they had come to the end of the road where the Setons' house stood.

"It is nice," said Elizabeth, with a happy sigh, "to think that we are going in to Father and Buff and tea. Have you got the paint-box all right ? Let me be there when you give it to him."

They walked along in contented silence, until Elizabeth suddenly laughed, and explained that she had remembered a dream Buff once had about Heaven.

"He was sleeping in a little bed in my room, and he suddenly sprang up and said, 'It's a good thing that's not true, any way.' I asked what was the matter, and he told me. He was, it seems, in a beautiful golden ship with silver sails, sailing away to Heaven, when suddenly he met another ship— a black, wicked-looking ship—bound for what Marget calls 'the Ill Place,' and to his horror he recognized all his family on board. 'What did you do, Buff ? ' I asked, and poor old Buff gave a great gulp and said, ' *I came on beside you.*' "

"Sound fellow ! " said Arthur.

CHAPTER XIII

" ' O tell me what was on yer road, ye roarin' norland wind,
  As ye cam' blowin' frae the land that's never frae my mind ? .
  My feet they traivel England, but I'm deein' for the North—'
  ' My man, I heard the siller tides rin up the Firth o' Forth.' "
                                                Songs of Angus.

SINCE the afternoon when Mr. Stewart Stevenson
had called and talked ballads with Mr. Seton he had
been a frequent visitor at the Setons' house. Something about it, an atmosphere homely and welcoming
and pleasant, made it to him a very attractive place.

One afternoon (the Thursday of the week of
Arthur Townshend's visit) he stood in a discouraged
mood looking at his work. As a rule moods troubled
Stewart Stevenson but little; he was an artist
without the artistic temperament. He had his light
to follow and he followed it, feeling no need for eccen-
tricity in the way of hair or collars or conduct.
He was as placid and regular as one of his father's
" time-pieces " which ticked off the flying minutes
in the decorous, well-dusted rooms of " Lochnagar."
His mother summed him up very well when
she confessed to strangers her son's profession.
" Stewart's a Nartist," she would say, half proud,
half deprecating, " but you'd niver know it."
Poor lady, she had a horror of artist-life as it was
revealed to her in the pages of the Heart's Ease

Library. Sometimes dreadful qualms would seize her in the night-watches, and she would waken her husband to ask if he thought there was any fear of Stewart being Led Away, and was only partially reassured by his sleepy grunts in the negative. " What's Art ? " she often asked herself, with a nightmare vision in her mind of ladies lightly clad capering with masked gentlemen at some studio orgy,—" What's Art compared with Respectability ? " though any one more morbidly respectable and less likely to caper with females than her son Stewart could hardly be imagined, and her mind might have been in a state of perfect peace concerning him. He went to his studio as regularly as his father went to the Ham and Butter place, and both worked solidly through the hours.

But, as I have said, this particular afternoon found Stewart Stevenson out of conceit with himself and his work. It had been a day of small vexations, and the little work he had been able to do he knew to be bad. Finally, about four o'clock, he impatiently (but very neatly) put everything away and made up his mind to take Elizabeth Seton the book-plate he had designed for her. This decision made, he became very cheerful, and whistled as he brushed his hair and put his tie straight.

The thought of the Setons' drawing-room at teatime was very alluring. He hoped there would be no other callers and that he would get the big chair, where he could best look at the picture of Elizabeth's mother above the fireplace. It was so wonderfully painted, and the eyes were the eyes of Elizabeth.

He was not quite sure that he approved of Elizabeth. His little mother, with her admiring " Ay, that's it, Pa," to all her husband's truisms, had

given him an ideal of meek womanhood which Elizabeth was far from attaining to. She showed no
deference to people, unless they were poor or very
old. She laughed at most things, and he was afraid
she was shallow. He distrusted, too, her power of
charming. That she should be greatly interested in
his work and ambitions was not surprising, but that
her grey eyes should be just as shining and eager
over the small success of a youth in the church was
merely absurd. It was her way, he told himself,
to make each person she spoke to feel he was the
one person who mattered. It was her job to be
charming. For himself, he preferred more sincerity,
and yet—what a lass to go gipsying through the
world with !

When he was shown into the drawing-room a
cosy scene met his eyes. The fire was at its best,
the tea-table drawn up before it ; Mr. Seton was
laughing and shaking his head over some remark
made by Elizabeth, who was pouring out tea ; his
particular big chair stood as if waiting for him.
Everything was just as he had wished it to be,
except that, leaning against the mantelpiece, stood a
tall man in a grey tweed suit, a man so obviously at
home that Mr. Stevenson disliked him on the spot.

" Mr. Townshend," said Elizabeth, introducing
him. " Sit here, Mr. Stevenson. This is very
nice. You will help me to teach Mr. Townshend
something of Scots manners and customs. His
ignorance is *intense*."

" Is that so ? " said Mr. Stevenson, accepting a
cup of tea and eyeing the serpent in his Eden (he
had not known it was his Eden until he realized
the presence of the serpent) with disfavour.

The serpent's smile, however, as he handed him
some scones was very disarming, and he seemed to

see no reason why he should not be popular with the new-comer. "My great desire," he confided to him over the table, "is to know what a 'U.P.' is?"

"Dear sir," said Elizabeth, "'tis a foolish ambition. Unless you are born knowing what a U.P. is you can never hope to learn. Besides, there aren't any U.P.'s now."

"Extinct?" asked Arthur.

"Well—merged," said Elizabeth.

"It's very obscure," complained Arthur. "But it is absurd to pretend that I know nothing of Scotland. I once stayed nearly three weeks in Skye."

"And," put in Mr. Seton, "the man who knows his Scott knows much of Scotland. I only wish Elizabeth knew him as you do. I believe that girl has never read one novel of Sir Walter's to the end."

"Dear Father," said Elizabeth, "I adore Sir Walter, but he shouldn't have written in such small print. Besides, thanks to you, I know heaps of quotations, so I can always make quite a fair show of knowledge."

Mr. Seton groaned.

"You're a frivolous creature," he said, "and extraordinarily ignorant."

"Yes," said his daughter, "I'm just, as some one said, a 'little brightly-lit stall in Vanity Fair'—all my goods in the shop-window. I suppose"—turning to Mr. Stevenson—"you have read all Scott?"

"Not quite all, perhaps, but a lot," said that gentleman.

"Yes, I had no real hope that you hadn't. But I maintain that the knowledge you gain about people from books is a very queer knowledge. In books and in plays about Scotland you get the idea that we ' pech ' and we ' hoast,' and talk constantly about ministers, and hoard our pennies. Now we are *not* hard as a nation——''

" Pardon me," broke in Arthur, " the one Scots story known to all Englishmen seems to point to a certain carefulness——"

" You mean," cried Elizabeth, interrupting in her turn, " that stupid tale, ' Bang gaed sixpence ' ? But do you know the end of the tale ? I thought not. ' *Bang gaed sixpence, maistly on wines and cigars.*' The honest fellow was treating his friends."

Arthur shouted with laughter, but presently returned to the charge. " But you can't deny your fondness for ministers, or at least for theological discussion, Elizabeth ? "

" Lizbeth ! " said her father, " fond of ministers ? This is surely a sign of grace."

" Father," said Elizabeth earnestly, " I'm not. You know I'm not. Ministers ! I know all kinds of them, and I don't know which I like least. There are the smug complacent ones with sermons like prize essays, and the jovial, back-slapping ones who talk slang and hope thus to win the young men. Then there is a genteel kind with long, thin fingers and literary leanings who read the Revised Version and talk about ' a Larger Hope ' ; and the kind who have damp hands and theological doubts—the two always seem to go together, and——"

" That will do, Lizbeth," broke in Mr. Seton. " It's a deplorable thing to hear a person so far from perfect dealing out criticism so freely."

" Oh," said his daughter, " I am only talking about *young* ministers. Old, wise padres, full of sincerity and simplicity and all the crystal virtues, I adore."

" Have you any more tea ? " asked Mr. Seton.
" I don't think I've had more than three cups."

" Four, I'm afraid," said Elizabeth ; " but there's lots here."

" These are very small cups," said Mr. Seton, as he handed his to be filled again. " You will have to add that to your list of the faults of the clergy— a feminine fondness for tea."

The conversation drifted back, led by Mr. Stevenson, to the great and radical differences between England and Scotland. To emphasize these differences seemed to give him much satisfaction. He reminded them that Robert Louis Stevenson had said that never had he felt himself so much in a foreign country as on his first visit to England.

" It's quite true," he added. " I know myself I'm far more at home in France. And I don't mind my French being laughed at, I know it's bad, but it's galling to be told that my English is full of Scotticisms. They laughed at me in London when I talked about ' snibbing ' the windows."

" They would," said Elizabeth, and she laughed too. " They ' fasten ' their windows, or do something feeble like that. We're being very rude, Arthur ; stand up for your country."

" I only wish to remark that you Scots settle down very comfortably among us alien English. Perhaps getting all the best jobs consoles you for your absence from Scotland."

" Not a bit of it," Elizabeth assured him. " We're homesick all the time : ' My feet they traivel England, but I'm *deein*' for the North.' But I'm afraid Mr. Stevenson will look on me coldly when I confess to a great affection for England. Leafy Warwick lanes, lush meadowlands, the lilied reaches of the Cherwell : I love the mellow beauty of it all. It's not my land, not my wet moorlands and wind-swept hills, but I'm bound to admit that it is a good land."

"Yes," said Mr. Stevenson, "England's a beautiful, rich country, but——"

"But," Elizabeth finished for him, "it's just the ' wearifu' South ' to you ? "

"That's so."

"You see," said Elizabeth, nodding at Arthur Townshend ; "we're hopeless."

"Do you know what you remind me of ? " he asked.

"Something disgusting, I can guess by your face."

"You remind me of a St. Andrew's Day dinner somewhere in the Colonies. . . . By the way, where's Buff ? "

"Having tea alone in the nursery, at his own request."

"Oh ! the poor old chap," said Arthur. "May I go and talk to him ? "

Buff, it must be explained, was in disgrace—he said unjustly. The fault was not his, he contended. It was first of all the fault of Elizabeth, who had once climbed the Matterhorn and who had fired him with a desire to be a mountaineer ; and secondly, it was the fault of Aunt Alice, who had given him on his birthday a mountaineering outfit, complete with felt hat with feather, rücksack, ice-axe, and scarlet-threaded Alpine rope. Having climbed walls and trees and out-houses until they palled, he had looked about for something more difficult, and one frosty morning, when sitting on the Kirkes' ashpit roof, Thomas drew his attention to the snowy glimmer of a conservatory three gardens away ; it had a conical roof and had been freshly painted. Thomas suggested that it looked like a snow mountain. Buff, never having seen a snow mountain, agreed, adding that it was very much the shape of the Matterhorn. They decided to make the ascent that very day. Buff said that as it was the first ascent of the season the thing to do was to take a priest with them to bless it. He had seen a picture of a priest blessing the real Matterhorn. Billy, he said, had better be the priest.

Thomas objected, " I don't think Mamma would like Billy to be a priest and bless things;" but he gave in when Buff pointed out the nobility of the life.

They climbed three garden-walls, and wriggled Indian-fashion across three back-gardens; then, roping themselves securely together, they began the ascent. All went well. They reached the giddy summit, and, perilously poised, Buff was explaining to Billy his duties as a priest, when a shout came from below—an angry shout. Buff tried to look down, slipped, and clutched at the nearest support, which happened to be Billy, and the next instant, with an anguished yell, the priest fell through the mountain, dragging his companions with him.

By rights, to use the favourite phrase of Thomas, they should have been killed, but except for scrapes and bruises they were little the worse. Great, however, was the damage done to glass and plants, and loud and bitter were the complaints of the owner.

The three culprits were forbidden to visit each other for a week, their pocket-money was stopped, and various other privileges were curtailed.

Buff, seeing in the devastation wrought by his mountaineering ambitions no shadow of blame to himself, but only the mysterious working of Providence, was indignant, and had told his sister that he would prefer to take tea alone, indicating by his manner that the company of his elders in their present attitude of mind was far from congenial to him.

" May I go and talk to him ? " Arthur Townshend asked, and was on his feet to go when the drawing-room door was kicked from outside, the handle turned noisily, and Buff entered.

In one day Buff played so many parts that it was difficult for his family to keep in touch with him. Sometimes he was grave and noble as be-fitted a knight of the Round Table, sometimes furtive and sly as a detective ; again he was a highwayman, dauntless and debonair. To-night he was none of these things ; to-night, in the re-bound from a day's brooding on wrongs, he was frankly comic. He stood poised on one leg, in his mouth some sort of whistle on which he performed piercingly until his father implored him to desist, when he removed the thing, and smiling widely on the company said, " But I must whistle. I'm ' the Wee Bird that cam'.' "

Elizabeth and her father laughed, and Arthur asked, " *What* does he say he is ? "

" It's a Jacobite song," Mr. Seton explained,— " ' A wee bird cam' tae oor ha' door.' He's an absurd child."

" Lessons done, Buff ? " his sister asked him.

" Surely the fowls of the air are exempt from lessons," Arthur protested ; but Buff, remembering that although he had allowed himself to unbend for the moment, his wrongs were still there, said in a dignified way that he had learned his lessons, and having abstracted a cheese-cake from the tea-table, he withdrew to a table in a corner with his paint-box. As he mixed colours boldly he listened, in

" Generous manners ! " said Mr. Seton. " I like the phrase. There are people who give one the impression of having to be sparing of their affection and sympathy because their goods are all, so to speak, in the shop-window, and if they use them up there is nothing to fall back upon. Others can offer one a largesse because their life is very rich within. But, again, there are people who have the wealth within but lack the power of expression. It is the fortunate people who have been given the generous manners—Friday's bairns, born loving and giving—others have the warm instincts but they are ' unwinged from birth.' "

Stewart Stevenson nodded his head to show his approval of the sentiment, and said, " That is so."

Elizabeth laughed. " There was a great deal of feeling in the way you said that, Mr. Stevenson."

" Well," he said, with rather a rueful smile, " I've only just realized it—I'm one of the people with shabby manners."

" You have not got shabby manners," said Elizabeth indignantly. " Arthur, when I offer a few light reflections on life and manners there is no need to delve—you and Father—into the subject and make us uncomfortable imagining we haven't got things. Personally, I don't aspire to such heights, and I flatter myself I'm rather a popular person."

" An ideal minister's daughter, I'm told," said Arthur.

" Pouf ! I'm certainly not that. I'm sizes too large for the part. I have positively to uncoil myself like a serpent when I sit at bedsides. I'm as long as a day without bread, as they say in Spain. But I do try very hard to be nice to the church folk. My face is positively stiff with grinning when I come home from socials and such like. An old woman said to me one day, 'A kirk is rale like a shop. In baith o' them ye've to humour yer customers !'"

"A very discerning old woman," said her father. "But you must admit, Elizabeth, that our 'customers' are worth the humouring."

"Oh ! they are—except for one or two fellows of the baser sort—and I do think they appreciate our efforts."

This smug satisfaction on his sister's part was too much for Buff in his state of revolt against society. He finished laying a carmine cloud across a deeply azure sky, and said :

"It's a queer thing that *all* the Elizabeths in the world have been nasty—Queen Elizabeth and—and "—failing to find another historical instance, he concluded rather lamely, pointing with his paintbrush at his sister—" you !"

"This," Mr. Townshend remarked, "is a most unprovoked attack !"

"Little toad," said Elizabeth, looking kindly at her young brother. "Ah, well, Buff, when you are old and grey and full of years and meet with ingratitude——"

"When I'm old," said Buff callously, "you'll very likely be dead !"

She laughed. "I daresay. Anyway, I hope I don't live to be *very* old."

"Why ?" Mr. Stevenson asked her. "Do you dread old age ? I suppose all women do."

"Why women more than men ?" Elizabeth's voice was pugnacious.

"Oh, well—youth's such an asset to a woman. It must be horrible for a beautiful woman to see her beauty go."

" ' Beauty is but a flower
Which wrinkles will devour,' "

Arthur quoted, as he rose to look at Buff's drawing.

Elizabeth sat up very straight.

" Oh ! if you look at life from that sort of ' from-hour-to-hour-we-ripe-and-ripe-and-then—from-hour-to-hour-we-rot-and-rot attitude, it is a tragic thing to grow old. But surely life is more than just a blooming and a decay. Life seems to me like a Road—oh ! I don't pretend to be original—a Road that is always going round corners. And when we are quite young we expect to find something new and delightful round every turn. But the Road gets harder as we get farther along it, and there are often lions in the path, and unpleasant surprises meet us when we turn the corners ; and it isn't always easy to be kind and honest and keep a cheerful face, and lines come, and wrinkles. But if the lines come from being sorry for others, and the wrinkles from laughing at ourselves, then they are kind lines and happy wrinkles, and there is no sense in trying to hide them with paint and powder."

" Dear me," Mr. Seton said, regarding his daughter with an amused smile. " You preach with vigour, Lizbeth. I am glad you value beauty so lightly."

" But I don't. I think beauty matters frightfully all through one's life, and even when one is dead. Think how you delight to remember beloved lovely people ! The look in the eyes, the turn of the head, the way they moved and laughed—all the grace of them. . . . But I protest against the littleness of mourning for the passing of beauty. As my dentist says, truly if prosaically, we all come to a plate in the end ; but I don't mean to be depressed about myself, no matter how hideous I get."

Mr. Townshend pointed out that the depression would be more likely to lie with the onlookers, and Buff, who always listened when his idol spoke, laughed loudly at the sally. "Haw," he said, "Elizabeth thinks she's beautiful!"

"No," his sister assured him, "I don't think I'm beautiful; but, as Marget—regrettably complacent—says of herself spiritually, 'Faigs! I'm no' bad!'"

They all laughed, then a silence fell on the room. Buff went on with his painting, and the others looked absently into the fire. Then Mr. Seton said, half to himself, "'An highway shall be there and a way . . . it shall be called the Way of Holiness . . . the wayfaring man though a fool shall not err therein.' Your Road, Lizbeth, and the Highway are one and the same. I think you will find that. . . . Well, well, I ought not to be sitting here. I have some visits to make before seven. Which way are you going, Mr. Stevenson? We might go together."

Stewart Stevenson murmured agreement and rose to go, very reluctantly. It had not been a satisfactory visit to him,—he had never even had the heart to produce the book-plate that he had taken such pains with, and he greatly disliked leaving Elizabeth and this stranger to talk and laugh and quote poetry together while he went out into the night. This sensible and slightly stolid young man felt, somehow, hurt and aggrieved, like a child that is left out of a party.

He shivered as he stood on the doorstep, and remarked that the air felt cold after the warm room. "Miss Seton," he added, "makes people so comfortable."

"Yes," Mr. Seton agreed, "Elizabeth has the knack of making comfort. The house always seems warmer and lighter when she is in it. She is such a sunny soul."

" Your daughter is very charming," Stewart Stevenson said with conviction.

When one member of the Seton family was praised to the others they did not answer in the accepted way, " Oh! do you think so? How kind of you!" They agreed heartily. So now Mr. Seton said, " *Isn't* she?"

Then he smiled to himself, and quoted:

> " ' A deal of Ariel, just a streak of Puck,
> And something of the Shorter Catechist.' "

Stewart Stevenson, walking home alone, admitted to himself the aptness of the quotation, and wondered what his mother would make of such a character. She would hardly value such traits in a daughter-in-law. Not, of course, that there was any question of such a thing. He knew he had not the remotest chance, and that certainly sent him in to the solid comfort of the Lochnagar dining-room feeling that the world was a singularly dull place, and nothing was left remarkable beneath the visiting moon.

* * * * * * *

" Are ye going out to-night, Stewart?" his mother asked him, as they were rising from the dining-table. There was just a note of anxiety in her voice: the Heart's Ease Library and the capering ladies were always at the back of her mind.

" It's the Shakespeare Reading to-night, and I wasn't at the last. I think I'll look in for an hour. I see that it's at Mrs. Forsyth's to-night."

Mrs. Stevenson nodded, well satisfied. No harm could come to a young man who went to Shake-

speare Readings. She had never been at one
herself, and rather confused them in her mind with
Freemasons, but she knew they were Respectable.
She had met Mrs. Forsyth that very day, calling at
another villa, and she had mentioned that it was
her evening for Shakespeare.

Mrs. Forsyth was inclined to laugh about it.

"I don't go in all the evening," she told Mrs.
Stevenson, "because you have to sit quiet and
listen; but I whiles take my knitting and go in to
see how they're getting on. There they all are, as
solemn as ye like, with Romeo, Romeo here and
somebody else there—folk that have been dead
very near from the beginning of the world. I
take a good laugh to myself when I come out. And
it's hungry work too, mind you. They do justice
to my sangwiches, I can tell you."

But though she laughed, Mrs. Forsyth had a great
respect for Shakespeare. Her son Hugh thought
well of him, and that was enough for her.

Stewart Stevenson was a little late, and the parts
had been given out and the Reading begun.

He stood at the door for a moment looking round
the room. Miss Gertrude Simpson gave him a
glance of recognition and moved ever so slightly,
as if to show that there was room beside her on
the sofa, but he saw Jessie Thomson over on the
window-seat—it was at the Thomsons' that he had
met Elizabeth Seton; the Thomsons went to Mr.
Seton's church; it was not the rose but it was
some one who at times was near the rose—and he
went and sat down beside Jessie.

That young woman got no more good of Shakespeare that evening. (She did not even see that it
was funny that Falstaff should be impersonated
by a most genteel spinster with a cold in her head,

7

who got continual shocks at what she found herself
reading, and murmured, " Oh ! I beg your pardon "
when she waded into the depths and could not save
herself in time.) The beauty and the wit of it passed
her unnoticed. Stewart Stevenson was sitting beside her.

There was no chance of conversation while the
reading lasted, but later on, over the " sangwiches "
and the many other good things that hearty Mrs.
Forsyth offered to her guests, they talked.

He recalled the party at the Thomsons' house
and said how much he had enjoyed it ; then she
found herself talking about the Setons. She told
him about Mrs. Seton, so absurdly pretty for a
minister's wife, about the Seton children who had
been so wild when they were little, and about Mr.
Seton not being a bit strict with them.

" It's an awful unfashionable church," she finished, " but we're all fond of Mr. Seton and Elizabeth, and Father won't leave for anything."

" Your father is a wise man. I have a great
admiration for Mr. Seton myself."

" Elizabeth's lovely, isn't she ? " said Jessie.
" So tall."   Jessie herself was small and round.

" Too tall for a woman," said Mr. Stevenson.

" Oh ! do you think so ? " said Jessie, with a
pleased thrill in her voice.

Before they parted Jessie had shyly told Mr.
Stevenson that they were at home to their friends,
" for a little music, you know," on the evenings of
first and fourth Thursdays ; and Mr. Stevenson,
while he noted down the dates, asked himself why
he had never noticed before what a sensible, nice
girl Miss Thomson was.

CHAPTER XIV

" Sir, the merriment of parsons is very offensive."
                                    DR. JOHNSON.

WHEN Mr. Seton had gone, and taken Stewart Stevenson with him, Elizabeth and Arthur sat on by the fire lazily talking. Arthur asked some question about the departed visitor.

" He is an artist," Elizabeth told him. " Some day soon, I hope, we shall allude to him as Mr. Stewart Stevenson *the* artist. He is really frightfully good at his job, and he never makes a song about himself. Perhaps he will go to London soon and set the Thames on fire, and become a fashionable artist with a Botticelli wife."

" I hope not," Arthur said. " He seems much too good a fellow for such a fate."

" Yes, he is. Besides, he will never need to think of the money side of his art—the Butter and Ham business will see to that—but will be able to work for the joy of working. Dear me ! how satisfactory it all seems, to be sure. My good sir, you look very comfortable. I hope you remember that you are going to a party to-night."

" *What !* My second last evening, too. What a waste ! Can't we send a telephone message, or

wire that something has happened ?   I say, do let's
do that."

Elizabeth assured him that that sort of thing
was not done in Glasgow. She added that it was
very kind of the Christies to invite them, and
having thus thrown a sop to hospitality she proceeded to prophesy the certain dullness of the
evening and to deplore the necessity of going.

" Why people give parties is always a puzzle to
me," Arthur said. " I don't suppose they enjoy
their own parties, and as a guest I can assure them
that I don't. Who and what and why are the
Christies ? "

" Don't speak in that superior tone. The Christies
are minister's folk like ourselves. One of the daughters, Kirsty, is a great friend of mine, and there is a
dear funny little mother who lies a lot on the sofa.
Mr. Johnston Christie—he is very particular about
the Johnston—I find quite insupportable ; and
Archie, the son, is worse. But I believe they are
really good and well-meaning—and, remember, you
are not to laugh at them."

" My dear Elizabeth ! This Hamlet-like advice——"

" Oh, I know you don't need lessons in manners
from me. It will be a blessing, though, if you can
laugh at Mr. Christie, for he believes himself to be
a humorist of a high order. The sight of him takes
away any sense of humour that I possess, and re-
duces me to a state of utter depression."

" It sounds like being an entertaining evening.
When do we go ? "

" About eight o'clock, and we ought to get away
about ten, with any luck."

Mr. Townshend sighed. " It will pass," he said,
" but it's the horrid waste that I grudge. Promise

that we shan't go anywhere to-morrow night—not even to a picture house."

"Have I ever taken you to a picture house? Say another word and I shall insist on your going with me to the Band of Hope. Now behave nicely to-night, for Mr. Christie, his own origin being obscure, is very keen on what he calls 'purfect gentlemen.' Oh! and don't change. The Christies think it side. That suit you have on will do very nicely."

Mr. Townshend got up from his chair and stood smiling down at Elizabeth.

"I promise you I shan't knock the furniture about or do anything obstreperous. You are an absurd creature, Elizabeth, as your father often says. Your tone to me just now was exactly your tone to Buff. I rather liked it."

.   .   .   .   .   .

At ten minutes past eight they presented themselves at the Christies' house. The door was opened by a servant, but Kirsty met them in the hall and took them upstairs. She looked very nice, Elizabeth thought, and was more demonstrative than usual, holding her friend's hand till they entered the drawing-room.

It seemed to the new-comers that the room was quite full of people, all standing up and all shouting, but the commotion resolved itself into Mr. Johnston Christie telling one of his stories to two clerical friends. He came forward to greet them. He was a tall man and walked with a rolling gait; he had a stupid but shrewd face and a bald head. His greeting was facetious, and he said every sentence as if it were an elocution lesson.

"Honoured, Miss Seton, that you should visit our humble home. How are you, sir? Take a chair. Take *two* chairs!!"

"Thank you very much," Elizabeth said gravely, "but may I speak to Mrs. Christie first?"

She introduced Mr. Townshend to his hostess, and then, casting him adrift on this clerical sea, she sat down by the little woman and inquired carefully about her ailments. The bronchitis had been very bad, she was told. Elizabeth would notice that she was wearing a shawl? That was because she wasn't a bit sure that she was wise in coming up to the drawing-room, which was draughty. (The Christies as a general rule sat in their dining-room, which between meals boasted of a crimson table-cover with an aspidistra in a pot in the middle of the table.) Besides, gas fires never did agree with her—nasty, headachy things, that burned your face and left your feet cold. (Mrs. Christie glared vindictively as she spoke at the two imitation yule logs that burned drearily on the hearth.) But on the whole she was fairly well, but feeling a bit upset to-night. Well, not upset exactly, but flustered, for she had a great bit of news. Could Elizabeth guess?

Elizabeth said she could not.

"Look at Kirsty," Mrs. Christie said.

Elizabeth looked across to where Kirsty sat beside a thin little clergyman, and noticed she looked rather unusually nice. She was not only more carefully dressed, but her face looked different; not so sallow, almost as though it had been lit up from inside.

"Kirsty looks very well," she said, "very happy. Has anything specially nice happened?"

"*She's just got engaged to the minister beside her,*" Mrs. Christie whispered hoarsely.

The whisper penetrated through the room, and Kirsty and her fiancé blushed deeply.

"Kirsty! *Engaged!*" gasped Elizabeth.

"Well," said her mother, "I don't wonder you're surprised. I was myself. Somehow I never thought Kirsty would marry, but you never know; and he's a nice wee man, and asks very kindly after my bronchitis—he's inclined to be asthmatic himself, and that makes a difference. He hasn't got a church yet, but Mr. Christie 'll do his best for him. *He's mebbe not a very good preacher.*" Again she whispered, to her companion's profound discomfort.

"I am sure he is," Elizabeth said firmly.

"*He's nothing to look at, and appearances go a long way.*"

"Oh! please don't; he hears you," Elizabeth implored, holding Mrs. Christie's hand to make her stop. "He looks very nice. What is his name?"

"Haven't I told you? Andrew Hamilton, and he's *three years younger than Kirsty.*"

"That doesn't matter at all. I do hope they will be very happy. Dear old Kirsty!"

"Yes," said Mrs. Christie, "but we can't look forward. We know not what a day may bring forth —nor an hour either, for that matter. Just last night I got up to ring the bell in the dining-room— I wanted Janet to bring me a hot-water bottle for my feet—and before I knew I had fallen over the coal-scuttle, and Janet had to carry me back to the sofa. I felt quite solemnized to think how quickly trouble could come. No, no, we can't look for- ward—— Well, well, here's Mr. M'Cann. Don't go away, Elizabeth; *I can't bear the man!*" Again that fell whisper, which, however, was drowned in the noise that Mr. Christie and the new-comer made in greeting each other. Mr. M'Cann was a large man with thick hands. He was an ardent poli- tician and the idol of a certain class of people. He boasted that he was a self-made man, though to a casual observer the result hardly seemed a subject for pride.

He came up to his hostess and began to address her as if she were a large (and possibly hostile) audience. Mrs. Christie shrank farther into her shawl and looked appealingly at Elizabeth, who would fain have fled to the other side of the room, where Arthur Townshend, with his monocle screwed tightly into his eye, was sitting looking as lonely as if he were on a peak in Darien, though the son of the house addressed to him a condescending remark now and again.

Mr. M'Cann spoke with a broad West Country accent. He said it helped him to get nearer the Heart of the People.

" Yes, Mrs. Christie," he bellowed, " I'm alone. Lizzie's washin' the weans, for the girrl's gone off in a tantrum. She meant to come to-night, for she likes a party—Lizzie has never lost her girrlish ways—but when I got back this evening—I've been down in Ayrshire addressin' meetin's for the Independent Candidate. What meetin's ! They just hung on my lips ; it was grand !—when I got back I found the whole place turned up, and Lizzie and the weans in the kitchen. It's a homely house ours, Miss Seton. So I said to her, ' I'll just wash my dial and go off and make your apologies,'—and here I am ! "

Here indeed he was, and Elizabeth wanted so much to know why he had not stayed at home and helped his little overworked wife that she felt if she stayed another moment she must ask him, so she fled from temptation, and found a vacant chair beside Kirsty.

Archie Christie strolled up to speak to her ;

he rather admired Elizabeth—" distangay-looking girl " he called her in his own mind.

" Frightfully clerical show here to-night," he said.

Elizabeth agreed ; then she pinched Kirsty's arm and asked her to introduce Mr. Hamilton.

It did not take Elizabeth many minutes to make up her mind that Kirsty had found a jewel. Mr. Hamilton might not be much to look at, but goodness shone out of his eyes. His quiet manner, his kind smile, the simple directness of his speech were as restful to Elizabeth after the conversational efforts of Mr. M'Cann as a quiet haven to a storm-tossed mariner.

" I haven't got a church yet," he told her, " though I've been out a long time. Somehow I don't seem to be a very pleasing preacher. I'm told I'm too old-fashioned, not ' broad ' enough nor ' fresh ' enough for modern congregations."

Elizabeth struck her hands together in wrath.

" Oh ! " she cried, " those hateful expressions ! I wonder what people think they mean by them ? When I hear men sacrificing depth to breadth or making merry-andrews of themselves striving after originality, I long for an old-fashioned minister— one who is neither broad nor fresh, but who magnifies his office. That is the proper expression, isn't it ? You see I'm not a minister's daughter for nothing ! . . . But don't let's talk about worrying things. We have heaps of nice things in common. First of all, we have Kirsty in common."

So absorbing did this topic prove that they were both quite aggrieved when Mr. Christie came to ask Elizabeth to sing, and with many fair words and set phrases led her to the piano.

" And what," he asked, " do you think of Christina's choice ? "

Elizabeth replied suitably ; and Mr. Christie continued :

" Quite so. A fine fellow—cultured, ye know, cultured and a purfect gentleman, but a little lacking in push. Congregations like a man who knows his way about, Miss Seton. You can't do much in this world without push."

" I daresay not. What shall I sing ? Will you play for me, Kirsty ? "

At nine o'clock the company went down to supper.

Mrs. Christie, to whom as to Chuchundra the musk-rat every step seemed fraught with danger, said she would not venture downstairs again, but would slip away to bed.

At supper Arthur Townshend found himself between the other Miss Christie, who was much engrossed with the man on her right, and an anæmic-looking young woman, the wife of one of the ministers present, who when conversed with said " Ya-as " and turned away her head.

This proved so discouraging that presently he gave up the attempt, and tried to listen to the conversation that was going on between Elizabeth and Mr. M'Cann.

" Let me see," Mr. M'Cann was saying, " where is your father's church ? Oh ay, down there, is it ? A big, half-empty kirk. I know it fine. Ay, gey stony ground, and if you'll excuse me saying it, your father's not the man for the job. What they want is a man who will start a P.S.A. and a band and give them a good rousing sermon. A man with a sense of humour. A man who can say strikin' things in the pulpit." (He sketched the ideal man, and his companion had no difficulty in recognizing the portrait of Mr. M'Cann himself.) " With the right man that church might be full.

Not, mind you, that I'm saying anything against your father, he does his best ; but he's not advanced enough, he belongs to the old evangelicals —congregations like something brighter."

Presently he drifted into politics, and lived over again his meetings in Ayrshire, likening himself to Alexander Peden and Richard Cameron, until Elizabeth, whose heart within her was hot with hate, turned the flood of his conversation into another channel by asking some question about his family.

Four children he said he had, all very young ; but he seemed to take less interest in them than in the fact that Lizzie, his wife, found it quite impossible to keep a " girrl." It was surprising to hear how bitterly this apostle of Freedom spoke of the " bit servant lasses " on whose woes he loved to dilate from the pulpit when he was inveighing against the idle, selfish rich.

Two imps of mischief woke in Elizabeth's grey eyes as she listened.

" Yes," she agreed, as her companion paused for a second in his indictment. " Servants are a nuisance. What a relief it would be to have slaves ! "

" Whit's that ? " said Mr. M'Cann, evidently not believing he had heard aright.

Elizabeth leaned towards him, her face earnest and sympathetic, her voice, when she spoke, honey-sweet, " like doves taboring upon their breasts."

" I said wouldn't it be delightful if we had slaves —nice fat slaves ? "

Mr. M'Cann's eyes goggled in his head. He was quite incapable of making any reply, so he took out a day-before-yesterday's handkerchief and blew his nose ; while Elizabeth continued : " Of course we wouldn't be cruel to them—not like Legree in *Uncle*

Tom's Cabin. But just imagine the joy of not having to tremble before them ! To be able to make a fuss when the work wasn't well done, to be able to grumble when the soup was watery and the pudding burnt—imagine, Mr. M'Cann, imagine having *the power of life and death over the cook !* "

Arthur Townshend, listening, laughed to himself ; but Mr. M'Cann did not laugh. This impudent female had dared to make fun of him ! With a snort of wrath he turned to his other neighbour and began to thunder platitudes at her which she had done nothing to deserve, and which she received with an indifferent " Is that so ? " which further enraged him.

Elizabeth, having offended one man, turned her attention to the one on her other side, who happened to be Kirsty's fiancé, and enjoyed snatches of talk with him between Mr. Christie's stories, that gentleman being incorrigibly humorous all through supper.

When they got up to go away, Kirsty went with Elizabeth into the bedroom for her cloak.

" Kirsty, dear, I'm so glad," Elizabeth said.

Kirsty sat solidly down on a chair beside the dressing-table.

" So am I," she said. " I had almost given up hope. Oh ! I know it's not a nice thing to say, but I don't care. You don't know what it means never to be first with any one, to know you don't matter, that no one needs you. At home—well, Father has his church, and Mother has her bronchitis, and Kate has her Girls' Club, and Archie has his office, and they don't seem to feel the need of anything else. And you, Lizbeth, you never cared for me as I cared for you. You have so many friends ; but I have no pretty ways, and I've a sharp tongue, and I can't help seeing through people, so I don't make friends. . . . And oh ! how I have wanted a house of my own ! That's not the proper thing to say either, but I have—a place of my own to polish and clean and keep cosy. I pictured it so often—especially, somehow, the store-room. I knew where I would put every can on the shelves."

She rubbed with her handkerchief along the smooth surface of the dressing-table. " Every spring when I polished the furniture I thought, ' Next spring, perhaps, I'll polish my own best bed-room furniture ' ; but nobody looked the road I was on. Then Andrew came, and—I couldn't be-lieve it at first—he liked me, he wanted to talk to me, he looked at me first when he came into the room. . . . He's three years younger than me, and he's not at all good-looking, but he's mine, and when he looks at me I feel like a queen crowned."

Elizabeth swallowed an awkward lump in her throat, and stood fingering the crochet edge of the toilet-cover without saying anything.

Then Kirsty jumped up, her own bustling little self again, rather ashamed of her long speech.

" Here I am keeping you, and Mr. Townshend standing waiting in the lobby. Poor man ! He seems nice, Lizbeth, but he's *awfully* English."

Elizabeth followed her friend to the door, and stooping down, kissed her. " Bless you, Kirsty," she said.

She was rather silent on the way home. She said Mr. Christie's jocularity had depressed her.

" I suppose *I* may not laugh," Mr. Townshend remarked, " but I think Fish would have ' lawffed.' That's a good idea of yours about slaves."

" Were you listening ? " she smiled ruefully. " It was wretched of me, when you think of that faithful couple, Marget and Ellen. That's the worst of this world, you can't score off one person without hurting some one quite innocent."

They found Mr. Seton sitting by the drawing-room fire. He had had a harassed day, waging warfare against sin and want (a war that to us seems to have no end and no victory, for still sin flaunts in the slums or walks our streets with mincing feet, and Lazarus still sits at our gates, "an abiding mystery," receiving his evil things), and he was taking the taste of it out of his mind with a chapter from *Guy Mannering*.

So far away was he under the Wizard's spell that he hardly looked up when the revellers entered the room, merely remarking, " Just listen to this." He read :

" ' I remember the tune well,' he said. He took the flageolet from his pocket and played a simple melody. . . . She immediately took up the song :

> ' Are these the links of Forth, she said ;
> Or are they the crooks of Dee,
> Or the bonny woods of Warrock Head
> That I so plainly see ? '

" ' By Heaven ! ' said Bertram, ' it is the very ballad.' "

Mr. Seton closed the book with a sigh of pleasure, and asked them where they had been.

Elizabeth told him, and " Oh yes, I remember now," he said. " Well, I hope you had a pleasant evening ? "

" I think Mr. Christie had, anyway. That man's life is one long soiree-speech. And I wouldn't mind if he were really gay and jolly and care-free ; but I know that at heart he is shrewd and calculating and un-simple as he can be. But, Father, the nicest thing has happened. Kirsty has got engaged to a man called Andrew Hamilton, a minister, a real jewel. You would like him, I know. But he hasn't got a church yet, although he is worth a dozen of the people who do get churches, and I was wondering what about Langhope ? It's the nearest village to Etterick," she explained to Arthur. " It's high time Mr. Smillie retired. He is quite old, and he has money of his own. and could go and live in Edinburgh and attend all the Committees. It is such a good manse, and I can see Kirsty keeping it so spotless, and Mr. Hamilton working in the garden —and hens, perhaps—and everything so cosy. There's a specially good store-room, too. I know, because we used to steal raisins and things out of it when we visited Mr. Smillie."

Mr. Seton laughed and called her an absurd creature, and Arthur asked if a good store-room was necessary to married happiness ; but she heeded them not.

" You know, Father, it would be doing Langhope a really good turn to recommend Mr. Hamilton as their minister. How do I know, Arthur ? I just know. His father was a Free Kirk minister, so he has been well brought up, and I know exactly the kind of sermons he will preach—solid well-reasoned discourses, with now and again an anecdote about the ' great Dr. Chalmers,' and with here and there a reference to ' the sainted Dr. Andrew Bonar ' or ' Dr. Wilson of the Barclay.' Fine Free Kirk discourses. Such as you and I love, Father."

Her father shook his head at her ; and Arthur, as he lit a cigarette, remarked that it was all Chinese to him. Elizabeth sat down on the arm of her father's chair.

" You had quite a success to-night, Arthur," she said kindly. " Mr. Christie called you a ' gentlemanly fellow,' and Mrs. Christie said, speaking for herself, she had no objection to the Cockney accent, she rather liked it ! And oh ! Father, your friend Mr. M'Cann was there. You know whom I mean ? He talked to me quite a lot. He has been politic-ing down in Ayrshire, and he told me that he rather reminds himself of the Covenanters at their best— Alexander Peden I think was the one he named."

Mr. Seton was carrying *Guy Mannering* to its place, but he stopped and said, " *The wretched fellow !* "

The utter wrath and disgust in his tone made his listeners shout with laughter, and Elizabeth said :

" Father, I love you. 'Cos why ? "

Mr. Seton, still sore at this defiling of his idols, only grunted in reply.

" Because you are not too much of a saint after all. Oh ! *don't turn out the lights !* "

CHAPTER XV

" There was a lady once, 'tis an old story,
    That would not be a queen, that would she not
    For all the mud in Egypt."

Henry VIII.

" IT is funny to think," Elizabeth said, " that last Friday I was looking forward to your visit with horror."

" Hospitable creature ! " Arthur replied.

" And now," she continued, " I can't remember what it was like not to know you."

They were sitting in the drawing-room after dinner. Mr. Seton had gone out, and Buff was asleep after such an hour of crowded life as seldom fell to his lot. He had been very down at the thought of losing his friend, and had looked so small and forlorn when he said his reluctant good-night, that Arthur, to lighten his gloom, asked him if he had ever taken part in a sea-fight, and being answered in the negative, had carried him upstairs shoulder-high. Then issued from the bathroom such a splashing of water, such gurgles of laughter and yells of triumph as Buff, a submarine, dashed from end to end of the large bath, torpedoing warships under Arthur's directions, that Elizabeth, Marget, and Ellen all rushed upstairs to say that if the performance did not stop at once the house would certainly be flooded.

As it was, fresh pyjamas had to be fetched, the pair laid out being put out of action by the wash of the waves. Then Arthur carried Buff to his room and threw him head-over-heels into bed, sitting by his side for quite half an hour and relating the most thrilling tale of pirates ; finally presenting him with two fat half-crowns, and promising that he, Buff, should go up in an aeroplane at the earliest opportunity.

Buff, as he lay pillowed on that promise, his two half-crowns laid on a chair beside him along with one or two other grubby treasures, and his heart warm with gratitude, wondered and wondered what he could do in return—and still wondering fell asleep.

Elizabeth was knitting a stocking for her young brother, and counted audibly at intervals ; Arthur lay in a large armchair and looked into the fire.

" Buff is frightfully sorry to lose you. *One two— one two.* This is a beautiful ' top,' don't you think ? Rather like a Persian tile."

" Yes," said Arthur rather absently.

There was silence for a few minutes ; then Elizabeth said, " There is something very depressing about last nights—we would really have been much better at the Band of Hope, and I would have been doing my duty, and thus have acquired merit. I hate people going away. When nice people come to a house they should just stay on and on, after the fashion of princes in fairy-tale stories seeking their fortunes. They stayed about twenty years before it seemed to strike them that their people might be getting anxious."

" For myself," said Arthur, " I ask nothing better. You know that, don't you ? "

"*One two—one two,*" Elizabeth counted. She looked up from her knitting with twinkling eyes. "Did you hate very much coming? or were you passive in the managing hands of Aunt Alice?"

He looked at her impish face blandly, then took out his cigarette case, chose a cigarette carefully, lit it, and smoked with placid enjoyment.

"Cross?" she asked, in a few minutes.

"Not in the least. Merely wondering if I might tell you the truth."

"I wouldn't," said Elizabeth. "Fiction is always stranger and more interesting. By the way, are you to be permanently at the Foreign Office now?"

"I haven't the least notion, but I shall be there for the next few months. When do you go to London?"

In the spring, she told him, probably in April, and added that her Aunt Alice had been a real fairy godmother to her.

"Very few ministers' daughters have had my chances of seeing men and cities. And some day, some day when Buff has gone to school and Father has retired and has time to look about him, we are going to India to see the boys."

"You have a very good time in London, I expect," Arthur said. "I can imagine that Aunt Alice makes a most tactful chaperon, and I hear you are very popular."

"'Here's fame!'" quoted Elizabeth flippantly. "What else did Aunt Alice tell you about me?"

Arthur Townshend put the end of his cigarette carefully into the ash-tray and leant forward.

"You really want to know—then here goes. She told me you were tall—like a king's own daughter; that your hair was as golden as a fairy tale, and your eyes as grey as glass. She told me of suitors waiting on your favours——"

Elizabeth dropped her knitting with a gasp.

"If Aunt Alice told you all that—well, I've no right to say a word, for she did it to glorify me, and perhaps her kind eyes and heart made her think it true ; but surely you don't think I am such a conceited donkey as to believe it."

"But isn't it true ?—about the suitors, I mean ? "

"Suitors ! How very plural you are ! "

"But I would rather keep them in the plural," he pleaded ; "they are more harmless that way. But Aunt Alice did talk about some particular fellow—I think Gordon was his wretched name."

"Bother ! " said Elizabeth. "I've dropped a stitch." She bent industriously over her knitting.

"I'm waiting, Elizabeth."

"What for ? "

"To hear about Mr. Gordon."

"Oh ! you must ask Aunt Alice," Elizabeth said demurely. "She is your fount of information." Then she threw down her knitting. "Arthur, don't let's talk any more about such silly subjects. They don't interest me in the least."

"Is Mr. Gordon a silly subject ? "

"The silliest ever. No—of course he isn't. Why do you make me say nasty things ? He is only silly to me because I am an ungrateful creature. I don't expect I shall ever marry. You see, I would never be a grateful wife, and it seems a pity to use up a man, so to speak, when there are so few men and so many women who would be grateful wives and may have to go without. I think I am a born spinster, and as long as I have got Father and Buff and the boys in India I shall be more than content."

"Buff must go to school soon," he warned her.

"Your brothers may marry; your father can't be with you always."

"Oh, don't try to discourage me in my spinster path. You are as bad as Aunt Alice. She thinks of me as living a sort of submerged existence here in Glasgow, and only coming to the surface to breathe when I go to London or travel with her. But I'm not in the least stifled with my life. I wouldn't change with anybody; and as for getting married and going off with trunks of horrid new unfamiliar clothes, and a horrid new unfamiliar husband, I wouldn't do it. I haven't much ambition; I don't ask for adventures; though I look so large and bold, I have but a peeping and a timorous soul."

She smiled across at Arthur, as if inviting him to share her point of view; but he looked into the fire and did not meet her glance.

"Then you think," he said, "that you will be happy all your life—alone?"

"Was it Sydney Smith who gave his friends forty recipes for happiness? I remember three of them," she counted on her fingers, "a bright fire, a kettle singing on the hob, a bag of lollipops on the mantelshelf—all easy to come at. I can't believe that I shall be left entirely alone—I should be so scared o' nights. Surely some one will like me well enough to live with me—perhaps Buff, if he continues to have the contempt for females that he now has; but anyway I shall hold on to the bright fire and the singing kettle and the bag of lollipops."

She sat for a moment, absent-eyed, as if she were looking down the years; then she laughed.

"But I shall be a frightfully long gaunt spinster," she said.

Arthur laughed with her, and said:

"Elizabeth, you aren't really a grown-up woman at all. You're a schoolboy."

"I like that 'grown-up,'" she laughed; "it sounds so much less mature than the reality. I'm twenty-eight, did you know? Already *airting* towards spinsterhood."

Arthur shook his head at her.

"In your father's words, you are an absurd creature. Sing to me, won't you? seeing it's my last night."

"Yes." She went to the piano. "What shall I sing? 'A love-song or a song of good life'?"

"A love-song," said Arthur, and finished the quotation. "'I care not for good life.'"

Elizabeth giggled.

"Our language is incorrigibly noble. You know how it is when you go to the Shakespeare Festival at Stratford? I come away so filled with majestic words that I can hardly resist greeting our homely chemist with 'Ho! apothecary!' But I'm not going to sing of love. 'I'm no' heedin' for't,' as Marget says. . . . This is a little song out of a fairy tale—a sort of good-bye song:

'If fairy songs and fairy gold
    Were tunes to sell and gold to spend,
Then, hearts so gay and hearts so bold,
    We'd find the joy that has no end.
But fairy songs and fairy gold
    Are but red leaves in Autumn's play.
The pipes are dumb, the tale is told,
    Go back to realms of working day.

The working day is dark and long,
    And very full of dismal things;
It has no tunes like fairy song,
    No hearts so brave as fairy kings.
Its princes are the dull and old,
    Its birds are mute, its skies are grey;
And quicker far than fairy gold
    Its dreary treasures fleet away.

But all the gallant, kind, and true
May haply hear the fairy drum,
Which still must beat the wide world through,
Till Arthur wake and Charlie come,
And those who hear and know the call
Will take the road with staff in hand,
And after many a fight and fall,
Come home at last to fairy-land.' "

  .   .   .   .   .   .

They were half-way through breakfast next morning before Buff appeared. He stood at the door with a sheet of paper in his hand, looking rather distraught. His hair had certainly not been brushed, and a smear of paint disfigured one side of his face. He was not, as Mr. Taylor would have put it, looking his " brightest and bonniest."

" I've been in Father's study," he said in answer to his sister's question, and handed Arthur Townshend the paper he carried.

" It's for you," he said, " a sea-fight. It's the best I can do. I've used up nearly all the paints in my box."

He had certainly been lavish with his colours, and the result was amazing in the extreme.

Mr. Townshend expressed himself delighted, and discussed the points of the picture with much insight.

" We shall miss you," Mr. Seton said, looking very kindly at him. " It has been almost like having one of our own boys back. You must come again, and to Etterick next time."

" Aw yes," cried Buff, " come to Etterick and see my jackdaw with the wooden leg." He had drawn his chair so close to Arthur's that to both of them the business of eating was gravely impeded.

" Come for the shooting," said Mr. Seton.

" Yes," said Elizabeth, as she filled out a third

cup of tea for her father, " and the fourth footman will bring out your lunch while the fifth footman is putting on his livery. Don't be so buck-ish, Mr. Father. Our shooting, Arthur, consists of a heathery hillside inhabited by many rabbits, a few grouse— very wild, and an ancient blackcock called Algernon. No one can shoot Algernon ; indeed, he is such an old family friend that it would be very ill manners to try. When he dies a natural death we mean to stuff him."

" But may I really come ? Is this a *pukka* invitation ? "

" It is," Elizabeth assured him. " As the Glasgow girl said to the Edinburgh girl, ' What's a slice of ham and an egg in a house like ours ? ' We shall all be frightfully glad to see you, except perhaps old Watty Laidlaw—I told you about him ? He is very anxious when we have guests, he is so afraid we are living beyond our means. One day last summer I had some children from the village to tea, and he stood on the hillside and watched them cross the moor, then went in to Marget and said in despairing accents, ' Pit oot eighty mair cups. They're comin' ower the muir like a locust drift.' The description of the half-dozen poor little stragglers as a ' locust drift ' was almost what Robert Browning calls ' too wildly dear.' "

" This egg's bad," Buff suddenly announced.

" Is it, Arthur ? " Elizabeth asked.

Mr. Townshend regarded the egg through his monocle.

" It looks all right," he said ; " but Buff evidently requires his eggs to be like Cæsar's wife."

" Don't waste good food, boy," his father told him. " There is nothing wrong with the egg."

" It's been a nest-egg," said Buff in a final manner, and began to write in a small book.

Elizabeth remarked that Buff was a tiresome little boy about his food, and that there might come a time when he would think regretfully of the good food he had wasted. " And what are you writing ? " she finished.

" It's my diary," said Buff, putting it behind his back. " Father gave it me. No, you can't read it, but Arthur can if he likes, 'cos he's going away ; " and he poked the little book into his friend's hand.

Arthur thanked him gravely, and turned to the first entry.

New Year's Day.

Good Rissolution.   Not to be crool to gerls.

The other entries were not up to the high level of the first, but were chiefly the rough jottings of nefarious plans which, one could gather, generally seemed to miscarry. On 12th August was printed and emphatically underlined the announcement that on that date Arthur Townshend would arrive at Etterick.

That the diary was for 1911 and that this was the year of grace 1913 troubled Buff not at all : years made little difference to him.

Arthur pointed this out as he handed back the book, and rubbing Buff's mouse-coloured hair affectionately, quoted :

" Poor Jim Jay got stuck fast in yesterday."

" But I haven't," Buff protested ; " I'll know it's 1914 though it says 1911."

He put his diary into his safest pocket and asked if he might go to the station.

" Oh, I think not," his father said. " Why go into town this foggy morning ? "

" He wants the ' hurl,' " said Elizabeth. " Arthur, that's a new word for you. Father, we should make Arthur pass an examination and see

what knowledge he has gathered.   Let's draw up a
paper :

> I. What is—
>> (a) A Wee Free ?
>> (b) A U.P. ?
> II. Show in what way the Kelvinside accent
>>   differs from that of Pollokshields.
> III. What is a ' hurl ' ?

I can't think of anything else.   Anyway, I don't
believe you could answer one of my questions, and
I am only talking for talking's sake, because we are
all so sad.   By the way, when you say Good-bye
to Marget and Ellen shake hands, will you ?   They
expect it."

" Of course," said Arthur.

The servants came in for prayers.

Mr. Seton prayed for " travelling mercies " for
the friend who was about to leave them to return
to the great city.

" Here's the cab ! " cried Buff, and rushed for
his coat.   His father followed him, and Arthur
turned to Elizabeth.

" Will you write to me sometimes ? "

Elizabeth stooped to pick up Launcelot, the cat.

" Yes," she said, " if you don't mind *prattle*.   I
so rarely have any thoughts."

He assured her that he would be grateful for anything she cared to send him.

" Tell me what you are doing ; about the church
people you visit, if the Peggy-child gets better, if
Mr. Taylor makes a joke, and of course about your
father and Buff.   Everything you say or do interests me.   You know that, don't you—Lizbeth ? "

But Elizabeth kept her eyes on the purring cat,

and—" Isn't he a polite young man, puss-cat ? " was all she said.

Buff's voice was raised in warning from the hall.

" Coming," cried Arthur ; but he still tarried.

Elizabeth put the cat on her shoulder and led the way.

" Launcelot and I shall see you off from the door-step. You mustn't miss your train. As Marget says, ' Haste ye back.' "

" You've promised to write. . . . There's loads of time, Buff." He was on the lowest step now. " Till April—you are sure to come in April ? "

" Reasonably sure, but it's an uncertain world. . . . My love to Aunt Alice."

an idle way, to the conversation that engaged his elders. It sounded to him dull, and he wondered, as he had wondered many times before, why people chose the subjects they did when there was a whole world of wonders to talk about and marvel at.

" Popularity ! " Elizabeth was saying. " It's the easiest thing in the world to be popular. It only needs what Marget calls ' tack.' Appear always slightly more stupid than the person you are speaking to ; always ask for information ; never try to teach anybody anything ; remember that when people ask for criticism they really only want praise. And of course you must never, never make personal remarks unless you have something pleasant to say. ' How tired you look ! ' simply means ' How plain you look ! ' It is so un-understanding of people to say things like that. If, instead of their silly, rude remarks, they would say, ' What a successful hat ! ' or ' That blue is delicious with your eyes ! ' and watch how even the most wilted people brighten and freshen, they wouldn't be such fools again. I don't want them to tell lies, but there is always *something* they can praise truthfully."

Her father nodded approval, and Arthur said, " Yes, but a popular man or woman needs more than tact. To be agreeable and to flatter is not enough—you must be tremendously *worth while*, so that people feel honoured by your interest. I think there is a great deal more in popularity than you allow. Watch a really popular woman in a roomful of people, and see how much of herself she gives to each one she talks to, and what generous manners she has. Counterfeit sympathy won't do, it is easily detected. It is all a question really of manners, but one must be born with good manners ; they aren't acquired."

CHAPTER XVI

" Then said he, I wish you a fair day when you set out for
Mount Zion, and shall be glad to see that you go over the river
dry-shod. But she answered, Come wet, come dry, I long to be
gone; for however the weather is on my journey, I shall have
time to sit down and rest me and dry me."
The Pilgrim's Progress.

" PURE religion and undefiled," we are told, " before
God and the Father is this, To visit the fatherless
and widows in their affliction and keep ourselves
unspotted from the world." If this be a working
definition of Christianity, then James Seton trans-
lated its letter as but few men do, into a spirit and
life of continuous and practical obedience. No
weary, sick, or grieved creature had to wait for his
minister's coming. The congregation was widely
scattered, but from Dennistoun to Pollokshields,
from Govanhill to Govan, in all weathers he trudged
—cars were a weariness to him, walking a pleasure
—carrying with him comfort to the comfortless,
courage to the faint-hearted, and a strong hope to
the dying.

On the day that Arthur Townshend left them he
said to his daughter:

" I wonder, Elizabeth, if you would go and see
Mrs. Veitch this afternoon ? She is very ill, and I
have a meeting that will keep me till about seven

o'clock. If you bring a good report, I shan't go
to see her till to-morrow."

"Mrs. Veitch who makes the treacle-scones?
I *am* sorry. Of course I shall go to see her. I
wonder what I could take her? She will hate to
be ill, indomitable old body that she is! Are you
going, Father? I shall do your bidding, but I'm
afraid Mrs. Veitch will think me a poor substitute.
Anyway, I'm glad it isn't Mrs. Paterson you want
me to visit. I so dislike the smug, resigned way
she answers when I ask her how she is : ' Juist
hingin' by a tack.' I expect that ' tack ' will last
her a good many years yet. Buff, what are you
going to do this afternoon? "

"Nothing," said Buff. He sat gloomily on a
chair with his hands in his pockets. " I'm as dull
as a bull," he added.

His sister did not ask the cause of his depression.
She sat down on a low chair and drew him on to her
lap, and cuddled him up and stroked his hair, and
Buff, who as a rule sternly repulsed all caresses,
laid his head on her shoulder and, sniffing dolefully,
murmured that he couldn't bear to have Arthur go
away, and that he had nothing to look forward to
except Christmas, and that was only one day.

"Nothing to look forward to! Oh, Buff!
Think of spring coming and the daffodils. And
Etterick, and the puppies you haven't seen yet.
And I'll tell you what. When Arthur comes, I
shouldn't wonder if we had a sea-fight on the mill-
pond—on rafts, you know."

Buff sat up, his grubby little handkerchief still
clutched in his hand, tears on his lashes but in his
eyes a light of hope.

"Rafts!" he said. He slid to the floor.
"*Rafts!*" he repeated. There was dizzy magic

in the word. Already, in thought, he was lashing spars of wood together.

Five minutes later Elizabeth, carrying a basket filled with fresh eggs, grapes, and sponge-cakes, was on her way to call on Mrs. Veitch, while at home Marget stood gazing, speechless with wrath, at the wreck Buff had made of her tidy stick-house.

When Elizabeth reached her destination and knocked, the door was opened by Mrs. Veitch's daughter Kate, who took her into the room and asked her to take a seat for a minute and she would come. Left alone, Elizabeth looked round the cherished room and noticed that dust lay thick on the sideboard that Mrs. Veitch had dusted so frequently and so proudly, and that the crochet antimacassars on the sofa hung all awry.

She put them tidy, pulled the tablecover even, straightened a picture, and was wondering if she might dust the sideboard with a spare handkerchief she had in her coat (somehow it hurt her to see the dust), when her attention was caught by a photograph that hung on the wall—a family group of two girls and two boys.

She went forward to study it. That funny little girl with the pulled-back hair must be Kate, she decided. She had not changed much ; it was the same good, mild face. The other girl must be the married daughter in America. But it was the boys she was interested in. She had heard her father talk of Mrs. Veitch's sons, John and Hugh. John had been his mother's stand-by, a rock for her to lean on , and Hugh had been to them both a joy and pride.

Elizabeth, looking at the eager, clever face in the faded old picture, understood why, even after twenty years, her father still talked sometimes of

Hugh Veitch, and always with that quick, involuntary sigh that we give to the memory of those ardent souls so well equipped for the fight, but for whom the drums ceased to beat before the battle had well begun.

John and his mother had pinched themselves to send Hugh to college, where he was doing brilliantly well, when he was seized with diphtheria and died. In a week his brother followed him, and for twenty years Mrs. Veitch and Kate had toiled on alone.

Elizabeth turned with a start as Kate came into the room. She looked round drearily. " This room hasna got a dust for days. I'm not a manager like ma mother. I can sew well enough, but I get fair baffled in the house when there's everything to do."

" Poor Kate ! Tell me, how is your mother ? "

" No' well at all. The doctor was in this morning, and he's coming up again later, but he says there is nothing he can do. She's just worn out, and can you wonder ? Many a time I've been fair vexed to see her toilin' with lodgers ; but you see we had just ma pay, and a woman's pay is no' much to keep a house on, and she wanted to make a few shillings extra. And, Miss Seton, d'ye know what she's been doing a' these years ? Scraping and hoarding every penny she could, and laying it away, to pay ma passage to America. Ma sister Maggie's there, ye know, and when she's gone she says I'm to go to Maggie. A' these years she's toiled with this before her. She had such a spirit, she would never give in." Kate wiped her eyes with her apron. " Come in and see ma mother."

" Oh, I don't think so. She oughtn't to see any one when she is so ill."

" The doctor says it makes no difference, and

she'll be vexed no' to see you. I told her you were in. She had aye a notion of you."

" If you think I won't do her harm, I should love to see her," said Elizabeth, getting up ; and Kate led the way to the kitchen. The fog had thickened, and the windows in the little eyrie of a kitchen glimmered coldly opaque. From far beneath came the sounds of the railway.

Mrs. Veitch lay high on her pillows, her busy hands folded. She had given in at last.

Elizabeth thought she was sleeping, but she opened her eyes, and, seeing her visitor, smiled slightly.

" Are ye collectin' the day ? " she asked.

" No," Elizabeth said, leaning forward and speaking very gently. " I don't want any money to-day. I came to ask for you. I am so sorry you are ill."

Mrs. Veitch looked at her with that curious appraising look that very sick people sometimes give one.

" Ay. I'm aboot by wi' it noo, and I em no' vexed. I'm terrible wearied."

" You are very wearied now," Elizabeth said, stroking the work-roughened hands that lay so calmly on the counterpane—all her life Mrs. Veitch had been a woman of much self-control, and in illness the habit did not desert her—" you are very wearied now, but you will get a good rest and soon be your busy self again."

" Na, I've been wearied for years. . . . Ma man died forty years syne, an' I've had ma face agin the wind ever since. That last nicht he lookit at the fower bairns,—wee Hugh was a baby in ma airms,—and he says, ' Ye've aye been fell, Tibbie. Be fell noo.' Lyin' here, I'm wonderin' what ma life's been—juist a fecht to get the denner ready, and a fecht to get the tea ready, an' a terrible trauchle on the washin'-days. It vexes me to think I've done so little to help ither folk. I never had the time."

"Ah! but you're forgetting," said Elizabeth. "The people you helped remember. I have heard —oh! often—from one and another how you did a sick neighbour's washing, and gave a hot meal to children whose mothers had to work out, and carried comforts to people in want. Every step your tired feet took on those errands is known to God."

The sick woman hardly seemed to hear. Her eyes had closed again, and she had fallen into the fitful sleep of weakness.

Elizabeth sat and looked at the old face, with its stern, worn lines. Here was a woman who had lived her hard, upright life, with no soft sayings and couthy ways, and she was dying as she had lived, " uncheered and undepressed " by the world's thoughts of her.

The fog crept close to the window.

Kate put the dishes she had washed into the press. The London express rushed past on its daily journey. The familiar sound struck on the dim ear, and Mrs. Veitch asked, " Is that ma denner awa' by ? "

Kate wiped her eyes. The time-honoured jest hurt her to-day.

" Poor mother ! " she said. " She's aye that comical."

" When I was a lassie," said Mrs. Veitch, " there was twae things I had a terrible notion of—a gig, an' a gairden wi' berries. Ma mither said, ' Bode for a silk goon and ye'll get a sleeve o't,' and

8

Alec said, ' Bide a wee, lassie, an I'll get ye them baith.' Ay, but, Alec ma man, ye've been in yer grave this forty year, an' I've been faur frae gairdens."

The tired mind was wandering back to the beginning of things. She plucked at the trimming on the sleeve of her night-dress.

" I made this goon when I was a lassie for ma marriage. They ca'ed this ' flowering.' I mind fine sittin' sewin' it on simmer efternunes, wi' my mither makin' the tea. Scones an' new-kirned butter an' skim-milk cheese. *I can taste that tea.* Naebody could mak' tea like ma mither. I wish I had a drink o' it the noo, for I'm terrible dry. There was a burn ran by oor door, an' twae muckle stanes by the side o' it, and Alec and me used to sit there and crack—and crack."

Her voice trailed off, and Elizabeth looked anxiously at Kate to see if so much talking was not bad for her mother ; but Kate said she thought it pleased her to talk. It was getting dark and the kitchen was lit only by the sparkle of the fire.

" I'd better light the gas," Kate said, reaching for the matches. " The doctor 'll be in soon."

Elizabeth watched her put a light to the incandescent burner, and when she turned again to the bed she found the sick woman's eyes fixed on her face.

" You're like your faither, lassie," said the weak voice. " It's one-and-twenty years sin' I fell acquant wi' him. I had flitted to this hoose, and on the Sabbath Day I gaed into the nearest kirk to see what kinna minister they hed. I've niver stayed awa' willingly a Sabbath sin' syne. . . . The first time he visited me he kent by ma tongue that I was frae Tweedside.

" ' Div 'ee ken Kilbucho ? ' I speired at him.

" ' Fine,' he says.

" ' Div 'ee ken Newby and the gamekeeper's hoose by the burn ? '

" ' I guddled in that burn when I was a boy,' he says ; and I cud ha' grat. It was like a drink o' cauld water. . . . I aye likit rinnin' water. Mony a time I've sat by that window on a simmer's nicht and made masel' believe that I could hear Tweed. It ran in ma ears for thirty years, an' a body disna forget. There's a bit in the Bible about a river . . . read it."

Elizabeth lifted the Bible and looked at it rather hopelessly.

" I'm afraid I don't know where to find it," she confessed.

" Tuts, lassie, yer faither would ha' kent," said Mrs. Veitch.

" There is a river," Elizabeth quoted from memory,—" there is a river the streams whereof shall make glad the city of God."

" Ay ! that's it." She lay quiet, as if satisfied.

" Mother," said Kate. " Oh ! Mother ! "

The sick woman turned to her daughter.

" Ay, Kate. Ye've been a guid lassie to me, and noo ye'll gang to Maggie in Ameriky. The money is there, an' I can gang content. Ye wudna keep me, Kate, when I've waited so lang ? I'll gang as blythe doon to the River o' Death as I gaed fifty years syne to ma trystin', and Alec will meet me at the other side as he met me then . . . and John, ma kind son, will be waitin' for me, an' ma wee Hughie——"

" And your Saviour, Mother," Kate reminded her anxiously.

Mrs. Veitch turned on her pillow like a tired child.

" I'll need a lang, lang rest, an' a lang drink o' the Water of Life."

" Oh! Mother!" said Kate. " You're no' going to leave me."

Elizabeth laid her hand on her arm. " Don't vex her, Kate. She's nearly through with this tough world."

The doctor was heard at the door.

" I'll go now, and Father will come down this evening. Oh! poor Kate, don't cry. It is so well with her."

That night, between the hours of twelve and one, at the turning of the tide, the undaunted soul of the old country-woman forded the River, and who shall say that the trumpets did not sound for her on the other side!

CHAPTER XVII

"He was the Interpreter to untrustful souls ;
The weary feet he led into the cool
Soft plains called Ease ; he gave the faint to drink :
Dull hearts he brought to the House Beautiful.
The timorous knew his heartening on the brink
    Where the dark River rolls.
He drew men from the town of Vanity,
Past Demas' mine and Castle Doubting's towers,
To the green hills where the wise shepherds be,
And Zion's songs are crooned among the flowers."

                                                    J. B.

THE winter days slipped past. Christmas came, bringing with it to Buff the usual frantic anticipations, and consequent flatness when it was borne in on him that he had not done so well in the way of presents and treats as he felt he deserved.

It was a hard winter, and there were more than the usual hardships among the very poor. James Seton, toiling up and down the long stairs of the Gorbals every day of the week and preaching three times on the Sabbath, was sometimes very weary.

Elizabeth, too, worked hard and laughed much, as was her way.

It took very little to make her laugh, as she told Arthur Townshend.

"This has been a nasty day," she wrote. "The rain has never ceased—dripping *yellow* rain. (By the way, did you ever read in Andrew Lang's *My Own Fairy Book* about the Yellow Dwarf who bled yellow blood ?   Isn't it a nice horrible idea ?)

"At breakfast it struck me that Father looked frail, and Buff sneezed twice, and I made up my mind he was going to take influenza or measles, probably both, so I didn't feel in any spirits to face the elements when I waded out to do my shopping.   But when I went into the fruit shop and asked if the pears were good and got the reply 'I'm afraid we've nothing startling in the pear line to-day,' I felt a good deal cheered.   Later, walking in Sauchiehall Street, I met Mrs. Taylor in her 'prayer-meeting bonnet,' her skirt well kilted, goloshes on her feet, and her circular waterproof draping her spare figure.   After I had assuaged her fears about my own health and Father's and Buff's, I complimented her on her courage in being out on such a day.

"'I hed to come,' she assured me earnestly ; 'I'm on ma way to the Religious Tract Society to get some *cards for mourners.*'

"The depressing figure she made, her errand, and the day she had chosen for it, sent me home grinning broadly.   Do you know that in spite of ill weather, it is spring ?   There are three daffodils poking up their heads in the garden, and I have got a new hat to go to London with some day in April.   What day, you ask, is some day ?   I don't know yet.   When Buff was a very little boy, a missionary staying in the house said to him, 'And some day you too will go to heaven and sing among the angels.'   Buff, with the air of having rather a good excuse for refusing a dull invitation, said, 'I can't go *some day* ; that's the day I'm going to Etterick.'"

But Elizabeth did not go to London in April.

One Sabbath in March, James Seton came in after his day's work admitting himself strangely tired.

" My work has been a burden to me to-day, Lizbeth," he said ; " I'm getting to be an old done man."

Elizabeth scoffed at the idea, protesting that most men were mere youths at sixty. " Just think of Gladstone," she cried. (That eminent statesman was a favourite weapon to use against her father when he talked of his age, though, truth to tell, his longevity was the one thing about him that she found admirable.) " Father, I should be ashamed to say that I was done at sixty."

Albeit she was sadly anxious, and got up several times in the night to listen at her father's door.

He came down to breakfast next morning looking much as usual, but when he rose from the table he complained of faintness, and the pinched blue look on his face made Elizabeth's heart beat fast with terror as she flew to telephone for the doctor. A nurse was got, and for a week James Seton was too ill to worry about anything ; but the moment he felt better he wanted to get up and begin work again.

" It's utter nonsense," he protested, " that I should lie here when I'm perfectly well. Ask the doctor, when he comes to-day, if I may get up to-morrow. If he consents, well and good ; but if he doesn't, I'll get up just the same. Dear me, girl," as Elizabeth tried to make him see reason, " my work will be terribly in arrears as it is."

Elizabeth and Buff were in the drawing-room when the doctor came that evening. It was a clear, cold march night, and a bright fire burned on the white hearth ; pots of spring flowers stood about the room, scenting the air pleasantly.

Buff had finished learning his lessons and was now practising standing on his head in the window, his heels dangerously near the plate glass. Both he and Elizabeth were in great spirits, the cloud of their father's illness having lifted. Elizabeth had been anxious, how anxious no one knew, but to-night she welcomed the doctor without a qualm.

" Come to the fire, Dr. Nelson," she said ; " these March evenings are cold. Well, and did you find Father very stiff-necked and rebellious ? He is going to defy you and get up to-morrow, so he tells me. His work is calling him—but I don't suppose we ought to allow him to work for a time ? "

Then the doctor told her that her father's work was finished.

With great care he might live for years, but there was serious heart trouble, and there must be no excitement, no exertion that could be avoided : he must never preach again.

.   .   .   .

A week later Elizabeth wrote to Arthur Townshend :

" Thank you for your letters and your kind thoughts of us. Aunt Alice wasn't hurt, was she ? that we didn't let her come. There are times when even the dearest people are a burden.

" Father is wonderfully well now ; in fact, except for occasional breathless turns, he seems much as usual. You mustn't make me sorry for myself. I am not to be pitied. The doctor says ' many years ' ; it is so much better than I dared to hope. I wonder if I could make you understand my feeling ? If you don't mind a leaf from a family journal, I should like to try.

" ' Tell me about when you were young,' Buff

sometimes says, and it does seem a long time ago
since the world began. . . . When I remember my
childhood I think the fairy pipes in Hans Andersen's
tale that blew every one into their right place must
have given us our Mother. She was the proper-est
Mother that ever children had. ' *Is Mother in ?* '
was always our first question when we came in from
our walks, and if Mother was in all was right with
the world. She had a notion—a blissful notion, as
you may suppose, for us—that children ought to
have the very best time possible. And we had it.
Funny little happy people we were, not penned up
in nurseries with starched nurses, but allowed to
be a great deal with our parents, and encouraged
each to follow our own bent.

" Our old nurse, Leezie, had been Father's nurse,
and to her he was still ' Maister Jimmie.' You said
when you were here that you liked the nursery with
its funny old prints and chintzes, but you should
have seen it with Leezie in it. She kept it a picture
of comfort, and was herself the most comfortable
thing in it, with her large clean rosy face and white
hair, her cap with bright ribbons, and her most
capacious lap. Many a time have I tumbled into
that lap crying from some childish ache—a tooth,
a cut finger, perhaps hurt feelings—to be comforted
and told in her favourite formula ' It 'll be better
gin morning.' She had no modern notions about
bringing up children, but in spite of that (or because
of that ?) we very rarely ailed anything. Once,
when Alan's nose bled violently without provocation, Mother, after wrestling with a medical book,
said it might be connected with the kidneys. ' *Na,
na,*' said Leezie, and gave her ' exquisite reason '
for disbelief, ' his nose is a lang gait frae his kidneys.'
In the evenings she always sat, mending, on a low

chair beside a table which held the mending basket
and a mahogany workbox, a gift to her from our
grandmother. As a great treat we were sometimes
allowed to lift all the little lids of the fittings, and
look at our faces in the mirror, and try to find the
opening of the carved ivory needlecase which had
come from India all the way. Our noise never
disturbed Leezie. ' Be wise, noo, like guid bairns,'
she would say when we got beyond reason ; and if
we quarrelled violently, she would shake her head
and tell herself, ' Puir things ! They'll a' gree when
they meet at frem't kirk doors,'—a dark saying
which seldom failed to quell even the most turbulent.

" On Sabbath evenings, when the mending basket
and the workbox were shut away in the cupboard,
the little table was piled with vivid religious
weeklies, such as *The Christian Herald*, and Leezie
pored over them, absorbed, for hours. Then she
would remove her glasses, give a long satisfied sigh,
and say, ' Weel, I hev read mony a stert-ling thing
this day.'

" Above the mantelshelf hung Leezie's greatest
treasure—a text, *Thou God seest me*, worked in
wool, and above the words, also in wool, a large
staring eye. That eye was, so to speak, a cloud on
my young life. I knew—Mother had taken it down
and I had examined it—that it was only canvas and
wool, but if I happened to be left alone in the room
it seemed to come alive and stare at me with a
terrible questioning look, until I was reduced to
wrapping myself up in the window curtains,
' trembling to think, poor child of sin,' that it was
really the eye of God, which seems to prove that,
even at a very tender age, I had by no means a
conscience ' void of offence.'

" We were brought up sturdily on porridge (I

can hear Leezie's voice now—' Bairns, come to yer porridges ') and cold baths, on the Shorter Catechism, the Psalms of David, and—to use your own inelegant phrase—great chunks of the Bible. When I read in books, where people talk of young men and women driven from home and from the paths of virtue by the strictness of their Calvinistic parents and the narrowness and unloveliness of their faith, I think of our childhood and of our father, and I ' lawff,' like Fish. Calvinism is a strong creed, too apt, as some one says, to dwarf to harsh formality, but those of us who have been brought up under its shadow know that it can be in very truth a tree of life, with leaves for the healing of the nations.

" Why do some families care so much more for each other than others ? Has it anything to do with the upbringing ? Is it the kind of mother one has ? I don't know, but I know we grew up adoring each other in the frankest and most absurd way. Not that we showed it by caresses or by endearing names. The nearest we came to an expression of affection was at night, when the clamour of the day was stilled and bedtime had come. In that evening hour Sandy, who fought ' bitter and reg'lar ' all day but who took the Scriptures very literally, would say to Walter and Alan, ' Have I hit you to-day ? Well, I'm sorry.' If a handsome expression of forgiveness was not at once forthcoming, ' Say you forgive me,' he warned them, ' or I'll hit you again.'

" When we were safely tucked away in bed, my door being left open that I might shout through to the boys, Sandy would say, ' Good-night, Lizbeth,' and then ' *Wee* Lizbeth,' and I would reply, ' Good-night, Sandy. *Wee* Sandy.' The same ceremony was gone through with Walter and Alan, and then, but not till then, we could fall asleep, at peace with all men.

"We were none of us mild or docile children, but Sandy was much the wickedest—and infinitely the most lovable. Walter and Alan and I were his devoted slaves. He led us into the most involved scrapes, for no one could devise mischief as he could, and was so penitent when we had to suffer the consequences with him. He was always fighting boys much bigger than himself, but he was all tenderness to anything weak or ugly or ill-used. At school he was first in both lessons and games, and as he grew up everything seemed to come easy to him, from boxing to sonnet writing.

"It isn't always easy to like beautiful, all-conquering sort of people, but I never heard of any one not liking Sandy. He had such a disarming smile and such kind, honest eyes.

"He was easily the most brilliant man of his year at Oxford ; great things were predicted for him ; he seemed to walk among us 'both hands full of gifts, carrying with nonchalance the seeds of a most influential life.' And he died—he died at Oxford, in his last summer-term, of a chill got on the river. Even now, after five years, I can't write about it ; my eyes dazzle. . . . Three months later my mother died.

"We hardly realized that she was ill, for she kept her happy face and was brave and gay and lovely to the end. Mother and Sandy were so like each other that so long as we kept Mother we hadn't entirely lost Sandy, but now our house was left unto us desolate.

"Of course we grew happy again. We found, almost reluctantly, that we could remember sad

things yet be gay! The world could not go on if
the first edge of grief remained undulled—but the
sword has pierced the heart and the wound remains.
On that June night when the nightingale sang, and
the grey shadow crept over Sandy's face, I realized
that nothing was too terrible to happen. Before
that night the earth had seemed a beautifully solid
place. I had pranced on it and sung the ' loud mad
song ' of youth without the slightest misgiving, but
after that I knew what Thomas Nash meant when
he wrote :

> ' Brightness falls from the air ;
> Queens have died young and fair ;
> Dust hath closed Helen's eyes,'

and I said, ' I will walk softly all my days.'

"Only Father remained to us. I clung to him as
the one prop that held up my world. Since then I
have gone in bondage to the fear that he might be
snatched from me as Mother and Sandy were.
When otherwise inoffensive people hinted to me
that my father looked tired or ill, I hated them for
the sick feeling their words gave me. So, you see,
when the doctor said that with care he might live
many years, I was so relieved for myself that I
could not be properly sorry for Father. It is hard
for him. I used to dream dreams about what we
would do when he retired, but I always knew at the
bottom of my heart that he would never leave his
work as long as he had strength to go on. If he had
been given the choice, I am sure he would have
wanted to die in harness. Not that we have ever
discussed the question. When I went up to his room
after the doctor had told me (I knew he had also
told Father), he merely looked up from the paper
he was reading and said, ' There is an ignorant
fellow writing here who says Scott is little read

nowadays,' and so great was his wrath at the
' ignorant fellow ' that such small things as the state
of his own health passed unremarked on.

" There is no point in remaining in Glasgow : we
shall go to Etterick.

" You say you can't imagine what Father will do,
forbidden to preach (he who loved preaching) ;
forbidden to walk except on level places (he who
wore seven-league boots) ; forbidden to exert himself (he who was so untiring in his efforts to help
others). I know. It will be a life of limitations.
But I promise you he won't grumble, and he won't
look submissive or resigned. He will look as if he
were having a perfectly radiant time—and what is
more, he will feel it. How triumphantly true it is
that the meek inherit the earth ! Flowers are left
to him, flowers and the air and the sky and the
sun ; spring mornings, winter nights by the fire,
and books—and I may just mention in passing those
two unconsidered trifles Buff and me ! As I write,
I have a picture in my mind of Father in retirement.
He will be interested in everything, and always apt
at the smallest provocation to be passionately angry
at Radicals. (They have the same effect on him as
Puritans had on gentle Sir Andrew Aguecheek—you
remember ?) I can see him wandering in the garden,
touching a flower here and there in the queer tender
way he has with flowers, listening to the birds, enjoying his meals, reading every adventure book he
can lay his hands on (with his Baxter's *Saints' Rest*
in his pocket for quiet moments), visiting the cottage
folk, deeply interested in all that interests them,
and never leaving without reminding them that
there is ' something ayont.' In the words of the
old Covenanter, ' He will walk by the waters of
Eulai, plucking an apple here and there,'—and we

who live with him will seem to hear the sound of his Master's feet."

Later she wrote :

" I don't suppose you ever ' flitted,' did you ? That is our Scots expression for removing ourselves and our belongings to another house—a misleadingly bird-like and airy expression for such a ponderous proceeding.

" Just at present all our household gods, and more especially the heavy wardrobes, seem to be lying on my chest. The worry is, we have far too much furniture, for Etterick is already furnished with old good things that it would be a shame to touch, so we can only take the things from here that are too full of associations to leave. We would hate to sell anything, but I wish we could hear of a nice young couple setting up house without much money to do it with, and we would beg of them to take our furniture.

" You would be surprised how difficult it is to leave Glasgow and the church people. I never knew how much I liked the friendly old place until the time came for leaving it ; it is like digging oneself up by the roots.

" And the church people are so pathetic. It never seems to have occurred to them that Father might leave them, and they are so surprised and grieved, and so quite certain that if he only goes away for a rest he will soon be fit again and able for his work.

" But I am not really sorry for them. I know quite well that in a few months' time, flushed with tea and in most jocund mood, they will be sitting at an Induction Soiree drinking in praise of their

new minister—and thank goodness I shan't be there
to hear the speeches ! Of course there are some to
whom Father simply made life worth living—it
hurts me to think of them.

" Life is a queer, confusing thing ! There are
one or two people in the church who have enjoyed
making things difficult (even in the most lamb-like
and pleasant congregations such are to be found),
and I have always promised myself that some day,
in a few well-chosen words, I should tell them what
I thought of them. Well, here is my opportunity,
and I find I don't want to use it ! After all, they
are not so complacent, so crassly stupid, so dead
to all fine feeling as I thought they were. They
are really quite decent folk. The one I disliked
most—the sort of man who says a minister is well
paid with ' three pounds a week and a free house '—
a Socialist, a leveller, this man came to see Father
the other night after he had ' cleaned hissel' ' after
the day's work. There were actually tears in his
suspicious small eyes when he saw Father so frail-
looking, and he talked in what was for him quite
a hushed small voice on uncontroversial subjects.
As he was going out of the room he stopped and
blurted out, ' I niver believed a Tory could be a
Christian till I kent you.' . . . I am glad I won't
have to say good-bye to Peggy. I saw her yesterday afternoon, and she didn't seem any worse, and
we were happy together. This morning they sent
up to tell me she had died suddenly in the night.
She went away ' very peaceably,' her father said.
It wasn't the word he meant, but he spoke more
truly than he knew. She went ' peaceably ' because
there was no resentment or fear in her child's heart.
To souls like Peggy's, innocent and quiet, God
gives the knowledge that Death is but His angel

a messenger of light in whom is no darkness at
all. . . .

"I have opened this to tell you a piece of news
that has pleased me very much. Do you remember my friend Kirsty Christie and her fiancé Mr.
Hamilton? Perhaps you have forgotten them,
though I expect the evening you spent at the
Christies' house is seared on your memory, and I
assure you your 'Cockney accent' has quite spoiled
Mrs. Christie for the plain Glasgow of her family
circle; well, anyway, Kirsty can't marry Mr.
Hamilton until he has got a church, and it so
happened that the minister at Langhope, the
nearest village to Etterick, was finding his work
too much and felt he must resign. Here was my
chance! (Oh for the old bad days of patronage!)
I don't say I didn't pull strings. I did. I pulled
about fifty, and tangled most of them; but the
upshot is that they have elected Mr. Hamilton to
be minister of Langhope. They are a wise and
fortunate people, for he is one of the best; and just
think of the fun for me having Kirsty settled near
us!

"It is the nicest thing that has happened for a
long time. I have just thought of another thing—
it is a solution of the superfluous furniture problem.

"Langhope Manse is large and the stipend small,
and I don't think Kirsty would mind taking our
furniture. I shall ask her delicately, using 'tack.'"

CHAPTER XVIII

THE END OF AN OLD SONG

The Setons left Glasgow in the end of May.

On the evening before they left Thomas and Billy made a formal farewell visit, on the invitation of Elizabeth and Buff, who were holding high revel in the dismantled house.

Mr. Seton had gone to stay with friends, who could be trusted to look after him very carefully, until the bustle and discomfort of the removal was over. Buff was to have gone with his father, but he begged so hard to be allowed to stay and help that, in spite of Marget's opposition (she held her own views on his helpfulness), his sister gave in.

He and his two friends had enjoyed a full and satisfying week among wooden crates and furniture vans, and were sincerely sorry that the halcyon time was nearly over ; in fact, Thomas had been heard to remark, " When I'm a man I'll flit every month."

Poor Thomas, in spite of the flitting, felt very low in spirits. He had done his best to dissuade the Setons from leaving Glasgow. Every morning for a week he had come in primed with a fresh

objection. Had Elizabeth, he asked, thought what
it meant to live so far from a station ? Had Elizabeth thought what it meant to be at the mercy of
oil-lamps ? " Mamma " said that six weeks of
Arran in the summer was more than enough of the
country. Had Elizabeth thought that she would
never get any servants to stay ?

He did not conceal from them that " Mamma "
thought the whole project very " daftlike." To
judge from Thomas, " Mamma " must have expressed herself with some vigour, and Elizabeth
could only hope that that placid lady would never
know the use her son had made of her name and
conversation.

But the efforts of Thomas had been unavailing,
and the last evening had come.

Thomas and Billy, feeling the solemnity of the
occasion needed some expression, did not open
the door and run in as was their custom, but
reached up and rang a peal at the bell, a peal that
clanged like a challenge through the empty house
and brought Ellen hurrying up the kitchen stairs,
expecting a telegram at the very least. Finding
only the familiar figures of Thomas and Billy, she
murmured to herself, " What next, I wonder ? "
and leading the way to the drawing-room, announced the illustrious couple.

Buff greeted them with a joyous shout.

" Come on. I helped to fry the potatoes."

The supper had been chosen by the boys themselves, and consisted of sausages and fried potatoes,
jam tartlets and tinned pine-apple, with home-made
toffee to follow ; also two siphons of lemonade.

It was spread on a small table, the tablecloth was
a kitchen towel, and there was only one tumbler
and the barest allowance of knives and forks ; but

Buff was charmed with his feast, and hospitably eager that his guests should enjoy it.

" Come on," he said again.

But Thomas, gripping Billy's hand, hung back, and it was seen that he carried a parcel.

" I've brought Buff a present," he announced.

" Oh, Thomas ! " said Elizabeth, " not another ! After that lovely box of tools."

" Yes," said Thomas firmly. " It's a book—a wee religious book." He handed it to Elizabeth. " It's about angels."

Elizabeth did not look at her young brother, but undid the paper, opened the book, and read :

> " It came upon the midnight clear,
>   That glorious song of old,
> From angels bending near the earth
>   To touch their harps of gold :
> ' Peace on the earth, good-will to men,
>   From heaven's all-gracious King ! '
> The world in solemn stillness lay
>   To hear the angels sing."

" How nice ! and the pictures are beautiful, Thomas. It's a lovely present. Look at it, Buff ! "

Buff looked at it, and then he looked at Thomas. " What made you think I wanted a book about angels ? " he demanded.

" Nothing in your behaviour, old man," his sister hastened to assure him. " D'you know you've never said Thank you ! "

Buff said it, but there was a marked lack of enthusiasm in his tone.

" I didn't buy it," Thomas said, feeling the present needed some explanation. " Aunt Jeanie sent it at Christmas to Papa, and Papa wasn't caring much about angels, and Mamma said I could give it to Buff ; she said it might improve him."

" I *knew* he didn't buy it ! " shouted Buff, passing over the aspersion on his character, " I knew it all the time. Nobody would *buy* a book like that : it's the kind that get given you."

" Aunt Jeanie sent me the *Prodigal Son*," broke in Billy in his gentle little voice (he often acted as oil to the troubled waters of Buff and Thomas). " I like the picture of the Prodigal eating the swine's husks. There's a big swine looking at him as if it would bite him."

" Should think so," Thomas said. " If you were a swine you wouldn't like prodigals coming eating your husks."

" I don't think, Billy," said Elizabeth, looking meditatively at him, " that you will ever be a prodigal, but I can quite see Thomas as the elder brother—— Ah ! here comes Ellen with the sausages ! "

It was a very successful party, noisy and appreciative, and after they had eaten everything there was to eat, including the toffee, and licked their sticky fingers, they had a concert.

Billy sang in a most genteel manner a ribald song about a " cuddy " at Kilmarnock Fair ; Buff recited with great vigour what he and Elizabeth between them could remember of " The Ballad of the Revenge " ; and Thomas, not to be outdone, thrust Macaulay's Lays into Elizabeth's hands, crying, " Here, hold that, and I'll do How Horatius kept the bridge."

At last Elizabeth declared that the entertainment had come to an end, and the guests reluctantly prepared to depart.

" You're quite sure you'll invite us to Etterick ? " was Thomas's parting remark. " You won't forget when you're away ? "

" Oh, Thomas ! " Elizabeth asked him reproachfully, " have I proved myself such a broken reed ?
I promise you faithfully that at the end of June I
shall write to Mamma and suggest the day and the
train and everything. I'll go further. I'll borrow
a car and meet you at the junction. Will that do ? "

Thomas nodded, satisfied, and she patted each
small head. " Good-bye, my funnies. We shall
miss you very much."

When Elizabeth had seen Buff in bed she came
downstairs to the dismantled drawing-room.

Ellen had tidied away the supper-table and made
up the fire, and pulled forward the only decent chair,
and had done her best to make the room look
habitable.

It was still daylight, but just too dark to read with
comfort, and Elizabeth folded her tired hands and
gave herself up to idleness. She had been getting
gradually more depressed each day, as the familiar
things were carried out of the house, and to-night
her heart felt like a physical weight and her eyes
smarted with unshed tears. The ending of an old
song hurts.

Sitting alone in the empty, silent room, a room
once so well peopled and full of happy sound, she
had a curious unsubstantial feeling, as if she were
but part of the baseless fabric of a vision and might
dissolve and " leave not a rack behind." . . .
The usually cheerful room was haunted to-night,
memories thronged round her, plucking at her to
recall themselves. It was in this room that her
mother had sung to them and played with them—
and never minded when things were knocked down
and broken. Over there, in the corner of the
ceiling near the window, there was still an ugly
mark made by Walter and a cricket-ball, and she

remembered how her father had said, so regretfully, " And it was such a handsome cornice ! " and her mother had laughed—peals of laughter like a happy schoolgirl, and taken her husband's arm and said, " You dear innocent ! " It was a funny thing to call one's father, she remembered thinking at the time, and did not seem to have any connection with the cornice. All sorts of little things, long forgotten, came stealing back ; the boys' funny sayings—Sandy, standing a determined little figure, assuring his mother, " *I shall always stay with you, Mums, and if any one comes to marry me I shall hide in the dirty clothes basket.*"

And now Sandy and his mother were together for always.

Elizabeth slipped on to the floor, and kneeling by the chair as she had knelt as a child—" O God," she prayed, " don't take anybody else. Leave me Father and Buffy and the boys in India. Please leave them to me—if it be Thy will. Amen."

She was still kneeling with her head on her folded arms when Marget came into the room carrying a tray. She made no comment on seeing the attitude of her mistress, but, putting the tray on the table, she went over to the window and, remarking that if they had to flit it was a blessing Providence had arranged that they should flit when the days were long, she proceeded to pull down the blinds and light the gas.

Then she leaned over her mistress and addressed her as if she were a small child.

" I've brocht ye a cup o' tea an' a wee bit buttered toast. Ye wud get nae supper wi' thae wild laddies. Drink it while it's hot, and get awa' to your bed, like a guid lassie."

Elizabeth uncoiled herself (to use her own phrase)

and rose to her feet. She blinked in the gaslight with her tear-swollen eyes, then she made a face at Marget and laughed :

" I'm an idiot, Marget, but somehow to-night it all seemed to come back. You and I have seen— changes. . . . You're a kind old dear, anyway ; it's a good thing we always have you."

" It is that," Marget agreed. " What aboot the men's breakfasts the morn's morning ? I doot we hevna left dishes to gang roond." She stood and talked until she had seen Elizabeth drink the tea and eat the toast, and then herded her upstairs to bed.

* * * * * * *

One day in the end of June, Elizabeth fulfilled her promise to Thomas, and wrote to Mrs. Kirke asking if her two sons could be dispatched on a certain date by a certain train, and arrangements would be made for meeting them at the junction.

It was a hot shining afternoon, and the Setons were having tea by the burn-side.

Mr. Jamieson (the lame Sunday-school teacher from the church in Glasgow) was staying with them for a fortnight, and he sat in a comfortable deck-chair with a book in his lap ; but he read little, the book of Nature was more fascinating than even Sir Walter. His delight in his surroundings touched Elizabeth. " To think," she said to her father, " that we never thought of asking Mr. Jamieson to Etterick before ! Lumps of selfishness, that's what we are."

Mr. Seton suggested that it was more want of thought.

" It amounts to the same thing," said his daughter. " I wonder if it would be possible to have Bob Scott out here ? You know, my little waif with the drunken father? Of course he would corrupt the whole neighbourhood in about two days, and be a horribly bad influence with Buff—but I don't believe the poor little chap has ever been in the real country. We must try to plan."

Mr. Seton sat reading the *Times*. He was greatly worried about Ulster, and frequently said "*Tut-tut*" as he read.

Buff had helped Ellen to carry everything out for tea, and was now in the burn, splashing about, building stones into a dam. Buff was very happy. Presently, Mr. Hamilton, the new minister at Langhope, was going to take him in hand and prepare him for school, but in the meantime he attended the village school—a haunt that his soul loved. He modelled his appearances and manners on the friends he made there, acquired a rich Border accent, and was in no way to be distinguished from the other scholars. At luncheon that day, he had informed his family that Wullie Veitch (the ploughman's son) had said, after a scuffle in the playground, "Seton's trampit ma piece fair useless;" and the same youth had summed up the new-comer in a sentence: "Everything Seton says is aither rideeclous or confounded," a judgment which, instead of annoying, amused and delighted both the new-comer and his family.

Things had worked out amazingly well, Elizabeth thought, as she sat with her writing-pad on her knee and looked at her family. Her father seemed better, and was most contented with his life. Buff was growing every day browner and stronger. The house was all in order after the improvements they had made, and was even more charming than she had hoped it would be. The garden was a riot of colour and scent, and a never-ending delight. To her great relief, Marget and Ellen had settled down with Watty Laidlaw and his wife in peace and quiet accord, and had even been heard to say that they *preferred* the country.

After getting Etterick into order, Elizabeth had worked hard at Langhope Manse.

The wedding had taken place a week before, and to-morrow Andrew Hamilton would bring home his bride.

Elizabeth, with her gift of throwing her whole self into her friends' interests, was as eager and excited as if she were the bride and hers the new home. True, much of it was not to her liking. She hated a dining-room " suite " covered in Utrecht velvet, and she thought Kirsty's friends had been singularly ill-advised in their choice of wedding presents.

Kirsty had refused to think of looking for old things for her drawing-room. She said in her sensible way that things got old soon enough without starting with them old ; and she just hated old faded rugs, there was nothing to beat a good Axminster.

She was very pleased, however, to accept the Setons' spare furniture. It was solid mid-Victorian, polished and cared-for, and as good as the day it was made. The drawers in the wardrobes and dressing-tables moved with a fluency foreign to the showy present-day " Sheraton " and " Chippendale " suites, and Kirsty appreciated this.

Elizabeth had done her best to make the rooms pretty, and only that morning she had put the finishing touches, and looked round the rooms brave in their fresh chintzes and curtains, sniffed the mingled odours of new paint and sweet-peas, and thought how Kirsty would love it all. The store-room she had taken especial pains with, and had even wrested treasures in the way of pots and jars from the store-room at Etterick (to Marget's wrath and disgust), and carried them in the pony-cart to help to fill the rather empty shelves at Langhope.

So this sunny afternoon, as Elizabeth rose from her writing and began to pour out the tea, she felt at peace with all mankind.

She arranged Mr. Jamieson's teacup on a little table by his side, and made it all comfortable for him. " Put away the paper, Father," she cried, " and come and have your tea, and help me to count our blessings. Let's forget Ulster for half an hour."

Mr. Seton obediently laid down the paper and came to the table.

" Dear me," he said, " this is very pleasant."

The bees drowsed among the heather, white butterflies fluttered over the wild thyme and the little yellow and white violas that starred the turf, and the sound of the burn and the gentle crying of sheep made a wonderful peace in the afternoon air. Marget's scones and new-made butter and jam seemed more than usually delicious, and—" Aren't we well off ? " asked Elizabeth.

Mr. Jamieson looked round him with a sigh of utter content, and Mr. Seton said, " I wish I thought that the rest of the world was as peaceful as this little glen." He helped himself to jam. " The situation in Ireland seems to grow more hopeless every day ; and by the way, Jamieson, did you see that the Emperor of Austria's heir has been assassinated along with his wife ? "

" I saw that," said Mr. Jamieson. " I hope it won't mean trouble."

"It seems a pointless crime," said Elizabeth. "Buff, come out of the burn, you water-kelpie, and take your tea."

Buff was trying to drag a large stone from the bed of the stream, and was addressing it as he had heard the stable-boy address the pony,—"Stan' up, ye brit! Wud ye, though?"—but at his sister's command he ceased his efforts and crawled up the bank to have his hands dried in his father's handkerchief.

It never took Buff long to eat a meal, and in a very few minutes he had eaten three scones and drunk two cups of milk, and laid himself face downwards in the heather to ruminate.

"Mr. Jamieson," he said suddenly, "if a robber stole your money and went in a ship to South Africa, how would you get at him?"

Mr. Jamieson, unversed in the ways of criminals, was at a loss.

"I doubt I would just need to lose it," he said.

This was feeble. Buff turned to his father and asked what course he would follow.

"I think," said Mr. Seton, "that I would cable to the police to board the ship at the first port."

Buff rejected this method as tame and unspectacular.

"What would you do, Lizbeth?"

"It depends," said Elizabeth, "on how much money I had. If it was a lot, I would send a detective to recover it. But sending a detective would cost a lot."

Buff thought deeply for a few seconds.

"I know what I would do," he said. "I would send a *bloodhound—steerage.*"

CHAPTER XIX

" How wilt thou do in the swelling of Jordan ? "

" As dying, and behold we live."

You know, of course, Gentle Reader, that there can be no end to this little chronicle ?

You know that when a story begins in 1913, 1914 will follow, and that in that year certainty came to an end, plans ceased to come to fruition—that, in fact, the lives of all of us cracked across.

Personally, I detest tales that end in the air. I like all the strings gathered up tidily in the last chapter and tied neatly into nuptial knots ; so I should have liked to be able to tell you that Elizabeth became a " grateful " wife, and that she and Arthur Townshend lived happily and, in fairy-tale parlance, never drank out of an empty cup ; and that Stewart Stevenson ceased to think of Elizabeth (whom he never really approved of) and fell in love with Jessie Thomson, and married her one fine day in " Seton's kirk," and that all Jessie's aspirations after refinement and late dinner were amply fulfilled.

But, alas ! as I write (May 1917) the guns still boom continuously over there in France, and there is scarce a rift to be seen in the war-clouds that obscure the day.

Jessie Thomson is a V.A.D. now and a very efficient worker, as befits the daughter of Mrs. Thomson. She has not time to worry about her mother's homely ways, nor is she so hag-ridden by the Simpsons. Gertrude Simpson, by the way, is, according to her mother, " marrying into the Navy —a Lieutenant-Commander, no less," and, according to Mrs. Thomson, is " neither to haud nor bind " in consequence.

Stewart Stevenson went on with his work for three months after war began, but he was thinking deeply all the time, and one day in November he put all his painting things away—very tidily— locked up the studio and went home to tell his parents he had decided to go. His was no martial spirit, he hated the very name of war and loathed the thought of the training, but he went because he felt it would be a pitiful thing if any one had to take his place.

His mother sits among the time-pieces in Lochnagar and knits socks, and packs parcels, and cries a good deal. Both she and her husband have grown much greyer, and they somehow appear smaller. Stewart, you see, is their only son.

It is useless to tell over the days of August 1914. They are branded on the memory. The stupefaction, the reading of newspapers until we were dazed and half-blind, the endless talking, the frenzy of knitting into which the women threw themselves, thankful to find something that would at least occupy their hands. We talked so glibly about what we did not understand. We repeated parrot-like to each other, " It will take all our men and all our treasure," and had no notion how truly we spoke or how hard a saying we were to find it. And all the time the sun shone.

It was particularly hard to believe in the war at Etterick. No khaki-clad men disturbed the peace of the glen, no trains rushed past crowded with troops, no aeroplanes circled in the heavens. The hills and the burn and the peeweets remained the same, the high hollyhocks flaunted themselves against the grey garden wall ; nothing was changed —and yet everything was different.

Buff and Thomas and Billy, as pleased and excited as if it were some gigantic show got up for their benefit, equipped themselves with weapons and spent laborious days tracking spies in the heather and charging down the hillside ; performing many deeds of valour for which, in the evening, they solemnly presented each other with suitable decorations.

Towards the end of August, when they were at breakfast one morning, Arthur Townshend suddenly appeared, having come up by the night train and motored from the junction.

His arrival created great excitement, Buff throwing himself upon him and demanding to know why he had come.

" Well, you know, you did invite me in August," Arthur reminded him.

" And when are you going away ? " (This was Buff's favourite formula with guests, and he could never be made to see that it would be prettier if he said, " How long can you stay ? ")

Arthur shook hands with Elizabeth and her father, and replied :

" I'm going away this evening as ever was. It sounds absurd," in answer to Elizabeth's exclamation, " but I must be back in London to-morrow morning. I had no notion when I might have a chance of seeing you all again, so I just came off when I had a free day."

"Dear me!" said Mr. Seton. "You young people are like Ariel or Puck, the way you fly about."

"Oh! *is* it to be the Flying Corps?" asked Elizabeth.

"No—worse luck! Pilled for my eyesight. But I'm passed for the infantry, and to-morrow I enter the Artists' Rifles. I may get a commission and go to France quite soon."

Ellen came in with a fresh supply of food, and breakfast was a prolonged meal; for the Setons had many questions to ask and Arthur had much to tell them.

"You're a godsend to us," Elizabeth told him, "for you remain normal. People here are all unstrung. The neighbours arrive in excited motorfuls, children and dogs and all, and we sit and knit, and drink tea and tell each other the most absurd tales. And rumours leap from end to end of the county, and we imagine we hear guns on the Forth—which isn't humanly possible—and people who have boys in the Navy are tortured with silly lies about sea-battles and the sinking of warships."

Before luncheon, Arthur was dragged out by the boys to admire their pets; but though they looked at such peaceful objects as rabbits, a jackdaw with a wooden leg, and the giant trout that lived in Prince Charlie's well, all their talk was of battles. They wore sacking round their legs to look like putties, their belts were stuck full of weapons, and they yearned to shed blood. No one would have thought, to hear their bloodthirsty talk, that only that morning they had, all three, wept bitter tears because the sandy cat from the stables had killed a swallow.

Billy, who had got mixed in his small mind between friend and foe, announced that he had, a few minutes ago, killed seven Russians whom he had found lurking among the gooseberry bushes in the kitchen garden, and was instantly suppressed by Thomas, who hissed at him, " You don't kill *allies*, silly. You inter them."

In the afternoon, while Mr. Seton took his reluctant daily rest, and the boys were busy with some ploy of their own in the stackyard, Elizabeth and Arthur wandered out together.

They went first to see the walled garden, now ablaze with autumn flowers ; but beautiful though it was it did not keep them long, for something in the day and something in themselves seemed to demand the uplands, and they turned their steps to the hills.

It was an easy climb, and they walked quickly, and soon stood at the cairn of stones that marked the top of the hill behind the house, stood breathless and glad of a rest, looking at the country-side spread out beneath them.

In most of the fields the corn stood in " stooks " ; the last field was being cut this golden afternoon, and the hum of the reaping-machine was loud in the still air.

Far away a wisp of white smoke told that the little branch-line train was making its leisurely journey from one small flower-scented station to another. Soon the workers would gather up their things and go home, the day's work finished.

All was peace.

And there was no peace.

The tears came into Elizabeth's eyes as she looked,

9

and Arthur answered the thought that brought the tears. " It's worth dying for," he said.

Elizabeth nodded, not trusting her voice.

They turned away and talked of trivial matters, and laughed, and presently fell silent again.

" Elizabeth," said Arthur suddenly, " I wish you didn't scare me so."

" *Do* I ? I'm very much gratified to hear it. I had no idea I inspired awe in any mortal."

" Well—that isn't at all a suitable reply to my remark. I wanted you to assure me that there was no need to be scared."

" There isn't. What can I do for you ? Ask and I shall grant it, even to the half of my kingdom."

" When we get this job over may I come straight to you ? "

Elizabeth had no coyness in her nature, and she now turned her grey eyes—not mocking now but soft and shining—on the anxious face of her companion and said :

" Indeed, my dear, you may. Just as straight as you can come, and I shall be waiting for you on the doorstep. It has taken a European war to make me realize it, but you are the only man in the world so far as I am concerned."

Some time later Arthur said, " I'm going away extraordinarily happy. By Jove, I ought to be some use at fighting now ; " and he laughed boyishly.

" Oh, don't," said Elizabeth. " You've reminded me, and I was trying to make believe you weren't going away. I'm afraid—oh ! Arthur, I'm horribly afraid, that you won't be allowed to come back, that you will be snatched from me——"

" I may not come back," said Arthur soberly,

" but I won't be snatched. You give me, and I give myself, willingly. But, Lizbeth, beloved, it isn't like you to be afraid."

" Yes, it is. I've always been scared of something. When I was tiny it was the Last Day. I hardly dared go the afternoon walk with Leezie in case it came like a thief in the night and found me far from my home and parents. I walked with my eyes shut, and bumped into people and lamp-posts, because I was sure if I opened them I should see the Angel Gabriel standing on the top of a house with a trumpet in his hand, and the heavens rolling up like a scroll, and I didn't know about parchment scrolls and thought it was a *brandy-scroll*, which made it so much worse."

" Oh, my funny Elizabeth ! " Arthur said tenderly. " I wish I could have been there to see you ; I grudge all the years I didn't know you."

" Oh," said Elizabeth, " it wouldn't have been much good knowing each other in those days. I was about five, I suppose, and you would be nine. You would merely have seen a tiresome little girl, and I would have seen a superior sort of boy, and I should probably have put out my tongue at you. I wasn't a nice child ; mine is a faulty and tattered past."

" When did you begin to reform ? " Arthur asked, " for it was a very sedate lady I found in Glasgow. Tell me, Lizbeth, why were you so discouraging to me then ? You must have known I cared."

" Well, you see, I'm a queer creature—affectionate but not very *loving*. I never think that ' love ' is a word to use much if people are all well and things in their ordinary. And you were frightfully English, you can't deny it, and a monocle, and everything very much against you. And then Aunt

Alice's intention of being a sort of fairy godmother was so obvious—it seemed feeble to tumble so easily in with her plans. But I suppose I cared all the time, and I can see now that it was very petty of me to pretend indifference."

" Petty ? " said Arthur in fine scorn. " *You* couldn't be petty. But I'm afraid I'm still ' frightfully ' English, and I've still got astigmatism in one eye—are you sure you can overlook these blemishes ? . . . But seriously, Lizbeth—if I never come back to you, if I am one of the ' costs,' if all you and I are to have together, O my beloved, is just this one perfect afternoon, it will still be all right. Won't it ? You will laugh and be your own gallant self, and know that I am loving you and waiting for you—farther on. It will be all right, Lizbeth ? "

She nodded, smiling at him bravely.

" Then kiss me, my very own."

.   .   .   .

The days drew in, and the Setons settled down for the winter. James Seton occupied himself for several hours in the day writing a history of the district, and found it a great interest. He said little about the war, and told his daughter he had prayed for grace to hold his peace ; but he was a comforter to the people round when the war touched their homes.

Elizabeth was determined that she would have busy days. She became the Visitor for the district for the Soldiers' and Sailors' Families Association ; she sang at war-concerts ; she amused her father and Buff ; she knitted socks and wrote letters. She went to Glasgow as often as she could be spared to visit her friends in the Gorbals, and came back laden with tales for her father—tales that made him laugh with tears in his eyes, for it was " tragical mirth."

To mothers who lost their sons she was a welcome visitor. They never felt her out of place, or an embarrassment, this tall golden-haired creature, as she sat on a wooden chair by the kitchen fire and listened and understood and cried with them. They brought out their pitiful treasures for her—the half-finished letter that had been found in " Jimmy's " pocket when death overtook him, the few French coins, the picture-postcard of his wee sister—and she held them tenderly and reverently while they told the tale of their grief.

" Oh ! ma wee Jimmie," one poor mother lamented to her. " Little did I think I wud never see him again. The nicht he gaed awa' he had to be at the station at nine o'clock, and he said none o' us were to gang wi' him. I hed an awfu' guid supper for him, for I thinks to masel', ' It's no' likely the laddie 'll ever see a dacent meal in France,' an' he likit it rare weel. An' syne he lookit at the time, an' he says, ' I'll awa' then,' an' I juist turned kinda seeck-like when he said it. He said guid-bye to the lasses an' wee John, but he never said guid-bye to me. Na. He was sic a man, ye ken, an' he didna want to greet—eighteen he was, ma wee bairn. I tell't the ithers to keep back, an' I gaed oot efter him to the stair-heid. He stood on the top step, an' he lookit at me, ' S'long, then, Mither,' he says. An' he gaed doon twa-three steps, an' he stoppit again, an' ' S'long, Mither,' he says. Syne he got to the turn o' the stair, an' he stood an' lookit as if he juist cudna gang,—I can see him noo, wi' his Glengarry bunnet cockit that gallant on his heid—and he cried, ' S'long, Mither,' an' he ran doon the stair—ma wee laddie."

It was astonishing to Elizabeth how quickly the women became quite at home with these foreign places with the strange outlandish names that swallowed up their men.

"Ay," one woman told her (this was later), "I sent oot a plum-puddin' in a cloth to ma son Jake— I sent twa o' them, an' I said to him that wan o' them was for Dan'l Scott—his mither was a neebor o' mine an' a dacent wumman an' she's deid—an' Jake wasna near Dan'l at the time, but the first chance he got he tuk the puddin' an' he rum'led a' roond Gally Polly until he fand him—and then they made a nicht o't."

Evidently, in her mind "Gally Polly" was a jovial sort of place, rather like Argyle Street on a Saturday night. As Elizabeth told her father, Glasgow people gave a homely, cosy feeling to any part of the world they went to—even to the blasted, shell-strewn fields of Flanders and Gallipoli.

The winter wore on, and Arthur Townshend got his commission and went to France.

Elizabeth sent him a parcel every week, and the whole household contributed to it. Marget baked cakes, Mrs. Laidlaw made treacle-toffee, Mr. Seton sent books, Buff painted pictures, and Elizabeth put in everything she could think of. But much though he appreciated the parcels he liked the letters more.

In November she wrote to him : "We have heard this morning that Alan's regiment has landed in France. He thinks he may get a few days' leave, perhaps next month. It would be joyful if he were home for Christmas.

"Poor old Walter, hung up in the Secretariat, comforts himself that his leave is due next year, and hopes—hopes, the wicked one !—that the war will still be going on then. Your letters are a tremendous interest. I read parts of them to Father and Buff, and last night your tale of the wild Highlander who was ' King of Ypres ' so excited them that Father got up to shut the door,—you know how he does when he is moved over anything,— and Buff spun round the room like a teetotum, telling it all over again, with himself as hero. That child gives himself the most rich and varied existence spinning romances in which he is the central figure. He means to be a Hero when he grows up (an improbable profession!), but I expect school will teach him to be an ordinary sensible boy. And what a pity that will be ! By the way, you won't get any more Bible pictures from him. Father had to forbid them. Buff was allowing his fancy to play too freely among sacred subjects, poor old pet !

" The war is turning everything topsy-turvy. You never thought to acquire the dignity of a second lieutenant, and I hardly expected to come down the social scale with a rattle, but so it is. I am a housemaid. Our invaluable Ellen has gone to make munitions and I am trying to take her place. You see, I can't go and make munitions, because I must stay with Father and Buff, but it seemed a pity to keep an able-bodied woman to sweep and dust our rooms for us when I could quite well do it. Marget waits the table now, and Mrs. Laidlaw helps her with the kitchen work.

" Ellen was most unwilling to go,—she had been five years with us, and she clings like ivy to people she is accustomed to,—but when her sister wrote about the opportunity for clever hands and that a place was open for her if she would take it, I un-

clung her, and now she writes to me so contentedly
that I am sure she is clinging round munitions.
We miss her dreadfully, not only for her work but
for her nice gentle self ; but I flatter myself that I
am acting understudy quite well.   And I enjoy it.
The daily round, the common task don't bore me
one bit.   True, it is always the same old work and
the same old dust, but *I* am different every day—
some days on the heights, some days in the *howes*.
I try to be very methodical, and I ' turn out ' the
rooms as regularly as even Mrs. Thomson, that
cleanest of women, could desire.   And there is no
tonic like it.   No matter how anxious and depressed
I may be when I begin to clean a bedroom, by the
time I have got the furniture back in its place, the
floor polished with beeswax and turpentine, and
clean covers on the toilet-table, my spirits simply
won't keep from soaring.   You will be startled to
hear that I rise at 6 a.m.   I like to get as much done
as possible before breakfast, and I find that when
I have done ' the nastiest thing in the day ' and get
my feet on to the floor, it doesn't matter whether it
is six o'clock or eight.   Only, my cold bath is very
cold at that early hour—but I think of you people
in France and pour contempt on my shivering self.
To lighten our labours we have got a vacuum cleaner,
one of the kind you stand on and work from side to
side.   Buff delights to help with this thing, and he
and I see-saw together.   Sometimes we sing ' A life
on the ocean wave,' which adds greatly to the hilarity
of the occasion.   By the time the war is over I expect
to be so healthy and wealthy and wise that I shall
want to continue to be a housemaid. . . .

   " I don't suppose life at the Front is just all you
would have our fancy paint ?   In fact, it must be
ghastly beyond all words, and how you all stand it

I know not. I simply can't bear to be comfortable by the fireside—but that is silly, for I know the only thing that keeps you all going is the thought that we are safe and warm at home. The war has come very near to us these last few days. A boy whom we knew very well—Tommy Elliot—has fallen. They have a place near here. His father was killed in the Boer War, and Tommy was his mother's only child. He was nineteen and just got his commission before war broke out. The pride of him ! And how Buff and Billy and Thomas lay at his feet ! He was the nicest boy imaginable— never thought it beneath his dignity to play with little boys, or be sweet to his mother. I never heard any one with such a hearty laugh. It made you laugh to hear it. Thank God he found so much to laugh at, and so little reason for tears.

" I went over to see Mrs. Elliot. I hardly dared to go, but I couldn't stay away. She was sitting in the room they call the ' summer parlour.' It is a room I love in summer, full of dark oak and coolness and sweet-smelling flowers, but cold and rather dark in winter. She is a woman of many friends, and the writing-table was heaped with letters and telegrams—very few of them opened. She seemed glad to see me, and was calm and smiling ; but the stricken look in her eyes made me behave like an utter idiot. When I could speak I suggested that I had better go away, but she began to speak about him, and I thought it might help her to have a listener who cared too. She told me why she was sitting in the summer parlour. She had used it a great deal for writing, and he had always come in that way, so that he would find her just at once. ' Sometimes,' she said, ' I didn't turn my head, for I knew he liked to " pounce "—a relic from the

little-boy days when he was a black puma.' Her
smile when she said it broke one's heart. 'If I
didn't happen to be here, he went from room to
room, walking warily with his nailed boots on the
polished floors, saying " Mother ! Mother ! " until
he found me.'

" *How are the dead raised up ? and with what
bodies do they come ?* I suppose that is the most
important question in the world to us all, and we
seek for the answer as they who dig for hid treasure.
But all the sermons preached and all the books
written about it help not at all, for the preachers
and the writers are as ignorant as everybody else.
My own firm belief is that God, who made us with
the power of loving, who thought of the spring and
gave young things their darling funny ways, will
not fail us here. He will know that to Tommy's
mother the light of heaven, which is neither of
the sun nor the moon but a light most precious,
even like a jasper stone clear as crystal, will matter
nothing unless it shows her Tommy in his old homespun coat, with his laughing face, ready to
' pounce '; and that she will bid the harpers
harping on their harps of gold still their noise
while she listens for the sound of boyish footsteps
and a voice that says ' Mother ! Mother ! ' . . .

" We read some of the many letters together.
They were all so kind and full of real sympathy, but
I noticed that she pushed carelessly aside those that
talked of her own feelings and kept those that
talked of what a splendid person Tommy was.

" There was one rather smudged-looking envelope
without a stamp, and we wondered where it had
come from. It was from Buff ! He had written
it without asking any one's advice, and had walked
the three miles to deliver it. I think that grimy

little letter did Mrs. Elliot good. We had read so many letters, all saying the same thing, all saying it more or less beautifully, one had the feeling that one was being sluiced all over with sympathy. Buff's was different. It ran :

" ' I am sorry that Tommy is killed for he had a cheery face and I liked him. But it can't be helped. He will be quite comfortable with God and I hope that some one is being kind to old Pepper for he liked him too.—Your aff. friend
                    " 'DAVID STUART SETON.

" ' P.S.—I'm not allowed to draw riligus pictures now or I would have shown you God being very glad to see Tommy.'

" ' Old Pepper ' is a mongrel that Tommy rescued and was kind to, and it was so like Buff to think of the feelings of the dumb animal.

" Tommy's mother held the letter in her hand very tenderly, and the only tears I saw her shed dropped on it. Then ' Let us go out and look for old Pepper,' she said, ' for " he liked him too." '

" I came home very heavy-hearted, trying to comfort myself concerning those splendid boys.

" To die for one's country is a great privilege— God knows I don't say that lightly, for any day I may hear that you or Alan have died that death —and to those boys the honour has been given in the very springtime of their days.

" Most of us part from our lives reluctantly : they are taken from us, and we go with shivering, shrinking feet down to the brink of the River, but those sons of the morning throw their lives from them and *spring* across. I think God will look very kindly at our little boys.

" And smug, middle-aged people say, ' Poor lads ! ' They dare to pity the rich dead. Oh ! the dull people dragging out their span of years without ever finding out what living means !

" But it breaks one's heart, the thought of the buried hopes. I have been thinking of the father, the man in business who was keeping things going until his boy would be through and ready to help him. There are so many of them in Glasgow, and I used to like to listen to them talking to each other in the car coming out from business. They boasted so innocently of their boys, of this one's skill at cricket, that one's prowess in the football field.

" And now this cheery business man has no boy, only a room with a little bed in the corner, a bookshelf full of adventure-stories and battered school-books, a cricket bat and a bag of golf clubs ; a wardrobe full of clothes, and a most vivid selection of ties and socks, for the boy who lies in France was very smart in his nice boyish way, and brushed his hair until it shone. Oh ! I wonder had anybody time to stroke just once that shining head before it was laid away in the earth ? remembering that over the water hearts would break with yearning to see it again.

" It isn't so bad when doleful people get sorrow, they at least have the miserable satisfaction of saying they had always known it would come, but when happy hearts are broken, when blythe people fall silent—the sadness of it haunts one.

" To talk of cheerier subjects. Aunt Alice is a heroine. Who would have thought of her giving up her house for a hospital ! Of course we always knew, didn't we ? that she was the most golden-hearted person in existence, but it has taken a European war to make her practical. Now she writes me long letters of advice about saving, and food values, and is determined that she at least won't be a drag on her country in winning the war.

" Talking about saving, I asked one of my women the other day if she had ever tried margarine. ' No,' she said earnestly, ' I niver touch it ; an' if I'm oot at ma tea an' no' verra sure if it's butter, I juist tak' jeely.' I said no more.

" And now, my very dear, it is perilously near midnight, and there is not the slightest sound in this rather frightening old house, and not the slightest sound on the moor outside, and I am getting rather scared sitting up all alone. Besides, six o'clock comes very soon after midnight ! I am so sleepy, with all my housework, that, like the herd laddie, I get no good of my bed.—Good-night,   E."

. . . .

A more contented woman than Kirsty Hamilton *née* Christie it would have been difficult to find. Andrew Hamilton and Langhope Manse made to her " Paradise enow." The little hard lines had gone from her face, and she bustled about, a most efficient mistress, encouraging the small maid to do her best work, and helping with her own capable hands. She planned and cooked most savoury, thrifty dinners, and made every shilling do the work of two ; it was all sheer delight to her. House-proud and husband-proud, she envied no one, and in fact sincerely pitied every other woman because she could not have her Andrew.

July, August, and September were three wonderful months to the Hamiltons. They spent them settling into the new house (daily finding new delights in it), working in the garden, and getting acquainted with the congregation.

After their one o'clock dinner, on good afternoons, they mounted their bicycles and visited out-
lying members. Often they were asked to wait for
tea, such a fine farmhouse tea as town-bred Kirsty
had never dreamed of ; and then they cycled home
in the gloaming, talking, talking all the time, until
they came to their own gate—how good that
sounded, *their own gate*—and having wheeled their
bicycles to the shed, they would walk round the
garden hand in hand, like happy children.

Andrew had generally something to show Kirsty,
some small improvement, for he was a man of his
hands ; or if there was nothing new to see, they
would always go and again admire his chief treasures
—a mossy bank that in spring would be covered
with violets, a stone dyke in which rock plants had
been encouraged to grow, and a little humpbacked
bridge hung with ferns.

The war did not trouble Kirsty much. She was
rather provoked that it should have happened, for it
hurt the church attendance and sadly thinned the
choir, and when Andrew had finished reading the
papers he would sometimes sit quite silent, looking
before him, which made her vaguely uneasy.

Her own family were untouched by it. Archie
had no thought of going to train, the notion seemed
to him ludicrous in the extreme, but he saw his way
to making some money fishing in the troubled
waters. The Rev. Johnston Christie confined his
usefulness to violent denunciations of the Kaiser
from the pulpit every Sunday. He had been much
impressed by a phrase used by a prominent Anglican
bishop about the Nailed Hand beating the Mailed
Fist—neat and telling he considered it, and used
it on every possible occasion.

One afternoon in late October the Hamiltons were

walking in their garden. They had been lunching at Etterick, and were going in shortly to have tea cosily by the study fire. It was a still day, with a touch of winter in the air—*back end*, the village people called it, but the stackyards were stocked, the potatoes and turnips were in pits, the byres were full of feeding cattle, so they were ready for what winter would bring them.

To Andrew Hamilton, country born and bred, every day was a delight.

To-day, as he stood with his wife by the low fence at the foot of the garden and looked across the fields to the hills, he took a long breath of the clean cold air, and said :

" This—after ten years of lodgings in Garnethill ! Our lines have fallen to us in pleasant places, Kirsty."

" Yes," she agreed contentedly. " I never thought the country could be so nice. I like the feel of the big stacks, and to think that the stickhouse is full of logs, and the apples in the garret, and everything laid in for winter. Andrew, I'm glad winter is coming. It will be so cosy the long evenings together—and only one meeting in the week."

Her husband put out his hand to stop her. " Don't, Kirsty," he said, as if her words hurt him.

In answer to her look of surprise, he went on :

" Did you never think, when this war was changing so much, that it would change things for us too ? Kirsty, my dear, I have thought it all out and I feel I must go."

Kirsty was apt to get cross when she was perturbed about anything, and she now said, moving a step or two away, " What in the world d'you mean ? Where are you going ? "

" I'm going to enlist, with as many Langhope men as I can persuade to accompany me. It's no use. I can't stand in the pulpit—a young strong man—and say Go. I must say Come ! "

Now that it was out, he gave a sigh of relief.

" Kirsty," he pleaded, " say you think I'm right."

But Kirsty's face was white and drawn.

" I thought you were happy," she said at last, with a pitiful little sob on the last word.

" So happy," said her husband, " that I have to go. Every time I came in and found you waiting for me with the kettle singing, when I went out in the morning and looked at the hills, when I walked in the garden and knew that every bush in it was dear to me—then I remembered that these things so dear were being bought with a price, and that the only decent thing for me to do was to go and help to pay that price."

" But only as a chaplain, surely ? "

Andrew shook his head.

" I'm too young and able-bodied for a chaplain. I'm only thirty-two, and though I'm not big I'm wiry."

" The Archbishop of Canterbury says the clergy *shouldn't* fight," Kirsty reminded him.

Andrew took her arm and looked very tenderly at her as he answered, laughing, " Oh ! Kirsty, since when did an Anglican bishop direct your conscience and mine ? " They walked slowly towards the house.

On the doorstep Kirsty turned.

" Andrew," she said, " have you thought it all out ? Have you thought what it may mean ? Leaving the people here—perhaps they won't keep your place open for you, for no man knows how long the war 'll last—leaving your comfortable home and your wife who—who loves you, and going away to a life of hardship and exposure, and in the end perhaps—death. Have you thought of this sacrifice you are making ? "

And her husband answered, " Yes, I have thought of all it may mean. I don't feel I am wrong leaving the church, because Mr. Smillie is willing to come back and look after the people in my absence. He will stay in the Manse and be company for you." Here poor Kirsty sniffed. " Oh ! my dear, don't think I am going with a light heart. ' Stay at home, then,' you say. ' Better men than you are will stay at home.' I know they will, and I only wish I could stay with them, for the very thought of war makes me sick. But because it is such a wrench to go, makes me sure that I ought to go. Love and sacrifice—it's the Way of the Cross, Kirsty. The ' young Prince of Glory ' walked that way, and I, one of His humblest ministers, will find my way by His footprints."

Kirsty said no more. Later, when Andrew was gone, her father came to Langhope and in no uncertain voice expressed his opinion of his son-in-law. That a man would leave a good down-sitting and go and be a private soldier seemed to him nothing short of madness.

" Andrew's a fool," he said, with great conviction.

" Yes," said Kirsty, " Andrew's a fool—a fool for Christ's sake, and you and I can't even begin to understand what that means in the way of nobility and courage and sacrifice, because we were born crawling things. Andrew has wings, and my only hope is that they will be strong enough to lift me with him—for oh ! I couldn't bear to be left behind." She ran from the room hurriedly, and left a very incensed gentleman standing on the hearth-rug.

Mr. Christie was accustomed to the adulation of females. He was a most welcome guest at the " At Home " days of his flock. He would drop in and ask in his jovial way for " a cup of your excellent tea, Mrs. So-and-so," make mild ministerial jokes, and was always, in his own words, " the purfect gentleman."

And his daughter had called him " a crawling thing " ! He was very cold to Kirsty for the rest of his visit, and when he went home he told his wife that marriage had not improved Christina.

His little invalidish wife looked at him out of her shrewd childish eyes and said, " That's a pity, now," but asked no questions.

The old minister, Mr. Smillie (who was not so very old after all), left his retirement and came back to Langhope, and preached with more vigour than he had done for ten years. Perhaps he had found Edinburgh and unlimited committees rather boring, or perhaps he felt that only his best was good enough for this time.

" Ay," said the village folk, " we've gotten the auld man back, and dod ! he's clean yauld ! Oor young yin's fechtin', ye ken ; " and they said it with pride. It was not every village that had a minister fighting.

The arrangement at the Manse worked very well. Kirsty, too, tried to do her best, and Mr. Smillie, who had been all his life at the mercy of house-keepers, felt he had suddenly acquired both a home and a daughter. When Andrew got his commission, Mr. Smillie went into every house in the village to tell them the news, and was almost as pleased and proud as Kirsty herself.

The Sabbath before he went to France Andrew Hamilton preached in his own pulpit. His text was, " Thou hast given a banner to them that fear Thee."

Two months later, Kirsty got a letter from him. He said : " I played football this afternoon in a match ' Officers *v.* Sergeants.' Perhaps you won't hear from me very regularly for a bit, for things may be happening ; but don't worry about me, I shall be all right. . . . I am going to a Company concert to-night to sing some Scots songs, and then, with their own consent, I am going to speak to my men alone of more serious things."

The next day he led his men in an attack, and was reported " Missing."

His colonel wrote to Kirsty : " I have no heart to write about him at this time. If he is gone, I know too well what it means to you, and I know what it means to the regiment. His ideals were an inspiration to the men he led. . . ."

The rest was silence.

Mr. Smillie still preaches, and Kirsty still sits in the Manse waiting and hoping. Her face has grown very patient, and I think she feels that if Andrew never comes back to her, she has wings which will some day carry her to him.

.   .   .   .

Alan Seton got leave at Christmas for four days.

The excitement at Etterick passed description. Marget cooked and baked everything she could think of, and never once lost her temper. Provisions were got out from Edinburgh ; some people near lent a car for the few days ; nothing was lacking to do him honour. The house was hung with holly from garret to basement, and in the most unexpected places ; for Buff, as decorator, was determined to be thorough.

Everything was Christmas-like except the weather. Buff had been praying very earnestly for snow and frost that they might toboggan, but evidently his expectations had not been great nor his faith of the kind that removes mountains, for when he looked out on Christmas Eve morning he said, " I *knew* it—raining ! "

They had not seen Alan for three years, and four days seemed a deplorably short span of time to ask all they wanted to know.

Buff was quite shy before this tall soldier-brother, and for the first hour eyed him in complete silence ; then he sidled up to him with a book in his hand, explaining that it was his chiefest treasure, and was called *The Frontiersman's Pocket-Book.* It told you everything you wanted to know if you were a frontiersman, which, Buff pointed out, was very useful. Small-pox, enteric, snake-bite, sleeping-sickness, it gave the treatment for them all and the cure—if there was one.

" I like the note on ' Madness,' " said Elizabeth, who was watching the little scene. " It says simply, ' Remove spurs.' Evidently, if the patient is not wearing spurs, nothing can be done."

Alan put his arm round his small brother. " It's a fine book, Buff. You will be a useful man some day out in the Colonies stored with all that information."

" Would—would you like it, Alan ? " Buff asked ; and then, with a gulp of resignation, " I'll give it you."

" Thanks very much, old man," Alan said gravely. " It would be of tremendous use to me in India, if you'll let me have it when I go back ; but over in France, you see, we are simply hotching with doctors, and very little time for taking illnesses."

" Well," said Buff in a relieved tone, " I'll keep

it for you ; " and he departed with his treasure, in case Alan changed his mind.

" I'm glad you didn't take it," said Elizabeth. " He would be very lonely without that book. It lies down with him at night and rises with him in the morning."

" Rum little chap ! " Alan said. " I've wanted him badly all the time in India. . . . Lizbeth, is Father pretty seedy ? You didn't say much in your letters about why he retired, but I can see a big difference in him."

" Oh ! but he's better, Alan," Elizabeth assured him,—" much better than when he left Glasgow ; then he did look frail."

" Well, it is good to be home and see all you funny folk again," Alan said contentedly, as he lay back in a most downy and capacious armchair. " We don't get chairs like this in dug-outs."

It was a wonderful four days, for everything that had been planned came to pass in the most perfect way, and there was no hitch anywhere.

Alan was in the highest spirits, full of stories of his men and of the life out there. " You don't seem to realize, you people," he kept telling them, " what tremendous luck it is for me coming in for this jolly old war."

He looked so well that Elizabeth's anxious heart was easier than it had been for months. Things couldn't be so bad out there, she told herself, if Alan could come back a picture of rude health and in such gay spirits. On the last night Alan went up with Elizabeth to her room to see, he said, if the fire were cosy, and sitting together on the fender-stool they talked—talked of their father (" Take care of him, Lizbeth," Alan said. " Father is a bit extra, you know. I've yet to find a better man "), of how things had worked out, of Walter in India, of the small Buff asleep next door—one of those fireside family talks which are about the most comfortable things in the world. " I'm glad you came to Etterick, I like to think of you here," Alan said. " Well—I'm off to-morrow again."

" Alan," said Elizabeth, " is it very awful ? "

" Well, it isn't a picnic, you know. It's pretty grim sometimes. But I wouldn't be out of it for anything."

" I'll tell you what I wish," said his sister. " I wish you could get a bullet in your arm that would keep you from using it for a long time. And we would get you home to nurse. Oh ! wouldn't that be heavenly ? "

Alan laughed.

" Nice patriotic creature you are ! But seriously, Lizbeth, if I do get knocked out—it does happen now and again, and there is no reason why I should escape—I want you to know that I don't mind. I've had a thoroughly good life. We've had our sad times—and the queer thing is that out there it isn't sad to think about Mother and Sandy : it's comforting, you would wonder !—but when we are happy we are much happier than most people. I haven't got any premonition, you know, or anything like that ; indeed, I hope to come bounding home again in spring, but just in case—remember, I was glad to go."

He put his hand gently on his sister's bowed golden head. Sandy had had just such gentle ways. Elizabeth caught his hand and held it to her face, and her tears fell on it.

" Oh ! Lizbeth, are you giving way to sentiment ? Just think how Fish would lawff ! " and Alan patted her shoulder in an embarrassed way.

Elizabeth laughed through her tears.

" Imagine you remembering Fish all these years ! We were very unsentimental children, weren't we ? And do you remember how Sandy stopped kissing by law ? "

They talked themselves back on to the level, and then Alan got up to go.

" Good-night, Lizbeth," he said, and then " *Wee* Lizbeth " ; and his sister replied as she had done when they were little children cuddling down in their beds without a care in the world :

" Good-night, Alan. *Wee* Alan ! "

The next morning he was off early to catch the London express.

It was a lovely spring-like morning such as some-times comes in midwinter, and he stood on the doorstep and looked over the country-side. All the family, including Marget and Watty Laidlaw and his wife, stood round him. They were loth to let him go.

" When will you be back, my boy ? " his father asked him.

" April, if I can work it," Alan replied. " After two hot weathers in India I simply pine to see the larches out at Etterick, and hear the blackbirds shouting. Scotland owes it to me. Don't you think so, Father ? "

The motor was at the door, the luggage was in, and the partings said—those wordless partings. Alan jumped into the car and grinned cheerily at them.

" Till April," he said. " Remember—Toujours Smiley-face, as we Parisians say——" and he was gone.

They turned to go in, and Marget said fiercely :

" Eh, I wull tak' it ill oot if thae Germans kill that bonnie laddie."

" I almost wish," said Buff, sitting before his porridge with *The Frontiersman's Pocket-Book* clutched close to comfort his sad heart,—" I almost wish that he hadn't come home. I had forgotten how nice he was ! "

It was in April that he fell, and at Etterick the blackbirds were " shouting " as the telegraph boy—innocent messenger of woe—wheeled his way among the larches.

CHAPTER XX

" The Poet says dear City of Cecrops, wilt thou not say dear
City of God ? "   MARCUS AURELIUS.

OUR story ends where it began, in the Thomsons'
parlour in Jeanieville, Pollokshields.

It was November then, now it is May, and light
long after tea, and in happier circumstances Mr.
Thomson would have been out in his shirt-sleeves
in the garden, putting in plants and sowing seeds,
with Mrs. Thomson (a white shawl round her
shoulders) standing beside him admiring, and Alick
running the mower, and Jessie offering advice, and
Robert sitting with his books by an open window
exchanging a remark with them now and again.
They had enjoyed many such spring evenings.
But this remorseless war had drawn the little
Thomsons into the net, and they sat huddled in
the parlour, with no thought for the gay green
world outside.

This was Robert's last evening at home. He
had been training since ever the war broke out, and
was now about to sail for the East. They feared
that Gallipoli was his destination, that ill-omened
place on whose alien shores thousands and thousands
of our best and bravest were to " drink death like
wine," while their country looked on in anguished
pride.

Mr. Chalmers, their new minister, had been in to tea. He had clapped Robert on the back and told him he was proud of him, and proud of the great Cause he was going to fight for. " I envy you, my boy," he said.

Robert had said nothing, but his face wore the expression " *Huch ! Away !* " and when the well-meaning parson had gone he expressed a desire to know what the man thought he was talking about.

" But, man Rubbert," his father said anxiously, " surely you're glad to fight for the Right ? "

" If Mr. Chalmers thinks it such a fine thing to fight," said Robert, " why doesn't he go and do it ? He's not much more than thirty."

" He's married, Rubbert," his mother reminded him, " and three wee ones. You could hardly expect it. Besides, he was telling me that if many more ministers go away to be chaplains they'll have to shut some of the churches."

" And high time, too," said Robert.

" Aw, Rubbert," wailed poor Mrs. Thomson, " what harm do the churches do you ? "

" Never heed him, Mamma," Mr. Thomson said. " He's just sayin' it."

Mrs. Thomson sat on her low chair by the fireside —the nursing chair where she had sat and played with her babies in the long past happy days, her kind face disfigured by much crying, her hands idle in her lap, looking at her first-born as if she grudged every moment her eyes were away from him. It seemed as if she were learning every line of his face by heart to help her in a future that would hold no Robert.

Jessie, freed for the night from her nursing, sat silently doing a last bit of sewing for her brother.

Alick was playing idly with the buckle of Robert's haversack, and relating at intervals small items of news culled from the evening papers, by way of cheering his family. Robert, always quiet, was almost speechless this last evening.

"I saw Taylor to-day," Mr. Thomson remarked, after a silence. "He asked to be remembered to you, Rubbert. In fact, he kinda hinted he would look in to-night—but I discouraged him."

"Wee Taylor! Oh, help!" ejaculated Alick.

"You were quite right, Papa," said his wife. "We're not wanting anybody the night, not even old friends like the Taylors."

Silence fell again, and Alick hummed a tune.

"Rubbert," said Mrs. Thomson, leaning forward and touching her son's arm, "Rubbert, promise me that you'll not do anything brave."

Robert's infrequent smile broke over his face, making it oddly attractive.

"You're not much of a Roman matron, wee body," he said, patting her hand.

"I am not," said Mrs. Thomson. "I niver was meant for a soldier's mother. I niver liked soldiers. I niver thought it was a very respectable job."

"It's the *only* respectable job just now, anyway, Mother," said Jessie.

"That's so," said her father.

"There's the bell," cried Alick. "I hear Annie letting somebody in."

"Dash!" said Robert, rising to fly. But he was too late; the door opened, and Annie announced "Mr. Seton."

At the sight of the tall familiar figure everybody rose to their feet and hastened to greet their old minister.

"Well, I niver," said Mrs. Thomson, "and me

just saying we couldn't put up with visitors the night."

" You see we don't count you a visitor," Mr. Thomson explained. " Rubbert's off to-morrow."

" I know," said Mr. Seton. " That is why I came. We are in Glasgow for a few days. I left Elizabeth and Buff at the Central Hotel. Elizabeth said you wouldn't want her to-night, but she will come before we leave."

" How is she ? " asked Mrs. Thomson. " Poor thing ! She'll not laugh so much now."

" Lizbeth," said her father, " is a gallant creature. I think she will always laugh, and like Charles Lamb she will always find this world a pretty world."

This state of mind made no appeal to Mrs. Thomson, and she changed the subject by asking about Mr. Seton's health. His face, she noticed, was lined and worn, he stooped more than he used to do, but his eyes were the same—a hopeful boy's eyes.

" Oh, I'm wonderfully well. You don't grudge me an hour of Robert's last evening ? I baptized the boy."

" Ye did that, Mr. Seton,"—the tears beginning to flow at the thought,—" and little did any of us think that this is what he was to come to."

" No," said Mr. Seton, " we little thought what a privilege was to be his. Robert, when I heard you had enlisted I said, ' Well done,' for I knew what it meant to you to leave your books. And I hear you wouldn't take a commission, but preferred to go with the men you had trained with."

Robert blushed, but his face did not wear the " affronted " look that it generally wore when people praised him as a patriot.

" Ah but, Mr. Seton," Alick broke in eagerly, " Robert's a sergeant ! See his stripes ! That's just about as good as an officer."

Robert made a grab at his young brother to silence him ; but Alick was not to be suppressed.

" I shouldn't wonder," he said in a loud, boastful voice (he had never been so miserable in all his fifteen years),—" I shouldn't wonder if he got the V.C. That would be fine—eh, Robert ? "

" I think I see myself," said Robert.

" Rubbert's a queer laddie," Mr. Thomson remarked, looking tenderly at his son. " He was objectin' to Mr. Chalmers sayin' he had a noble Cause."

Robert blushed again.

" There's nothing wrong with the Cause,' he grumbled, " but I hate talking about it."

" ' Truth hath a quiet breast,' " quoted Mr. Seton.

There was a silence in the little parlour that looked out on the garden. They were all thinking the same thing—would they ever sit here together again ?

So many had gone away ! So many had not come back. Mrs. Thomson gave a choking sob and burst out : " Oh ! Mr. Seton, your boy didn't come back ! "

" No," said Mr. Seton gently, " my boy didn't come back ! "

" And oh ! the bonnie laddie he was ! I can just see him as well ; the way he used to come swinging into the church in his kilt, and his fair hair, and his face so full of daylight. And I'm sure it wasna for want of prayers, for I'm sure Papa there niver missed once, morning and night, and in our own private prayers too—and you would pray just even on ? "

" Just even on," said Mr. Seton.

" *And He never heeded us,*" said Mrs. Thomson.

Mr. Seton smiled at the dismayed amazement in her tone.

" Oh, yes, He heeded us. He answered our prayers beyond our asking. We asked life for Alan, and He has given him length of days for ever and ever."

" But that wasna what we meant," complained Mrs. Thomson. " Oh ! I whiles think I'm not a Christian at all now. I *cannot* see why God allows this war. There's Mrs. Forsyth, a neighbour of ours—you wouldn't meet a more contented woman, and that proud of her doctor son, Hugh. It was the biggest treat you could give her just to let her talk about him, and I must say he was a cliver, cliver young man. He did wonders at College, and he was gettin' such a fine West End practice when the war began ; but nothing would serve but he would away out to France to give his services, and he's killed—*killed !* " Her voice rose in a wail of horror that so untoward a fate should have overtaken any friend of hers. " And oh ! Mr. Seton, how am I to let Rubbert go ? All his life I've taken such care of him, because he's not just that awfully strong ; he was real sickly as a bairn and awful subject to croup. Many's the time I've left ma bed at nights and listened to his breathing. Papa used to get fair worried with me, I was that anxious-minded. I niver let the wind blow on him. And now . . ."

" Poor body ! " said Mr. Seton. " It's a sore job for the mothers." He turned to Mr. Thomson. " Perhaps we might have prayers together before I go ? "

Mr. Thomson brought the Bible, and sat down close beside his wife.

Jessie and Robert and Alick sat together on the sofa, drawn very near by the thought of the parting on the morrow. Mr. Seton opened the Bible.

"We shall sing the Twenty-third Psalm," he said.

Sing? The Thomsons looked at their minister. Even so must the Hebrews have looked when asked to sing Zion's songs by the waters of Babylon. But James Seton, grown wise through a whole campaign of this world's life and death, knew the healing balm of dear familiar things, and as he read the words they dropped like oil on a wound :

> " The Lord's my Shepherd, I'll not want.
>   He makes me down to lie
> In pastures green : He leadeth me
>   The quiet waters by.
>
> My soul He doth restore again ;
>   And me to walk doth make
> Within the paths of righteousness,
>   Ev'n for His own name's sake.
>
> Yea, though I walk in death's dark vale,
>   Yet will I fear none ill :
> For Thou art with me ; and Thy rod
>   And staff me comfort still.
>   .   .   .   .   .
> Goodness and mercy all my life
>   Shall surely follow me ;
> And in God's house for evermore
>   My dwelling-place shall be."

It is almost the first thing that a Scots child learns, that the Lord is his Shepherd, that he will not want, that goodness and mercy will follow him—even through death's dark vale.

Death's dark vale, how trippingly we say it when we are children, fearing " none ill."

Mrs. Thomson's hand sought her husband's.

She had been unutterably miserable, adrift from all her moorings, bewildered by the awful march of events, even doubting God's wisdom and love ; but as her old minister read her childhood's psalm she remembered that all through her life the promise had never failed ; she remembered how stars had shone in the darkest night, and how even the barren plain of sorrow had been curiously beautified with lilies, and she took heart of comfort.

God, Who counteth empires as the small dust of the balance, and Who taketh up the isles as a very little thing, was shaking the nations, and the whole earth trembled. But there are some things that cannot be shaken, and the pilgrim souls of the world need fear none ill.

Goodness and mercy will follow them through every step of their pilgrimage. The way may lie by " pastures green," or through the sandy, thirsty desert, or through the horror and blood and glory of the battlefield, but in the end there awaits each pilgrim that happy place whereof it is said " sorrow and sighing shall flee away."

" We shall sing the whole psalm," said Mr. Seton. " The tune is ' French.' "

THE END

PRINTED IN GREAT BRITAIN AT
THE PRESS OF THE PUBLISHERS